A DARKER SHADE

LAURA K. CURTIS

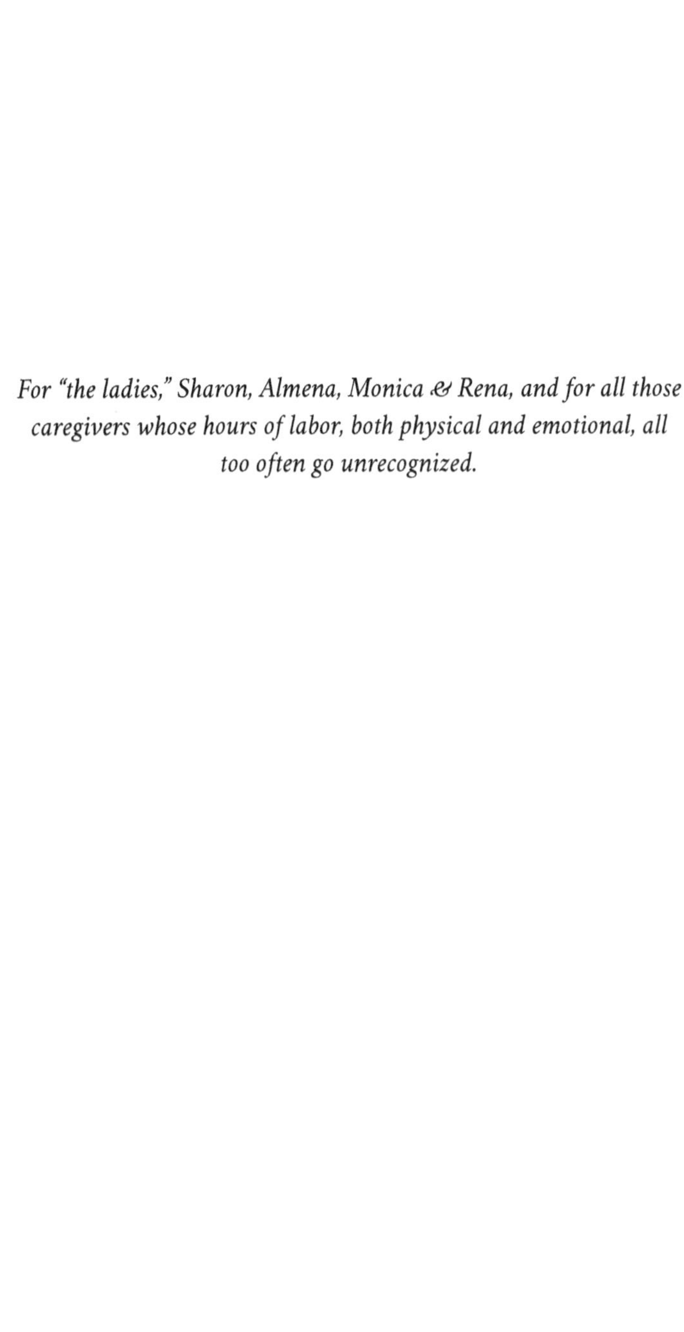

For "the ladies," Sharon, Almena, Monica & Rena, and for all those caregivers whose hours of labor, both physical and emotional, all too often go unrecognized.

CHAPTER 1

*I*f my mother had been alive, she would never have allowed me to take the job. But then, if my mother had been alive, I wouldn't have been on my fourth night of rice and beans, struggling to pay the rent for the portion of the two-bedroom apartment Ali and I shared with our aunt, uncle, and two cousins. Instead, I would have gotten my Master's. I'd be working in a career I loved. Or at least, that was the dream, and while Mama lived all dreams were possible, no matter how grim our circumstances. Em Allworth believed her children could conquer the world and for far too brief a time, we believed it, too.

I'd buried that confidence along with Mama, however, and when I recognized the care service number on my cell phone, I almost wept with relief. I held up a hand, waving for quiet in the chaos of the apartment while I answered. I could have taken my cell into the hallway, but our whole building lived as we did, with only the thinnest of walls and doors between us, and I would have no more peace in the cold and uncomfortable stairwell than on our cozy couch.

"He's looking for an au pair and tutor for his twelve-year-

"

old daughter and fourteen-year-old niece," Sandy explained. "It's a big house, and his sister-in-law lives there, too. He has a housekeeper five days a week so you don't have to clean, but you'll be responsible for some of the cooking. The thing is, it's in the middle of nowhere, Maine. He tried a service out of Boston first, and they sent two candidates who couldn't cut it more than a few months. And that was in the summer. Come winter, you won't be able to leave the property at all. Apparently they're surrounded by woods and don't bother to plow the road out."

Never live in. It was one of Em Allworth's cardinal rules. If you lived in, you lost your autonomy, lost any chance of having your own life, keeping your own traditions. But as far as I was concerned, living in meant no more rent. Even being shut away from the world entirely and disobeying my mother's prime dictate wasn't enough to balance out the financial incentives. Besides, most of our traditions had died years before, when my father's murder forced us to move to Connecticut.

"Not a problem." I had given my little sister our Honda, which was almost as old as she was, to use at college. Bright, beautiful, brilliant Ali would not lose her dream. She would conquer the world, if I had to die to make it happen. She had a full-ride scholarship to a university in Missouri that covered food, housing, books... everything but transportation, and St. Louis wasn't Hartford—she needed a vehicle. Even if there'd been a hundred places to go in Maine, I wouldn't have had a way to get to them.

"What does it pay?" Even if it weren't much, without me around, Aunt Nadya and Uncle Bo could rent out the room Ali and I usually shared, so I wouldn't owe rent.

A long silence came over the phone, echoing into the apartment as my relatives waited to hear the answer. The Allworths survived as a unit. If I got paid, everyone benefited. I had been out of work for two weeks, and we were all eating rice and beans, goulash, and peanut butter and jelly.

"It's an unusual setup," Sandy said finally.

"Unusual how?" A hard lump formed between my shoulders.

"As I explained, you'll be the third woman who's gone up there. The first two he paid a regular salary without restrictions, but he's reluctant to do it again. So he's offering a sliding scale. The first three months you'll get a thousand a month. The second three months, two thousand a month, the third, three, the fourth, four. If you make it there a year, your pay will stay at four thousand a month with six month contract renewals. He'll also pay for the minimum standard state health insurance. If you leave before the end of six months, however, you'll be responsible for paying what he owes me out of your pocket."

Four thousand a month plus insurance and room and board. I had never even imagined earning that kind of money. Not without an advanced degree. Still, it sounded too good to be true and I drilled for the inevitable downside.

"That's more than Sharon or Almena make on their live-ins."

"Desperation premium," Sandy replied tartly. "Plus, Sharon and Almena have easy situations. There's a small hitch on this one."

Because of course there was. For those who lived as Ali and I did, there was always one more hitch. A job too far away, an employer who changed their mind, our mother's cancer… nothing came easy to the Allworth sisters.

"The daughter is uncommunicative."

"Uncommunicative as in sullen, or uncommunicative as in mute?"

"It's not that she can't speak, it's that she doesn't. Her mother died two years ago and apparently Liza became quieter and quieter until she stopped talking altogether. Mr. Prescott doesn't expect you to work miracles. The other girl, Hailey, requires a regular tutor, but you just need to do what you can with Liza. And if you can get her talking, there's a bonus in it for you. Ten thousand dollars."

My heart tripped. Literally skipped a beat. I whispered a prayer I'd learned at my father's knee as my fingers tightened on the phone. Ten thousand dollars. Ali could apply directly to medical school. She wouldn't have to take some job cleaning houses with our aunt or doing elder care or child care for Sandy, putting her educational goals on hold. If I could see her off with some combination of cash and scholarship money, I might be able to return to my own long-deferred ambitions without betraying the promise I'd made my mother.

I shook off the dream. I had only a rudimentary education in child psych, the few courses I'd taken in college before my mother's diagnosis derailed my plans for a career as a school counselor. My chances of coaxing a truly damaged girl out of her silence were slim. "Is that why she's being home-schooled?"

I could hear Sandy breathing on the other end of the line, but she did not answer.

"Sandy?"

"You understand that even if you refuse this job, you are prevented from discussing the circumstances by the non-disclosure agreement you signed when you came to work for me?"

"Of course."

"Good. You'll likely have to sign another—Mr. Prescott made the others he hired sign them. He doesn't want his daughter labeled crazy—but the gist of it is that he pulled Liza out of school because she told anyone who would listen that she could talk to her mother's ghost. Of course, that was before she stopped speaking altogether."

Sandy was too professional to mock a client, too ladylike to snort, but even over the phone line I could hear her eyes rolling. I made a noncommittal sound, shaking off the little shiver that ran over my skin. I might have been first generation American on my mother's side, but my father's grandfather had arrived well before World War II, and I put my faith in psychology. Still, my heritage would not let me dismiss the spiritual altogether. Spirits, if not actual ghosts, lived among the Romani, as well as in the Catholic church my mother had insisted we attend before my father's death and her falling out with God. For what were saints but benevolent spirits?

"She's been under a psychiatrist's care," Sandy continued, "but with winter coming that may have to be put on hold. Since the girl won't talk, it's all art therapy and play therapy and nonsense like that, anyway." Typical Sandy—no more patience with psychiatry than with the paranormal.

"As long as her father understands that I'm not capable of taking the psychiatrist's place, it should be fine."

"You're certain? As I said, it's remote. Very little cell phone access, so you'll have to give your sister the house number, and even that goes down in big storms. My reputation is on the line here. I can't afford to send someone out there who won't stick."

"I'm certain. Send me the paperwork."

THE MORNING I LEFT, Aunt Nadya drove me to the bus station, passing along a steady stream of advice the whole time.

"Keep your head down and your chin up," she finished as I

hugged her goodbye in front of the long, low building. This was one of her favorite sayings and I'd never worked up the courage to ask her how such a thing might be possible. Maybe in another twenty years, when she'd lost a little of her stiff-spined, intimidating posture to age, I'd find my nerve. For the moment, I appreciated all her advice, no matter how contradictory.

As the bus pulled away from the station, I glanced back only once. Twenty years there, and nothing called to me from Hartford. I still remembered every detail, all the smells and sounds and sights of the tiny apartment I'd shared with my parents in Queens before my father's murder sent us north to his family, and bringing it to mind sent a pang of longing through me even now. It was as if, still tied to New York, my heart had never made the move.

At least homesickness would not be an issue as it had been for Prescott's earlier hires. I glanced around the interior of the bus. Only a dozen people shared the space, so I had a row to myself. The next row up and across the aisle, two women in their forties had taken out flasks and were sipping from them and giggling as they looked at the screen of a tablet. In the front, a man in a suit had unpacked an entire office-worth of supplies onto the seat beside him and tapped away at a laptop. A couple in their twenties squished as close together as possible, her long hair tangling in his beard as they snuggled. Others minded their own business, reading, sleeping, staring mindlessly out windows. Time to get to know my new charges.

I pulled out the slim file Sandy had given me when I went into the office to sign my contract and the non-disclosure agreement. The front page listed the household members. Nothing unexpected there; Nathaniel Prescott, age thirty-five, and his daughter, twelve-year-old Liza. He would sign my paycheck, but I was also responsible to his sister-in-law, Jennifer Brahms Prescott because her daughter, Hailey, was my second student. The housekeeper, Mrs. Irene Vogel, came in five days a week. Her husband, Henry, was a local cab driver and did light repair work around the house. He would meet me at the station in Portland and drive me to the house.

The second page of the packet was the "plan of care." Sandy had come to childcare from elder care, where such plans were common. A plan of care went over all a caregiver's responsibilities, the weaknesses and difficulties of the client, the problems she might encounter. Unlike the typical elder care plan, which consisted of a series of bullet points like "assist with bathing," Sandy had chosen a a narrative format for this page.

The Prescotts are a family in crisis and will need to be handled as such. Liza's mother, Marianne Prescott, died two years ago. Instead of recovering from that death, the child has become increasingly disturbed and closed off, to the point that she no longer speaks. Evaluating her learning will be difficult, but her father says she is an eager student.

Daniel Prescott, Nathaniel's brother and Hailey's father, died in a car accident six months ago. His wife was injured in the wreck and now uses a cane but is self-sufficient and does not need the attention of a medical aide. Hailey had been slated to go to a very competitive boarding school, but Jennifer Prescott felt that after the accident the child was too anxious and too emotionally fragile to be sent away immediately. Mother and daughter moved into the Prescott house in Maine to recover. Hailey will need intense education if she is to keep up with the coursework at the boarding school.

While your essential responsibility is to educate the girls and keep them occupied and entertained, the Prescotts may call on you to do anything they need to keep the house—known as Rook's Rest —running smoothly. Prescott runs his boatbuilding business out of the home, and his sister-in-law frequently assists him. Mrs. Vogel does the majority of the cooking and cleaning, but the girls cannot simply run wild or they will ruin his business.

In short, both girls need to be educated, trained, molded as they mature. According to Jennifer Prescott, neither girl likes to get up particularly early. You will want to discuss the schedule in detail with her because if her daughter is returning to a regular school next year she may wish to get her on a particular plan. Liza is overly imaginative and believes in ghosts. She must be cured of this if she is to grow into a successful adult member of society. If you can eliminate this particular fantasy, there is a good chance she will speak again.

A sticky note attached to the page at this point reminded me of the bonus for convincing Liza to talk. As if I could forget.

The idea of a house with a name captivated me, pulling my mind from its usual endless circle of worries. Pemberley. Manderley. Brideshead Castle. I knew such places from my reading, but I'd never imagined living in one. Combined with the generous salary, the house's name brought pictures of rolling, perfectly manicured lawns and fountains sparkling under endless sunlight.

The bus rolled on, wheels swishing against the pavement, and I pulled out the notebook I used as an auxiliary brain. As usual, the file touched only on the facts of the job. I always had dozens of questions left unaddressed. Before I could begin this particular job, I would need a curriculum for each girl, for example. But a more pressing issue, at least to me, was the nature of Liza's paranormal experiences. On the phone, Sandy had said that Liza had spoken to her mother's ghost, but surely that was not enough to label her "damaged." I'd certainly called out to my father after his murder, and had half-imagined him answering. Nor would my mother have been particularly surprised had I come to her certain I'd seen him, heard him, even years after his passing. But the spirit world lived with us, with my mother's side of the family if not the Allworths. From Mr. Prescott's reaction—moving his daughter all the way to Maine to eliminate his wife's continued presence in her life—I doubted the spirits of the departed formed a valid part of his culture.

FOR ALL THE differences at first glance when I stepped off the bus in Portland with my fellow travelers, I might have gone round trip. The smell of diesel hung thick in the air and the rumble of engines drowned out the city's native soul. But then, I imagined bus stations were much the same everywhere, with none terribly cheerful. The driver hauled my duffel from the bay beneath the bus and handed it to me and when I turned, a small, wizened, winter apple of a man had appeared at my elbow.

"Miss Allworth? I'm Henry Vogel. I'm to bring you to Rook's Rest."

I shouldered the duffel and followed him out to a boxy Volvo station wagon idling at the curb. He popped the back and I stuffed the duffel in.

"I c'n give you a quick tour if you like. Show you downtown. There's not much to it. Portland's a small town."

"That would be wonderful."

Henry was right. Portland was small. And short. It occurred to me that with every move, I'd literally come "down" in life—from New York's skyscrapers to Hartford's multi-level skyline, to Portland's squatter buildings with only the occasional tall spire. But if the buildings were smaller, the sky was bigger. Blue-white with puffy clouds decorating the high dome, an upside-down bowl spilling clean, salty air over us as we drove.

"It's beautiful." I sucked in a deep breath of the sea-fresh air from the open window.

"Ayup."

We turned off the small streets and onto a highway of sorts that wound through the woods. The deciduous trees were already turning here, though they were still green in Connecticut. Fiery gold and bloody red they fluttered as we passed, overhanging the road and blocking out the sun.

"Your wife works at Rook's Rest, right?" I leaned forward to speak to Henry Vogel.

"Ayup."

"Is it a very grand place?"

He grunted. Not much of a talker.

"How did it get its name? Do you know?" That had been bothering me. I knew several meanings for the word rook.

"Dunno," Henry said. "Suppose it's from the crows. There's always been crows at the Rest."

We slammed into a pothole and I was thrown back into my seat. So much for conversation.

THE ROAD WOUND DEEPER into the country and the woods closed in around us, the birches with their white trunks like ghostly sentinels among the evergreens and fiery-colored deciduous trees slowly dropping their leaves. A child of concrete and glass, I had never lived outside of a city. In my experience, nature was carefully bottled up in parks and zoos, constrained by walls, gates, and cages. Here it edged so close to the tarmac that it seemed ready to break through, as if at any moment we might take a blind curve and find the road buckled by the gnarled roots of giant trees.

I shivered as Henry turned off the road onto a private drive. As we broke from the trees, a single bird of prey circled overhead. Henry had spoken of crows, but this was a hawk, or even an eagle, its wingspan as large as my arms, and as I watched it swooped, a dark and deadly shadow, on some hapless prey. But then the car bumped to a stop and my attention was pulled to the house.

No English country manor this. The house rose up from the ground in a swift, vertical shear. An abundance of peeling gingerbread decorated narrow windows, and separate mansard roofs over a taller tower and two stepped-back bits made it look as if it were tilting forward, hunching over. A slightly sagging porch ran along the front and right sides of the house, and a wing stuck out perpendicular to the left side, held up by hefty columns. Before it, a brick patio was set with cast iron furniture. A wide window took up two-thirds of the wing. Movement flickered briefly behind the glass and I started. But the moment passed and the front door opened and a black-clad woman stepped out, drawing my attention.

Here we go. For a moment, fear knifed through me and I wanted to run. But this was the job of a lifetime. The job that would return both me and Ali to the paths we had been on before cancer stole our mother and slashed our dreams. Whatever might happen, I would succeed; I had no other option. I pushed open the car door and climbed out.

"You're Maloney Allworth?" the woman asked. Her steel-gray hair was knotted behind her head with a few wisps fluttering out to soften her round, lined face. But no such softening showed in her cool, assessing eyes.

"Molly, please. No one calls me Maloney." I held out a hand and she took it, her grip firm and steady.

"I'm Mrs. Vogel, the housekeeper." She focused over my shoulder. "Bring her things in, Henry."

He hefted my duffel out of the back of the Volvo.

"That's all you brought?" Mrs. Vogel frowned.

It was everything I owned. "I don't need much."

Mrs. Vogel sniffed as if to say *you don't fool me, girl.* "Come along, then."

The atrium had the same run down elegance as the outside. The center hall extended up all three stories, with narrow, precipitous staircases and balconies on each level looking down over the parquet floor. The rails and balusters were worn but gleamed with the shine of real wax. Dark wood panels extended midway up the walls, with slightly stained, butter yellow wallpaper above the chair rail.

Paintings hung everywhere. Pastoral landscapes, beautiful but eerie, with indeterminable light sources. In each, the earth cracked open—sometimes in a corner, sometimes at the center—spilling unnatural hues of electric blue, neon orange, blood red.

"Mrs. Marianne painted those," explained Mrs. Vogel.

"I've never seen anything like them." It was the most diplomatic answer I could come up with. In truth, the paintings gave me the creeps. The whole house did. There was no denying that the place had a certain faded glory, but for a child who saw ghosts, it must be a nightmare. Even I could feel the presence of generations. Nathaniel Prescott should have taken an apartment in town, a clean, new one, without the history this one had. But of course, he wouldn't see it that way.

"Liza's upstairs," Mrs. Vogel said. "Mr. Prescott will be home shortly. He had to run to Boston last night for a meeting."

"And the others?"

"Mrs. Jennifer and Hailey are in town shopping."

The front door burst open and a man strode in. He stopped in the middle of the hallway, his black eyes scraping over me in a single encompassing glance.

Nathaniel Prescott was as angular and forbidding as his

house. Dark hair swept back from a tall forehead in a sharp widow's peak and bony shoulders poked through his heavy wool coat. I knew from the packet that he was only thirty-five years old, but already fine lines fanned out beside hollowed eyes and fine silver threads shot through his dark hair and shone even in the dim light of the foyer.

"My God," he said. "You'll never do. I'll have Henry pick you up."

"Excuse me?"

Those eyes pinned me. "I am sending you back." Each word was punctuated with a period, as if he were speaking to an idiot and I repressed a snarl. *Never show emotion, never let them see your spine.* That was my Aunt Nadya, who'd taught me how to get on in the world when I shifted from conqueror to conquered. "I don't see how I could have made myself clearer to your boss, but apparently she didn't take me seriously."

"We have a contract." I squared my shoulders and kept my tone calm despite the pit of panic that had opened beneath my stomach. "It's not my fault you don't like the look of me. You approved my qualifications and agreed to employ me. You signed the contract."

He could break it. I wasn't so naive as to believe a man with his kind of money couldn't get out of anything he wanted. But damned if I'd let him do so without at least giving me a chance.

Sharp lips thinned into a straight line. "And when you decide to run? Do I hold you to your end of that contract?"

My end. The end that said I would pay Sandy's fees out of my own pocket.

"I won't run." But I wanted to. Already. And the job had not even begun. I was accustomed to dismissive employers, snobby ones, desperate ones...working in care, I'd seen all kinds of families. Some were grateful for the help, but many resented having to ask for it and took their frustrations out on the very people they'd hired to ease their burden. I understood Prescott's reaction but not my own sick feeling that the house stank of psychological rot. There was a festering here, hidden behind the wallpaper and beneath the carpet. My mother would have felt it. Aunt Nadya, on the other hand, would tell me to buck up, that it was nothing a bit of bleach couldn't take care of. She'd never had any patience with her sister-in-law's superstitions, and had done her best to stomp them out entirely once we moved north to live near her.

A squeak above from above drew my attention to the second floor. A child sat on the top step, watching us through owl's eyes. Dark hair hung in long, untamed ropes around her face and she was perched to run. I remembered Ali at that age, her hair in braids that fell below her shoulder blades, her bright eyes curious, and my heart thumped. If I abandoned this child, I would be abandoning my own sister; my salary kept us together as my mother wanted, as we wanted.

I glanced at Prescott to see him staring up at his daughter as if he could, by sheer force of will, compel her to meet his gaze. But her eyes, as dark as her father's, remained fixed on me. Her lips parted and all of us in that hallway held our breaths. Would she speak? Her eyes slid to the side as if someone had called her, and she rose and darted away into the shadows.

"My daughter," said Prescott. "Your charge, should you stay."

I swallowed. "I'm staying."

CHAPTER 2

"We don't use the third floor at all," Mrs. Vogel explained as she led me up the creaking stairs. "All the bedrooms are on the second. The master is down the end behind us."

Despite the size of the house, the hallways were narrow, and were I inclined to claustrophobia, I would have had a panic attack just standing there. Heavy paneled doors lined both walls, and the hall turned off to the right at the end

"That's the access to the new wing," Mrs. Vogel explained. "Where the playroom is. You can see it when you're standing outside the house. The one with the big window." Where Liza had watched my arrival. "That's where you'll have your study time. Your room and Liza's are on this side, with a connecting door. Hailey's is down the end, with a connection to her mother. Bathroom is across the hall from you, next to Mrs. Jennifer. You'll share it with the girls."

I tried to imagine why anyone would have built a house with so many attached bedrooms, but despite my love of literature I hadn't read much about architecture. Perhaps one had been a nursery? Plenty of books discussed those, but only younger children needed nurseries. Didn't Liza resent having a series of strangers only a door away? And how did Hailey feel about having a room that connected to her mother's? In fact, why had her mother decided that living in the middle of nowhere was a good idea for her teenaged daughter? Until I'd seen the place, I hadn't appreciated the warning Sandy was trying to give me. How would a fourteen-year-old find friends in a place like this? My stomach twisted. I had been so caught up with Liza's situation I hadn't properly considered Hailey's.

"Has Hailey always been home-schooled?" I asked.

"Oh, no. They were living in Boston when Mr. Daniel died. But the tragedy was very hard on the poor child, so they moved up here with Mr. Nathaniel. She'll go back to school next year once she and her mother find their feet again. This is just for one year." She opened a door to let me into the bedroom. "You can set your bag down and I'll take you to Liza."

I had a mere moment to admire the elegance of the room that was to be mine. I could take in only the heavy, canopied bed that dominated the space, standing on a giant tapestry-style area rug beneath it before Mrs. Vogel urged me down the hall and into the new wing. Thick, tweedy carpet covered the playroom floor, a concession to the needs of active children, I imagined, as I had not seen it anywhere else in the house. A low bookcase ran beneath the wide window, forming a bench, its single shelf stuffed with books shoved in every which way. Shadows clung to both ends of the bench where it ended beneath steep eaves. From one, a cluster of dolls stared at me, sizes ranging from about six inches to nearly three feet tall. I'd never been a fan of dolls, and an uncomfortable shudder ran over me at the sight of all those blank, unblinking eyes.

Opposite the dolls, scrunched into the far corner of the bench, hiding beneath the eave, deep in shadow, sat Liza.

"Come say hello to Miss Molly," Mrs. Vogel said.

The girl blinked a couple of times, then unfolded herself and came forward. She held out a hand and I took it, feeling her long, bony fingers cold against my skin.

"I'll be downstairs if you need me," said Mrs. Vogel. "Dinner's at seven and everyone's expected to be prompt. Mrs. Jennifer and Hailey will be back before then, though, so you'll have a chance to meet them." Her duties discharged, she made her escape.

I took a deep breath. The room smelled of all the raw wood in the exposed beams and unfinished shelving, overlaid with a fair amount of dust. If we were going to be spending our days here, I'd be scrubbing it down it myself.

"Well," I said to Liza, "I guess it's just you and me. I understand you may not feel like talking to me yet, but I hope you don't mind if I talk to you. Before this, I lived with my little sister, my aunt and uncle, and two cousins, so I'm not used to the quiet."

I wrinkled my nose. "It's dusty in here, don't you think? My aunt and uncle clean houses and before she died, my mom helped them out. I've been cleaning houses all my life, it seems like, so I'm a little picky. Do you think you could help me try to put this room in order? You don't think Mrs. Vogel will be upset if we clean in here, do you? She won't think we're criticizing her housekeeping skills?"

Liza didn't answer, but I'd seen a spark behind the dark, watchful stare when I mentioned my mother. Let her chew on it for a while. Maybe she would ask me an actual question at some point.

"I'm supposed to be doing a bit of cooking, too, according to my contract, but I'll tell you a secret." I looked her up and down. "Yes, you look as if you could keep a secret. So here it is: I don't know how to cook. My sister and I ate a lot of really basic food. Mac and cheese out of a box, rice and beans, stews and soups. I don't think that would make your dad happy. So I am going to have to go to town and buy a couple of cookbooks. Unless there are cookbooks here? Do you know?"

She squinted, then very slowly shook her head.

"You don't know, or there aren't any?"

She shook her head again. I wasn't going to get a word out of her so easily, but the head shaking was more than I'd expected. When Sandy had said "uncommunicative," I'd pictured a child who actively refused any overture, not simply one who did not speak. I could work with nods.

"Okay. We'll have to go shopping, then. I hope you'll come with me so we can pick at least one that has recipes that appeal to you."

Liza shifted on her feet, eyes making that same sideways slip I'd noticed earlier, then darted over to the window to peer outside. I followed.

A shiny Range Rover was pulling up in front of the house. How had Liza heard it when I'd noticed nothing at all? She put her hand on the window, laying it flat against the glass. A blonde girl exploded from the passenger side door, her hands full of shopping bags. The driver followed more slowly, also blonde. She reached into the back of the vehicle and withdrew a cane and a single bag before following her daughter—for, surely, these were Jennifer and Hailey Prescott—into the house. A moment later, Mrs. Vogel came out, started up the SUV and drove it out of sight.

FOOTSTEPS THUNDERED up the stairs and down the hall and Hailey Prescott burst into the playroom. Blonde curls bounced around glowing cheeks and a bright purple tunic covered striped leggings. She was as different from her cousin as two children could be.

"Ohmigod," she said, "Liza, you totally missed out. I got the cutest outfits! And I got us a PlayStation game.

"Hi! I'm Hailey!"

It took a second for me to realize she was addressing me.

"Hi, Hailey. I'm Molly."

She looked me over and I had the distinct impression she found me lacking. But someone had schooled her to politeness. "It's nice to meet you. You're going to be my tutor?"

"I am."

"There's a packet." She rolled blue eyes so high they almost disappeared and I had to smother a laugh.

"I know. I've gotten them before." The packets were from home school authorities. They listed textbooks, lesson plans, resources. This would be my first actual homeschooling charge, but I'd taken on areas of instruction with younger children when I cared for them.

"My mom has it. I think she's afraid I'd rip it up if she didn't keep it in her room." Again the rolled eyes, this time accompanied by a deep sigh.

"I'm sure she just wants to have a chance to go over it with me before you get started on it." I glanced over to Liza. "We'll have to come up with lessons for you, too."

"Oh, she has them," said Hailey. "She's way better at studying than I am. Aren't you, Liza? Just 'cause she doesn't talk, doesn't mean she's stupid."

Was that a tightening at the corners of Liza's eyes? Had I heard an undercurrent of resentment beneath Hailey's supportive comment? Or was I letting my imagination run away with me?

"Actually," I said, "I'm well aware that it doesn't. We've already had a lovely conversation about cookbooks, haven't we Liza?" I invited her to share the humor and imagined her lips lifted slightly at the corners when she inclined her head a fraction. "I only meant that I hadn't seen a packet for her yet, either, and surely your mom isn't afraid you'd rip hers up."

"Nah. But Liza doesn't need a packet. She's ahead for her age, so she does my packet with me."

"Well, that does make things simpler, doesn't it?"

An uneven squeak-and-thump walk announced Jennifer Prescott's arrival. She shared all her daughter's features, from the snub nose and wide blue eyes to the long neck and narrow shoulders. Jennifer, however, had a decidedly more subdued sense of fashion. A creamy sweater topped a gray pencil skirt. Where Hailey jumped about in bright purple high-tops with green laces, her mother wore low-heeled pumps. They presented an odd picture with her cane, but I could not imagine the woman in flats. Odds were, she'd been the stiletto type before the accident and this was as much of a concession as she was willing to make to her injury.

"You must be Molly." She switched her cane to her left hand so she could take my right in a no-nonsense grip. "I'm Jennifer Prescott."

Her visual assessment was more circumspect, but no less thorough than her daughter's.

"It's nice to meet you." I gave her my best smile.

"Thane says you plan to stay."

Thane? It took a minute for me to connect the name with Nathaniel Prescott. "Yes, I do." I remembered Prescott's comment about running and looked her dead in the eye. "I realize I don't look terribly hardy, Mrs. Prescott, but I am."

"Oh, please. Call me Jennifer. And I know better than to judge a book by its cover." She shifted her gaze to the girls. "Liza, honey, I bought you a sweater. There's already a nip in the air and I think it will look marvelous on you. Come here and let me hold it up to see whether it will fit."

In that maddeningly slow way that even after only a brief time in the house I understood to be an expression of displeasure, Liza obeyed. Stiffly, she stood before her aunt while Jennifer held up a blue and gray Fair Isle sweater. The colors were lovely, but the style suited Jennifer or Hailey better than Liza.

"Perfect," Jennifer said. "I'll just tuck it into your sweater drawer." She folded the sweater and put it back into the shopping bag. "You're welcome, Liza."

Although Liza's expression remained utterly flat, a chill shivered through the still playroom air. I wanted to get Jennifer, with her pretty sweater and perfect hair, out of the room, though who I was protecting with that instinct I had no idea.

"Hailey says you have the girls' homeschool packet," I said.

"Yes, I do." Jennifer checked her watch. "There are only a couple of hours until dinner, so I can't go over it with you now. But if you'd like to look it over tonight, we could chat after breakfast."

"That sounds fine. Shall I come with you and get it now?"

"Certainly." She cast a warning glance at the girls—what kind of trouble did she think they were apt to get in?—then led me out of the room.

As Mrs. Vogel had mentioned, Jennifer's room lay at the far end of the corridor. It was even larger than mine, and it had been remodeled to add a private bathroom. A gorgeous, dark vanity that had been transformed into a writing desk stood in the corner, and Jennifer reached into the single drawer and pulled out a hefty folder of papers.

"Here you go." She tucked the folders into the shopping

bag with the sweater. "You can put that away, too, since your room connects to Liza's."

Right, because all twelve-year-old girls wanted complete strangers going through their things. That would absolutely get me off on the wrong foot. I would keep the sweater in my own room and offer it to Liza later on.

"I'll see you for dinner," said Jennifer. "I don't know whether Thane told you exactly what's expected of you or not, but if he didn't we can hash that out tomorrow, too. I don't have time right now."

I bit back the childish urge to tell Jennifer she was wasn't my boss, that I'd been hired by Nathaniel Prescott and I'd talk to him until he said otherwise. Antagonizing one of the few people I would be spending the foreseeable future with was a bad idea, however, especially if it turned out that "Thane" did intend for her to be my supervisor. Old Mrs. Sutter, my last charge, had regularly screamed epithets at me that would make a sailor blush, and I'd stuck it out with her until her family moved her into a facility; I could cope with Jennifer Prescott's haughty dismissiveness.

When I got back to the playroom, the girls were sitting in front of the television in the corner playing tennis on the PlayStation. In my opinion, actual tennis would be a better use of their time, but the sun was already on the downslope and soon enough it would be time for them to wash up for dinner. A single evening in front of the screen wouldn't hurt them, but I resolved to encourage as many outdoor activities as we could fit in before the weather turned.

"Hi, Molly." Hailey looked away from the screen for a minute. "I'm kicking Liza's ass. Do you want a turn?"

Was she allowed to use language like that? It didn't bother me, but I somehow couldn't imagine Jennifer Prescott finding it amusing. I'd have to clarify language parameters with both Jennifer and Nathaniel. And the phrasing...surely she hadn't meant to make it sound as if she were inviting me to take a turn humiliating her cousin.

"No, thanks. Eye-hand coordination is not my strong suit. I rather think Liza would slay me in any video game." Not that it seemed to me Liza cared much about her score. But the girl was wrapped so tightly inside herself that I couldn't make any real judgment.

"Okay. But I'm going to my room." Hailey chucked Liza on the shoulder. "See ya."

I took the vacated spot on the small couch in front of the television. "Do you want me to play a game with you? It doesn't have to be tennis. Is there one you like better?"

She flipped off the television, which I took as a decided no, and picked up a book.

OVER MRS. VOGEL'S excellent beef stroganoff, Jennifer filled in Prescott on her day with Hailey. He listened with half an ear, answering only when he was asked a direct question, his attention fixed on his daughter. For her part, Liza ignored us all, cutting her food into tiny pieces and chewing each bite thoroughly. I did my best to emulate her so as not to gobble down the savory dish, which was so far beyond anything we ate in my house even in the best of times that I feared making an ass of myself in front of the others.

"Matthew finished his case," Jennifer said, "so he'll be coming tomorrow." She turned to me. "Matthew is my brother. He's a lawyer. He's coming to stay for a few days. We'd thought he wouldn't be here until Thursday, so this is excellent news."

"I'd better re-stock the bourbon." Prescott raised an eyebrow at Jennifer. I couldn't tell whether he was serious, but she laughed.

"Don't be silly. Matthew doesn't drink that much. And if he did, he's perfectly capable of providing for himself. He'll only be here a week."

"A week?" I considered the house's layout. "I thought the third floor was closed off?"

"It's not actually shut off, but we don't use it. He won't stay in the main house. There's a very spacious apartment over the garage. You can see it from the kitchen or from Thane's room."

I remembered Mrs. Vogel driving the Range Rover around the back of the house. So there was a garage. A substantial one, if it had a big apartment above it.

As Mrs. Vogel cleared the plates, Prescott turned his attention to me. "And you, Miss Allworth? Is everything at Rook's Rest to your liking?"

All eyes, including Liza's, swung toward me and I repressed a shudder. So much for avoiding scrutiny.

"Her name is Molly," said Hailey.

Prescott's lips twitched in a half-smile. "So it is."

"It's very nice here," I said, "though I haven't had much chance to explore. I'm hoping Liza and Hailey will show me the grounds while the weather's still nice enough."

"Of course they will." Jennifer touched her daughter's hand. "Won't you, girls?"

"Yes, mom. We'll show you all the good stuff, Molly."

"Tomorrow I'd like to take Liza—and Hailey if she wants to come—into Portland. Is there a car I can use?"

Prescott's dark eyes narrowed. "Why would you want to do that?"

"Is it a problem? I told Liza she could help me pick out cookbooks since she's going to have to eat whatever I make."

His jaw went slack for a second, but he recovered quickly. "I'll take you."

Considering that the trip was meant to help me get close

to Liza, having her father along would be less than ideal. But I could not contradict him in front of the girls.

"That sounds fine. Perhaps after lunch?"

He nodded.

"Also, if you have time tonight, I'd like a word." I held my breath, hoping Jennifer would let it pass. She didn't.

"I told you. I'll go over everything with you in the morning."

"And I appreciate that. I do. But Mr. Prescott is my employer."

"His name is Thane." Hailey scrunched up her face, clearly put out that neither her uncle nor I were observing the rules she had for us.

"You're absolutely right," I said. "But he's not my uncle, so I have to be a bit more formal."

"No." Prescott winked at Hailey before turning back to me. "I don't want to undermine your authority with the girls, Miss Allworth—Molly—but there's no need for formality. Thane will do nicely."

My cheeks heated and I was glad of the dim light. "Thank you."

Mrs. Vogel served fresh fruit and chocolate chip cookies for dessert. This, at least, Liza dug into with enthusiasm.

After dinner, I helped tidy away the dishes, but Mrs. Vogel turned down my offer to wash them.

"I'm staying late tonight because it's your first night. Normally, Henry and I leave between five and six. There will be plenty of time for you to learn the cleaning later."

I almost laughed aloud at the idea of learning to clean. When Mama first got sick, while I still had to finish school, I'd cleaned houses for Aunt Nadya. Even then, no one had had to teach me. No, I'd told Liza the truth when I said I'd been cleaning houses my entire life. Once, when I was about her age and I'd complained about having to make my bed every morning when I was just going to crawl back into it at night, Mama had explained the world to me.

"Only the rich can afford to be slobs," she'd said. "If you're rich, other people pick up after you. And if they don't, if you don't have someone like Nadya to make your bed and empty your wastebaskets, then you're eccentric. When you're poor, no one calls you eccentric. They call you lazy, filthy, and they look at you out of the corners of their eyes as if you might be stealing from them or giving their children diseases."

A night off dishes was a treat, and I left Mrs. Vogel with my thanks and joined the family in the living room. Heavy, overstuffed furniture cluttered the space, but in one corner cushions had been piled on the floor next to a painted chest. Hailey opened the chest and both girls peered inside, shuffling through the contents.

"We always play a board game after we eat," Jennifer explained. "It's been a bit more challenging with Liza, but family time is the most important thing."

I had the absurd urge to laugh. It had never occurred to me that people needed to schedule time with their loved ones. But I supposed it only became an issue when your whole family didn't share a single bathroom.

"Why don't you get the girls started while Miss Allworth and I have our discussion," Nathaniel suggested

Jennifer's smile stiffened into a rictus. Did Prescott realize he'd just undercut her assertion by placing our conversation above the game? But she hesitated only a moment before nodding and removing herself to join the girls.

I followed Prescott across the atrium, his hard soles clicking a rapid tattoo on the parquet floor. He'd set up his office in what must originally have been the ballroom. Two large oriental rugs divided the enormous room into separate spaces. One part had been organized into a seating area with a large leather sofa and a pair of armchairs set around a coffee table. The other half of the room, farther back from the door, had been modernized into a working space. In the dim light I could make out the shape of a heavy desk, steel file drawers, a drafting table, and some ergonomic chairs.

Prescott was a boat builder. I knew that from the packet I'd read on the train. He'd run his business out of both Boston and Portland before his wife's death, but had shifted the whole thing up to Maine when he decided Liza needed to be there.

"Well, Molly." He gestured to the sofa. "Shall we sit?"

I chose one of the big chairs while he took his place catty-corner to me on the couch and flicked on a floor lamp between us.

"It's your show," he said.

I took a deep breath, let it out slowly. "I read the paper-work you sent. It was very bare bones. I'm going to assume, given your history, that you didn't trust that I would stick around, so didn't want to go into too much detail."

For the first time, I saw a hint of actual amusement slide across his face.

"You're very direct."

"I don't believe in wasting time. Your daughter needs help." I squelched down the internal voice calling *phony, phony, phony. You can't help a girl like that, you're not qualified.* "If you expect me to help her, you have to be candid with me about precisely what I'm facing."

All amusement vanished from his features. "What are you accusing me of hiding?"

Step carefully. Vanity has no place in service. "In the packet you sent, it said that your wife died."

His jaw was so tense the words had a hard time escaping. "She did."

"Let me tell you something that's not in my employment file, Mr. Prescott." Despite his earlier remark to appease his niece, he didn't correct the formal address when we were alone. "My father died when I was eight."

Even after all these years, the story was hard to tell. It had been a Saturday morning when they'd found him. Bright and bitterly cold. My mother had made us cinnamon raisin French toast for breakfast, a rare treat, and the whole house smelled sweet and spicy. The police had come to the door as she was bundling Ali into snow pants to take us to the zoo. I pushed away the emotions and stiffened my spine. *Keep it professional.*

"My sister wasn't even a year old. We were living in Queens and my dad was driving a taxi on the night shift. He was killed one night when someone decided that a cab driver made an easy target."

"I'm sorry." The light cast a golden glow across the bottom of his face, but his eyes were dark, shadowed mysteries. He probably wondered why the hired help was bothering him with her history.

"I'm not telling you to get your pity." This was the important part, and I found myself leaning toward him, as if simple proximity could force him to understand. "Sudden death is very different for a child than one she has time to plan for. My mother was diagnosed with inoperable cancer when I was in my senior year of college. My sister was fifteen. We had three months with Mama. Three months to say goodbye, to let her tell us all the things she needed to say. It wasn't enough. No amount of time is ever enough. But it was a completely different experience than what we had with Dad.

"Right now, the single biggest turning point in your daughter's life is her mother's death. Not just the fact of it, but because you changed your whole way of life afterwards. I need to know all I can about that if I'm to help her at all."

He leaned back against the shiny, slightly cracked leather of the couch, his jaw working. Had none of the others asked for this information? Or had all of them, wearing him out with telling the same story over and over to people who never stuck around?

At last he took a deep breath and forcibly relaxed his shoulders. "Marianne was never the strongest woman. She'd give you the shirt off her back, would do absolutely anything for absolutely anyone, but she suffered from depression and would sometimes lock herself into her room for days at a time. After Liza was born, she seemed to get better. As if Liza gave her a focus. I wasn't a great father. I spent a lot of time at work. We were living in Boston, and using this as a summer home, the same way my parents did with me and

Danny. In fact, the playroom was built for me and Danny. So every summer, we'd come up here, Liza, Marianne, and I. That was the time I really got to know my daughter. Danny and Jenn would come up, too, with Hailey.

"Then two years ago, twenty-six months, to be exact, right after we moved back down to Boston for the school year, I got a call from Liza's school saying Marianne hadn't picked up Liza. It wasn't the first time. Marianne was an artist—you'll see her work around the house; she said this place inspired her—and sometimes she'd get caught up in a painting and forget the world. I went by the school and got Liza and brought her home, got her settled in the kitchen with her homework and went to the studio to see what was keeping Marianne."

The stark lines of his face hollowed even further. I knew what was coming, but I was powerless to open my mouth and tell him he didn't need to continue.

"She'd taken a bottle of pills and washed them down with a bottle of bourbon. I don't know where she got the drugs and she didn't even like bourbon. She always said it smelled like turpentine when I drank it."

"What did you tell Liza?"

"What was I supposed to say? I told her mommy had a heart attack. She wasn't old enough to hear the truth."

But she knew it. I felt absolutely certain, though I could not put my finger on why.

"Why did you move here? Your business was in Boston. Wouldn't it have made more sense to stay there?" Rather than here, surrounded by her dead mother's work, where spirits hung in dark corners and a lonely little girl would have no opportunity to make new friends.

"Do you think I didn't try? The true circumstances of my wife's death were in the papers. People talked. Eventually, Liza's classmates found out. They were… less than kind. So I withdrew her from school and tried to homeschool her in Boston. But she kept asking to spend time in her mother's studio. She called it 'spending time with mommy.' I indulged her at first, but she became more and more insistent, more and more reclusive. When she locked herself in there and I had to break the door down, I realized we needed to make a radical change."

"Is that when she started talking about ghosts?"

He nodded.

"So you brought her up here."

"Yes. The Boston au pair backed out once she saw the living conditions. She was a city girl. But even so, this seemed the right place for Liza. Here, she had only happy memories of her mother and me. I always took time in the summer to spend with them when we were at the house. She was speaking less and less, but she seemed happier away from the memories of her mom's death. And then my brother died, and Jenn and Hailey needed a place, so they came up here, too. I thought the company would be good for Liza."

Two lonely, mourning children instead of one. It made a certain kind of sense, though it wasn't the direction I would have chosen.

"You don't agree."

"It's not that." At least, that wasn't all. "Do Jennifer and Hailey know about the ghosts?"

"I had to tell Jenn. I wasn't sure she'd want Hailey exposed to Liza's ideas, but she said she didn't mind. In the long run, I don't know that either Jenn or Liza said a word about spirits to Hailey. It wasn't long after they arrived that Liza quit talking altogether."

I filed that away for later. Had Liza been retreating more every day, or did she suddenly cut herself off because of the new arrivals?

"Did you tell Liza that the ghosts weren't real?"

"Of course!" He glared. "For Christ's sake. You don't think we should play along with her little fantasy?"

Never criticize the choices your employers make. This time, the voice in my head was Sandy's. I had never realized how much alike she and my Aunt Nadya were in their worldview. *They won't thank you for it.*

"I'm not sure what I think. Not yet. But what if the ghosts were just her way of telling you things? What if by telling her you didn't believe her about the ghosts, you were shutting the conversational doorway she was trying to open?"

"You want me to lie to her? To tell her I believe spirits are talking to her?" A muscle popped in his jaw. It was amazing he could even get the words out.

"No." *Never criticize.* But he'd asked for my opinion. I couldn't waste this chance to give it. "I do think, however, that you should to ask her to tell you about them and promise to listen with an open heart. If ghosts are the only thing she wants to talk about, isn't that better than not talking at all?"

He ran a hand through his hair. "I gave her every opportunity, Miss Allworth. I asked her before she stopped talking what she thought her mom wanted, showing up as a ghost. She shrugged and said she didn't know. She was shutting me out long before she quit speaking."

I could hear the weariness in his voice. I thought about watching my mother fade away despite all her efforts to stay with us and tried to imagine how I would feel if she'd done it deliberately. But as sorry as I felt for Nathaniel Prescott, I could help him only by getting close to his daughter.

I took a deep breath. "Please let me take Liza into Portland tomorrow without you. Find an excuse to back out."

"Why would I do that?"

"Because you want me to connect with Liza. And right now, you're not someone she's comfortable talking to."

"I'm her father."

There was so much pain in that statement I almost got up from my chair and went to him. But I was his employee, not his friend.

"I know you want Liza to trust you, to lean on you, but you've just told me she's not ready yet. You have to show her you believe in her before she can believe in you."

"The psychiatrist said exactly the opposite. That she had to trust me because I was showing her the truth, not buying into her fantasy. I realize this sounds cruel, but I think he's a bit more reliable than you are. Sandra Martin said you were hoping to get a degree in child psychology one day, but you've a ways to go. So for the moment I'll follow the advice of the actual expert."

I hadn't expected any other response.

"Still, since I am trying to connect with Liza, do you mind terribly if I take her on my own?"

He grunted. "Fine. Take the Range Rover. Find an excuse that won't make her hate me even more than she already does."

I LEFT the family playing Monopoly and dragged myself up the narrow and creaking staircase. Before I could get ready for bed, however, I had to clean up the bathroom. The girls' stuff was spread out everywhere—I counted four separate shampoos, two conditioners, a giant bucket of makeup, acne cream, and moisturizer, multiple hairbrushes, combs, and hair ties...we definitely needed to have a chat about shared space. The best idea would be to find some totes while we were in town so the girls could bring what they wanted into the bathroom, use it, and take it back to their bedrooms.

After a quick shower, I pulled on my pajamas, wrapped my hair in a peony-covered bath towel, and stuck my head out into the hall. Liza was coming up the stairs and she stopped when she saw me. I touched my tall, flowered terrycloth turban.

"It looks ridiculous, right?"

An actual smile lit her face. I stepped fully into the hallway.

"My hair's a nightmare. I have to wash it, comb out the tangles, and braid it while it's wet or it hatches an evil plan to take over the world. My sister usually does the braiding when she's home because it's hard for me to get the back straight otherwise. Do you want to help?"

A flare of interest, but she shook her head.

"Okay, then. I'll see you in the morning. If you need anything during the night, the door between our rooms is unlocked. You don't have to knock."

She blinked a couple of times, then brushed by me into the bathroom. I heard water running and the scent of mint flowed on the air.

As I sat on the edge of my bed combing out my hair, I heard her get into the shower. A few minutes later—a very few minutes, we were going to have to have a talk about washing behind the ears—the hair dryer came on. And shortly after that, I heard her scamper into her own room.

But her door did not close.

Once my hair was braided into a tight queue, I began to flip through the homeschool packet . Most of my previous charges were under eight or over eighty, so there were a number of subjects I would have to brush up on before seeing to Hailey and Liza's educations.

I looked up when I heard the bathroom door slam. *Hailey.*

This shower was longer. It was still going on when more footsteps came up. Not Jennifer's, these were even and heavy, without the thump of Jennifer's cane.

Prescott. Even in my head, I could not think of him as Thane. It was too intimate, too emotionally fraught.

He stopped in front of Liza's door, tapped on it, and entered. I heard him talking to her—not the words, but the tone, including the rising inflection of questions—and assumed he would soon be gone. But he stayed. I could hear him speaking, more a mumble than anything, and could not resist slipping from my bed to eavesdrop. I tiptoed across the floor, wincing when it squeaked a betrayal, to stand next to the connecting door. Pressing one ear against the wall, I covered the other with my hand and listened.

He was reading aloud, and it took only a few lines for me to recognize the book: *Little Women*. It had been one of my mother's favorites, and I'd read it to Ali night after night while mom dozed in her sickbed, but it seemed an odd choice for Liza being so focused on motherhood. Had it been her decision? Perhaps she thought it might tell her about what it was like to have a mother, but I would have thought she would choose a more modern story. Or maybe it was already here in the house and she merely found it among the old books in the playroom.

If it had not been for Liza's silence, I could have convinced myself in that moment that this was a completely ordinary job. But the longer he read, the longer no childish exclamations interrupted him, the more obvious the wrongness became.

I hung on to the memories of my mother for a few minutes longer, then crept back to bed.

THE FOLLOWING MORNING, Jennifer and I remained at the dining table with coffee and the homeschool packet when the others had gone their separate ways after breakfast. I had more on my mind than coursework, but I hadn't figured out exactly how to approach the issue of either girl's emotional well-being.

"Don't bother Thane with questions about their schooling." Jennifer plunged right into the packet as soon as we were alone. "He doesn't have any idea what they're supposed to learn. I have been teaching the girls since the last tutor left, so if you run into any issues with the work, I can help you. They can take this week off and start up again once my brother leaves."

"I looked the packet over last night and I don't think the workload will be a problem. I do have a few concerns about Liza reading *Heart of Darkness* at twelve, though."

"She doesn't have to." Jennifer waved slender fingers, dismissing my concerns. "Between the two of us women, Molly, we can be frank. Liza is not likely ever to go back to a normal school. Hailey, however, was accepted to boarding school before the accident. They're holding a spot for her for next year, but she has to keep up with the work. *Heart of Darkness* is part of that curriculum. If you need me to grade a paper on it or discuss it while you deal with Liza, just let me know."

I was offended on my own behalf but also on Liza's, so I took a sip of coffee to give myself a moment to modulate my tone. "I can handle it."

I also had reservations about Romeo and Juliet for a child whose mother had killed herself, but Shakespeare came toward the end of the list. If Liza had chosen to speak by then, discussing the tragedy might actually help her. If she remained silent, I'd swap in another play. Either way, I was pretty sure Jennifer didn't want to hear my concerns about

Liza's well-being just at the moment. I could address them later on, when Hailey was secure on her path.

"Hailey is a reluctant student." It was as if Jennifer read my thoughts. "She needs to be motivated. You can't simply tell her she has to do the work, you have to make her want to do it. She likes attention, so if you spend time with her, she'll work hard for you."

"That's good to know." I did not need Sandy or Nadya to tell me to keep my opinion on Hailey's future prospects to myself. How Jennifer expected her to survive in boarding school as a reluctant, attention-seeking student was not my business.

"What is your plan for the school day?"

"I understand the girls don't care for getting up early. That's not unusual, and one of the advantages to home-schooling is that we don't have to force them into traditional class hours. Unless you'd prefer it, given that Hailey is going to start back at a regular school next fall?"

"No, she can adjust when it happens."

"Good. Then I think we can manage with a school day that runs from nine-thirty to three, with a break for lunch. I'd like them to have plenty of activity time in the afternoons, and we should organize planned physical activity from three to four or five. I don't want them stagnating in front of the television when their studies are over."

"I agree." Jennifer poured herself another cup of coffee from the carafe that remained on the table. "The grounds are quite extensive. Once the freeze comes, they can ice skate, too. Have you had thoughts about visual arts?"

"I don't have the skill to teach ceramics or painting. Where did the course list in the packet come from? Because I'm afraid many of those classes I'm simply not capable of teaching."

"Oh, don't worry. Just cross those off. That's the course

catalog for the school Hailey will be going to next year. They require one visual arts class, so I need her to take something this year. Pick out the ones you think you can teach and then let her choose one. We'll order whatever books or supplies you need."

I made a note. Maybe I could get a sense from Liza while we were in town what she would like to study. Despite Jennifer's attitude, I was certain that if I could get her to speak, she had a good chance of returning to a mainstream school.

CHAPTER 4

I drove Liza to town in the big, shiny Range Rover, which had a fancy GPS system in it. Old Mrs. Sutter had never gone anywhere but the doctor, and her family had driven her to those appointments, but before her I'd worked for a family with a pair of rambunctious four-year-olds. The Range Rover was about the same size as their minivan had been, but the wheel beneath my hands hummed with power and the car practically leapt forward with every touch of the gas pedal.

Before we'd left, Prescott had taken me aside and pressed a roll of bills into my hand. "You get her whatever she wants," he said. "And if there's something you need, something you want, get that, too."

I was not up to another fight, so I smiled and nodded. I needed Liza's trust and that could not be bought. No matter how meek one had to be with employers, being a pushover with one's charges always turned out for the worst.

The road unfurled through the trees, wet tarmac shining black like the tongue of a naughty child after a licorice feast. Liza sat stone silent beside me, but her body vibrated more than the smooth ride accounted for. Did she often go into town, or did her father keep her isolated?

"I don't know whether your father told you," I said, "but I grew up in New York City and then Hartford. I've never been this far north. When the driver brought me up to your house, he passed through Portland first so I could get a look at it, but I didn't have a chance to see much. We have plenty of time today, though, so if there's someplace you want to go after the bookstore, you just let me know."

She did not react.

"One place I'd like to visit is the yarn store I saw. The last lady I worked for taught me to knit, and my mom used to crochet. Your aunt wants Hailey to learn some kind of art or craft and fiber arts was on the list of possibilities. Do you think you'd like to learn to work with yarn?"

Liza shrugged.

"I think we should get both knitting needles and crochet hooks," I continued as if she'd replied. You can pick out what kind of yarn and what color you want for yourself and for Hailey. Since she elected not to come with us, she'll just have to use whatever you choose for her."

At that, Liza turned to stare at me. Clearly, she was not used to making decisions for Hailey. I glanced over and winked before focusing again on the road.

I could have spent the whole afternoon at the bookstore and Liza would likely have been perfectly happy. She helped me choose two cookbooks, both filled with pictures for making rather simple meals, then disappeared among the shelves. I found a book on color theory and one on the history of fashion that I thought Hailey might enjoy as part of her studies, then went to look for Liza.

She had seated herself cross-legged on the carpeted floor in the New Age/Religion/Spirituality section and was deeply entranced in the book in her lap.

"Liza?"

She did not raise her head, so I squatted next to her. "What did you find?"

Her lips thinned and her eyes narrowed in challenge. In that moment, she looked more wholly present—and more like her father—than I had seen her. She flipped up the book so I could see the cover: *Hauntings: Communicating With Unquiet Spirits* by Delilah Holt.

Nathaniel Prescott would lose his mind if I bought such a book, and Liza clearly knew it.

I stalled. "May I look?"

She handed over the book and I flipped through it, considering my options. Prescott had as much as told me not to encourage Liza's beliefs. But he'd offered a huge bounty if I could get her to speak. If I sided with him on this issue, I risked losing not only that bounty, but any chance of helping Liza.

I closed the book, wincing at the rather lurid cover. Liza had folded her arms across her chest and was waiting for my decision.

"I'll tell you what," I said. "This is pretty gruesome stuff. I'll buy it, because I know you really want it, but only on the condition that we read it together. It stays in my room, not yours, okay?"

Her features pinched up a little, but she nodded. Then she laid one hand on my arm and, when I looked at her, put a finger over her lips.

"You don't want me to tell anyone about this?"

Her dark eyes bore into mine.

"Honey, I have to tell your dad. We can't hide it from him. But I won't tell your aunt or your cousin."

Her hand squeezed on my arm and her skinny chest heaved as she sucked in breaths. If she'd been psychologically capable of speech, she would have spoken then.

"You don't want to upset him."

A nod.

"It's okay. I'll talk to him. He won't be angry at you." No, his fury would have another focus. Luckily for me, I was his last resort—he was as desperate for my help as I was for his job.

~

LIZA and I lost track of time in the yarn store and as we returned to Rook's Rest the sun was dying a bloody death in the western sky. As we headed to the house with our bags, a silver SUV pulled up. A tall blond man jumped out of the driver's seat and strode over.

"Let me." He took the bag of books from my hand and the yarn shop bag from Liza. "Hi, Liza, how you doing?" He opened the front door and held it for us. "I'm Matthew Brahms."

"Molly Allworth."

"Uncle Matt!" Hailey barreled down the stairs. "You're here!"

Matt swung his niece up and around. "How you doin', Sprite?"

The door to the ballroom office popped open and Nathaniel stuck his head out, black brows beetling and a scowl on his sharp features. Whatever he was working on, he wasn't pleased to be interrupted and I had no intention of adding to the aggravation by mentioning the ghost book. I'd broach the topic when he was more relaxed.

"Matthew," he said. "You made it."

"Of course. I just didn't get out of town as early as I thought."

"Where is it?" Hailey frowned at his hands, empty now

that he had set down my packages. "You said you were bringing me something!"

"It's in the car. But I told you it's for both you and Liza."

"Of course." She danced on her tiptoes and Matt winked at her.

"You guys want to come help me get it out of the car?"

"Sure!"

I figured he'd brought them a sled or the like. I couldn't have been more wrong. A second later, Hailey squealed and a small, black form leapt from the SUV, and dashed for the front door.

"Grab him!" Matthew yelled.

I reached out and the little black dog jumped into my arms, all quivering muscles, pointy ears, and bulging eyes.

"He's so cute!" Hailey took the pup from me. "Thanks, Uncle Matt."

"What were you thinking, Matthew?" Jennifer's question cut through her daughter's excitement. "This is Thane's house. He might not want a dog in it."

Prescott shrugged. "We've always had dogs. I figured I'd get one eventually. Though I must admit I was thinking more along the lines of a Lab or shepherd."

"This will only make the transition to boarding school more difficult for Hailey."

"I told you I'm not going to boarding school, mom."

"We are not having this conversation right now. Please tell me that dog is at least housebroken?"

"He is. He's almost three years old and fully trained. Or as fully trained as a Boston terrier is likely to get—he's a little excitable and sometimes he loses control. I got him from a client. His name's Rocky and as you can see he loves people. His crate and leash and food and toys are in the truck."

Liza stroked the little dog's smooth fur as Hailey cuddled him.

"He's going to sleep with me," Hailey said.

"If he's crate trained, he'll sleep in the kitchen," Prescott corrected her. "Otherwise he'll become crate trained. Dogs don't sleep in people beds."

"Uncle Thane—"

"No."

Hailey huffed. "Come on, Liza, let's take him up to the playroom."

"Take him out first," I said. "Get his leash from your uncle and give him a nice walk. He's had too much excitement to settle down." I'd been peed on by Old Mrs. Sutter's poodle every time company came to the house. I didn't know a whole lot about dogs, but I knew about excitement.

Matthew took the girls to the SUV to get the leash and walk the pup.

"I'm sorry, Thane." She turned accusing eyes on her brother. "I had no idea he was planning this."

Prescott choked on what might have been a laugh. "That was pretty clear. Don't worry about it. Matt means well, he's just impulsive. Always has been. I really was planning to get Liza a dog before you and Hailey decided to move in. The company will be good for her."

Of course, Liza having a dog and Liza and her cousin sharing one were two completely different things. Why couldn't Prescott, Jennifer, or Matt foresee the problems that would arise from such an arrangement? If Hailey had her way, the dog would go off with her and her mother whenever they moved out, which would be one more loss for Liza. If Jennifer sent Hailey off to school when she left and the dog stayed with Liza, it would be Hailey who suffered.

I wanted to yell at them that it wasn't merely Matt who was shortsighted, but I knew better. Leashing my tongue, I picked up the bags Matt had abandoned on the bottom step and carried them up to my room. At least maybe the novelty of the dog would distract Liza from the ghost book.

DINNER WITH MATT was considerably more fun than it had been without him. He kept all of us entertained with stories from life at court, making his career seem an endless parade of laughs. I suspected he was exaggerating some of the tales if not making them up out of whole cloth, but I appreciated the effort.

After a game of Jenga, Prescott took the girls out to walk Rocky. Jennifer went along, leaving me alone with her brother. Matt poured himself a glass of bourbon from the bar table in the corner of the living room.

"Anything for you?"

"No, thanks." I should go upstairs, but it would be rude to leave the man alone. He settled onto the couch and stretched his legs out in front of him.

"So, Molly Allworth, tell me about yourself. Jenn tells me you're from Hartford. This has to be a big change."

"It is. But it's beautiful here."

He grimaced. "Wait until it snows. Winter is brutal."

"Town's not that far away."

"No. But unless it's an emergency, you can't get there. The Prescotts used this as a summer house for several generations. Jenn said Thane bought a snowmobile when he decided to move here year round, but that's just in case he needs to go for a doctor. You can't exactly run into town for groceries on it."

"So this is the first year anyone's actually lived here?" My stomach sank. It was one thing for me to be out of my depth —I was used to that on a job—but the families I worked for were supposed to have their systems in place when I got there.

"Well, not the first. But the first in a while. Changing your mind about sticking it out?"

"Not at all."

"Your family's not concerned about you?"

"You sound as if this is the end of the known universe. It's only Maine."

He gave me a rueful grin. "Sorry. That's the New Yorker in me. It feels a bit like the end of the known universe. And I do worry about Jenn and Hailey being here, so I thought your family might feel the same."

"That's kind of you. But no, my parents are long dead and my sister's in college in the Midwest. She's not happy that the phone may go out and she won't be able to reach me, but I wouldn't say she was worried. If anything, I worry about her, not the other way around."

The words were out before I thought about it. Matt Brahms was remarkably easy to talk to. Probably part of his legal training. He also had a quick mind. I would have to watch myself with him or I'd spill the negative opinions that occasionally snuck into my head. This was an aspect of living in I hadn't considered. I was accustomed to going home after a twelve-hour shift and chatting with my relatives without fear of censure.

"So you've been her mother. No wonder another child without a mom lured you in." There was no appropriate response, so I remained silent. Matt studied the amber liquid in his glass as if it held all the answers to the universe. "Are you going to fix my niece?"

"I don't think she's broken. But if you mean am I going to help her regain her voice, I hope so."

"Oh, bravo. Nicely said." The words had bite, but he smiled as he spoke.

"I say what I mean."

"Do you?"

Well, no. Once upon a time, maybe. But I'd grown up, grown out of that kind of incautious outburst. Learned restraint.

He laughed when I did not answer. "I thought not. To be fair, you wouldn't last long if you did. I adore my sister, but she wouldn't tolerate an outspoken tutor. She doesn't take well to being contradicted."

"And yet you brought a dog. You had to know she wouldn't approve."

He grinned. "Of course I did. But I'm her brother. She wouldn't turn on me any more than she'd turn on Thane."

He was trying to tell me something, but I couldn't determine what. To tread carefully with Jennifer? I'd figured that much out on my own, though it was sweet of him to try to protect me.

AFTER A TUSSLE over who got to pet the dog last, I ushered the girls upstairs. Hailey opted to use her mother's bathroom while Liza showered in the shared one, so it all went quickly enough. I had hoped that Liza would have forgotten about the ghost book in the excitement over the dog and her uncle's arrival, but instead of going to her own room when she was through in the bathroom, she slipped into mine.

"What's up?" I knew what she wanted, but she needed to learn to ask, even if she would not use words. Anger flashed over her sharp features, but she was almost as practiced at hiding her resentment as I was. She glanced around until she saw the shopping bags tucked neatly up against the wardrobe and then went over, pulled out the book, and held it out to me.

"Not tonight." I took the book and tapped it against my knee. Her eyes followed the move instead of meeting mine. "I haven't had a chance to talk to your dad about it, and I don't want to start until he knows what we're doing."

She crossed her arms, cocked her head, and glared.

"Sorry. We'll do it tomorrow. Is he coming up to read to you tonight?"

Her head snapped back. Had I blundered? Was the reading with her father a secret? "I won't say anything about it to anyone if you don't want. I heard him last night and thought I might corner him if he was coming up tonight and mention the new book to him."

She didn't respond. I would have to put the book out of her reach, though it would be hard. At twelve, she was nearly my height; any place I could get to, so could she. With anything else, I would have trusted her. She didn't seem the type of child to sneak around, but the book was clearly too important to leave within easy reach.

"Good. So that's the plan. We can start reading tomorrow if you like. Your aunt says you don't have to start official school until after your uncle Matt leaves, so if you'd like to read together for an hour or so during the day, we can do that. That way it won't interfere with your time with your father."

She nodded slowly and, with a long look at the book in my hand, left the room. Instead of going to clean up myself, I propped the pillows up against the heavy wooden headboard and leaned back against them to see what the book had to say.

It began with a brief history of séances, spiritualism, and mediumship, then dove into the story of John D. Fox and his family in Hydesville, New York. Fox's was the earliest studied case of intentional conversation with a disturbed spirit in America. Fox had two daughters, fifteen and eleven.

So close to Hailey and Liza that my fingers tingled and my neck prickled reading about them.

> *Working out a code of tapping and knocking, the family began to speak with their unwelcome resident using a single knock for yes and two for no. Then they developed an alphabet to use with him for more complex communication. At first, the ghost spoke only to the daughters, but eventually he was convinced to communicate with others, including residents of the town, to whom he told secrets no living being should know about their lives.*
>
> *He was, he said, a peddler who had been brutally murdered by one of the house's previous occupants. According to some sources, bones found buried in the basement of the Foxes' home proved the claims of the ghost, though other sources refute the claim.*
>
> *As an adult, Margaret Fox claimed that she and her sister had made up the haunting, conspiring to frighten their mother by rapping, cracking their knuckles, and dropping objects to simulate the ghost communicating with them. However, skeptics—including the third, older sister, who had left the family by the time they moved into the haunted home—were never able to recreate the sounds heard by family, friends, and investigators of the time, even using the methods Margaret said she and Catherine had used.*
>
> *And Margaret herself, in later years, retracted her claim, saying she had made it only to take the spotlight off herself.*

What had I agreed to, promising Liza I would read this with her? I glanced over at the door separating my room from hers and was dismayed to notice that the space beneath was dark. I considered going back downstairs but could not imagine what excuse I would give to Matt and Jennifer for needing to speak to Prescott so soon. Absorbed in the book, I'd missed my chance to tell him I'd bought it.

CHAPTER 5

Given my choice of reading material, it was perhaps no surprise that my mother should visit me that night. She had done so often in the dreams that consumed the early weeks after her death, reminding me of my responsibilities and generally making a pain of herself. In those days, she never showed the ravages of illness. Her eyes were bright and piercing, her skin unlined, dusky and beautiful, and her indomitable will clear in every sharp movement.

The Em Allworth who arrived that night, however, was a different woman. She hovered over Liza's bed rather than mine, and when I tried to call to her she laughed at me in a hollow, screeching tone I'd never heard. Her hair, loose, oily, and wild, flew about her head in a filthy halo. Her hands had become the gaunt claws I recognized from her last days. But perhaps worst of all, black mirrors hid her warm brown eyes so that when she looked at me I saw not my mother's love but a shrouded, heartless reflection of myself.

She reached for Liza and I knew, with the surety of a dream, that the moment those claws made contact with the child's fair skin I would lose her. Would lose them both. That the tiny, frail flame of vitality left in Liza would transfer itself to the horror that had once been my mother.

I flung myself at the mother-thing and reached for her arm. I half expected mist and was shocked when I grabbed bone that snapped in my hands and cut the skin of my fingers, while the rest of her dissolved into a cloud of choking smoke. Surrounded by the bitter, ashy remnants of my own mother, I could see nothing. The smoke smothered me and just as I became convinced I had breathed my last, I woke, choking on my own cries.

Liza stood over my bed, looking down at me, and I let out an undignified yelp at the sight of her pale skin and dark eyes hanging there in the darkness.

My pulse was racing and my heart hammered unsteadily, so it took a moment for me to find my voice. And when it came, I still felt ash in my throat.

"What's going on, Liza?"

She blinked.

"Are you okay?"

Her eyes narrowed and she studied me. The silence that frustrated me during the day was far stranger and more oppressive in the dark room.

"Did I wake you?"

She nodded.

"I'm sorry. It was just a nightmare."

Which, of course, it had been. No matter what Liza believed, dead mothers did not come calling on their children after midnight.

MY ALARM BEAT like a jackhammer against my aching head mere seconds after I closed my eyes. Desperate for coffee, I made my way downstairs to find Matt and Prescott bent over a stack of papers.

"I told you she wouldn't go for it," said Matt.

Prescott grunted. They both glanced up at my entrance and Matt sprang to his feet.

"Good morning, Molly." He squinted. "Or is it? You don't look as if you got much sleep."

"I'm fine. It's just a new place. You know how it is."

"No he doesn't." Prescott slid the papers into a manila folder. "Matt's never met a stranger and he's utterly comfortable wherever you put him."

Matt shrugged. "Guilty as charged."

"Are the girls up yet?" I poured a mug of coffee, drank a long draught and refilled it. Food could wait. Coffee could not.

"Not likely." Matt grinned. "You have to drag Hailey out of bed kicking and screaming. Her mother was like that as a kid, too."

"Has anyone walked Rocky?"

"I did," Prescott assured me. "He's in the kitchen until breakfast is cleared."

The dog situation still troubled me, but there was nothing to be done about it at the moment and I had more immediate problems. "Mr. Prescott, can you spare me a few minutes this morning?"

Matt's blonde eyebrows practically disappeared beneath the hair that flopped over his forehead. "Mr. Prescott? That's a mouthful, Thane, really."

"I did tell her to call me Thane," Prescott said.

I took a sip of my coffee. "I assumed that was for the children. Since Hailey was so insistent."

"*Hailey* was?"

I laughed at Matt's shocked expression and some of the

night's gloom faded. "She was quite the little hostess the first night I was here."

Matt looked to Prescott for confirmation and he shrugged. "I wasn't paying any attention."

Matt's eyes twinkled. "Clearly."

Prescott rose. "I'll be in the office. Molly, come in whenever it's convenient. Don't knock. I wear earbuds most of the time and won't hear you."

"He's not a morning person," Matt said when Prescott had left and I'd filled a bowl with yogurt and fruit. "Or an afternoon or evening person, to be completely honest. He was always the more withdrawn, but between Marianne's death and Danny's, he's gotten even grimmer. It can't be easy for Liza living here with him."

"Always? You've known the Prescott family for a long time?"

"Oh, sure. We grew up together. Jenn dated Thane for a while in high school."

"Awkward for family reunions." The words were out before I thought about them and Matt laughed.

"It might have been if either of them had cared, but they didn't. They were just passing the time and the minute they went off to college, Jenn found someone new."

"Daniel Prescott."

"Oh, no. Danny came later." He leaned back and craned his neck to look out the door toward the stair. Satisfied that he would not be overheard, he lowered his voice. "Jen married Danny when Hailey was almost five. She never told the family who Hailey's father was."

I tried to wrap my mind around the idea. Pregnancy happened, of course, but Jennifer Prescott was so stiff and buttoned up and starched that I had a hard time imagining her getting carried away to such an extent. But maybe the starch had come later, maybe she felt she needed to make up for the wildness of her youth. Births, like deaths, could reverse a person's path.

"And now she's a single mother again." The papers I'd been given were no more detailed with regard to Daniel Prescott's death than they had been about Marianne's.

"Yes. There was a car accident. Apparently, a bee became trapped inside with him and Jenn. Danny had a lot of allergies, including to bee stings. The car had every safety measure, so Jenn only shattered her knee. Danny died from anaphylaxis, not the accident itself."

"That's terrible. No wonder she decided to take a year away. She's lucky they could come here."

He made a noncommittal sound, then grinned. "But they're all lucky you're here. And so am I. I suspect I'll be visiting often."

My cheeks heated and I could hear my aunt's voice in my head: *keep your head down and don't cause a fuss*. I rather imagined flirting with Jennifer Prescott's brother qualified for causing a fuss.

BEFORE BEARDING Prescott in the office, I darted upstairs, the ancient steps betraying my progress through moans and creaks. I knew he was the type who would not be content to rely on my description of the book. He would want to examine it for himself before coming to any kind of decision. I had secreted it between my mattress and box spring, but once I removed it I faced another problem. Should anyone see me carrying it downstairs, I would be breaking my promise to Liza. I grabbed my carryall tote and stuffed a few random items in with the book as camouflage.

Just as well, for as I stepped into the hall, Hailey confronted me.

"What were you doing in my room last night?"

"What do you mean?" For a second, in the dim hallway light, my mind flashed to the nightmare of my dying mother standing over Liza's bed and I had to repress a shudder.

"I was awake. I saw you."

"Hailey, I wasn't in your room. Why would I be?"

"I don't know. That's why I asked."

"You must have been dreaming."

Her mouth set in a flat, defiant line. "I wasn't dreaming. I saw you."

"Let's try this. What was I doing when you saw me?"

For the first time, Hailey hesitated. She shrank away slightly. "You were in the corner. Kind of…swaying."

No wonder she was upset. Such a dream would certainly have freaked me out. "That's terrible. I can understand why you'd be angry, but stop and think for a second. Does that sound like something I would do?"

She shrugged. "Maybe."

"Hailey, be honest."

"Okay, maybe it was a dream. But you stay out of my room."

"No problem. I promise, I won't spy on you in your sleep."

On my way down the stairs, I wondered whether Hailey, who had been through her own share of loss, had ever seen a therapist. Dream interpretation was far from my forte—I'd had only a brief introduction to it in my psych classes—but I imagined a specialist would have interesting things to say about the image of the swaying woman.

With the office door in front of me, I took a deep breath and let it out slowly, reorganizing my thoughts to focus on Liza instead of Hailey.

Despite the sun shining outside, the ballroom was little brighter than it had been the night before. Heavy, emerald velvet drapes at each of the tall windows kept the space gloomy. On the far side of the room, a trio of long-necked chrome floor lamps, shockingly modern and out of place now that they were lit, illuminated Nathaniel's desk. He did not look up even when I stepped into his spotlight.

Cords trailed down from his ears, bright white against the tan of his skin. I reached out to touch his shoulder, then hesitated. I never touched my employers. My clients, old and young, absolutely. Physical contact was part of the job. But they were not the ones paying the bills. I clenched my fingers together for a moment, then waved a hand through his field of vision. He pulled the earbuds from his ears and glanced up at me.

"Ah, Miss Allworth. What can I do for you?" He gestured to one of the web-backed office chairs and I seated myself.

"I need to talk to you about yesterday's trip to Portland."

"What happened?" His eyes narrowed and his voice roughened.

"Nothing. Nothing like that, I mean. Nothing bad. I think Liza had a pretty good time, though it's hard to tell because I haven't spent enough time with her yet to read her moods."

"So then why this meeting?"

"She wanted to buy this." I drew the book from my bag and handed it to him.

He scanned the cover, sharp lips curling into a scowl of distaste.

"And you agreed?" Ice flaked from the words and prickled the skin of my cheeks. "Did I not make myself perfectly clear on this subject? I will not have you encouraging my daughter's descent into superstition!" He yanked open a drawer, shoved the book inside, and slammed it shut. "If you cannot follow that simple rule, you can pack your bags and Henry will drive you to the bus this afternoon."

Cold sweat beaded along my hairline at the threat, but indignation heated my blood and tinged my words with acid though I tried to keep it out. "I did not say I was planning to encourage her. But in my opinion, pretending she doesn't have these beliefs is a mistake. You can't ignore them. You have to help her face them."

"And that New Age tripe, that's how you plan to help her face her delusions?"

"It's not the method I'd have chosen, but since she picked it I'm willing to go along. I told her when I agreed to buy it that she couldn't read it without me, that we'd do it together, and only if you allow it."

He leaned back the chair tilting beneath his weight as he bounced thoughtfully for a few seconds. "So you abdicated. 'Sure, honey, I'll do what you want, but only if mean old dad says it's okay?'"

I flushed. I hadn't considered that aspect of the conversation.

"All right," he said at last. He retrieved the book from its drawer and handed it to me. "But I'll expect a report after every session."

"You could join us." The words popped out of their own accord and as soon as I heard them I wished I could suck them back in. His disdain and disbelief would not help Liza.

"No," he said slowly and I had the uncomfortable feeling that he could read my reservations in my face. "I'll leave that to you. At least for now."

WHEN I LEFT THE OFFICE, I heard Hailey chattering in the dining room, with Matt's deep voice providing counterpoint. I peeked inside and saw that Liza, too, was eating. Her eyes met mine then shifted to the bag on my shoulder. I tapped the bag and nodded. A little twitch of her lips showed me she understood.

Before I could make my escape, Matt caught sight of me.

"Molly! Come in! Did you get a chance to talk to Thane?"

"I did."

"Great. Then you're free. Since the sun's out and it's warm, or warm for Maine in October, we've been making plans to show you around the property. Right, girls?"

Both girls nodded but Hailey's petulant expression didn't lighten. She hadn't gotten over her dream yet. Fair enough, I hadn't entirely gotten over my own.

"I'd love to see the property. How big is it?"

"Officially, about eight acres. But it's backed by greenbelt so there are no neighbors to speak of."

"The isolation drove our last tutor crazy." Hailey put in. "Stark, raving bonkers."

"Hailey—" Matt tried to interrupt.

"She attacked Uncle Thane," the girl continued. "Went after him with a knife."

I clamped my lips shut over the gasp trying to escape. The file Sandy had given me contained no such incident. Had he concealed it from her? Or had she left it out to make the job more attractive to me? After all, if the money was good for me, it was good for her, too. And supplying a caregiver for a difficult case would raise her profile. How many people were manipulating the situation at Rook's Rest to their own ends?

"Are you going to go nuts?" asked Hailey.

"Hailey! For God's sake!"

I ignored Matt's outburst. "I sincerely doubt it. I'm a pretty stable person. If I get lonely, I'll write letters to my family."

Matt seized on the change of subject. "Do you have a big family?"

"Big enough. My little sister is at college in Missouri. I need to write to her at least once a week anyway, or she worries, especially since the cell coverage here is so bad."

"What's she studying?" asked Matt.

"Pre-med." A little swell of pride washed through me at the words. My job, this job, would make Ali's dream come true.

"You just have one sister?" asked Hailey.

"She's my only sibling. But my Aunt Nadya and my Uncle Bo live in Hartford and they'll want to hear from me. And their children, Milosh and Walther. We're very close."

"Russian?" asked Matt.

"Romani. Eastern European descent, though that side of the family has been here for several generations."

Hailey straightened up in her seat. "You're a *Gypsy*?"

"Rom," I corrected her. "Gypsy is fine when it's used within the community, but it's considered rude for outsiders to use it. It comes from 'Egyptian' and only the uneducated believe that the Rom came from Egypt. Plus, here in the U.S., when you feel you've been cheated, you say you've been 'gypped,' which isn't a kind thing to say about a whole group of people. You can see why the Rom don't like being called Gypsies."

She shrugged off my explanation. "Did Uncle Thane know that when he hired you?"

"I can't imagine why it should matter." In fact, I had a good idea of why it mattered. Ali's background was helping her pay for college. She'd won a scholarship for an essay she'd written on being Romani and the grandchild of a Holocaust survivor. Plus, checking the "other" box for ethnicity on her application put her into a different category. She hadn't wanted to do it—we were, after all, Caucasian—but the way I saw it, that box was about whether you were a persecuted minority, and we absolutely were. After all, every positive has a negative, and I was always careful never to reveal my heritage to my elderly clients. No matter how liberal they appeared, sooner or later when they discovered my heritage, they accused me of stealing from them. I'd even been fired over it once.

"Does my mom know?"

"You'll have to ask her."

Hailey looked at her uncle. "I think we should keep it a secret, don't you, Uncle Matt?"

Matt's blue eyes clouded over. "Not a bad idea, Hails. You know your mom can be a bit rigid in her ideas."

Hailey nodded and my head pounded. Minutes earlier, I'd have sworn the girl wanted me gone. Now she seemed to be my ally. I shrugged off the discomfort as much as I could and suggested we all meet in the atrium in half an hour to go exploring.

I RETURNED the book to its hiding place, pulled my warm fleece sweatshirt from its drawer, and made sure the girls had made at least a token attempt at tidying the bathroom. They had not, which made me a few minutes late to meet them downstairs. Cleaning up was not on the curriculum advised by Hailey's boarding school, but it was absolutely on my educational agenda.

"Come on!" Hailey called as she saw me at the top of the stairs. "Let's go!" Rocky danced impatiently at the end of his leash and Matt grinned. Liza kept her head bent, her hands in the pockets of her Barbour jacket. Whether she wanted to go outside or not was anyone's guess.

"Over that way is the pond," Matt said as our little party rambled around the side of the house toward the expanse of the back yard. "This time of year, the ducks and geese are leaving because in November it freezes hard. It's great for ice skating then, but not so good for the birds. In the summer, though, you can come down with a loaf of bread and the ducks will take pieces right out of your hand."

"You'll like that, Rocky, won't you?" Hailey said. The little dog, intently sniffing at a hole in the grass, paid her no mind.

"In that direction, there's an old structure and a covered over swimming pool. The kids aren't allowed near it because it's not safe."

"Why'd you have to tell her that?" Hailey grimaced.

"Am I lying?"

"No, but—"

"No buts. That building was already shuttered when I was your age. It was just as tempting and just as forbidden for me as it is for you. And it's twice as dangerous now as it was then."

Down an overgrown flagstone path littered with leaves and weeds I could see the outline of a little brick cottage. "Why hasn't anyone torn it down if it's been out of use for so long?"

Matt glanced at Liza, who had wandered a few feet from us and was crouched down, poking at something on the ground. He lowered his voice. "Marianne loved swimming. Thane planned to renovate the whole pool section of the property for her. He got a new pool in—the old one was completely trashed, irreparable—and was in the process of bringing architects out to bid on turning the pool house into a guest cottage and studio as well when she…died."

A studio and guest cottage. Even though they already had the apartment over the garage. Perhaps it was meant to be a place for Marianne to live without entirely leaving her husband and child? Marital problems could explain both Liza's emotional distress—children sensed such things no matter how hard their parents tried to hide them—and Nathaniel's guilt.

"Let's show Molly the graveyard!"

"Graveyard?"

"It's totally awesome." Hailey was off, Rocky tripping along beside her, leaving the rest of us to follow.

"It's not as bad as it sounds," Matt assured me. "It's a small private cemetery. We used to dare each other to camp out in it overnight as kids. Even Linda, Thane's mom, couldn't remember anyone ever being buried there. The graves go back to the mid 19th century, but the most recent one with an actual date is 1937."

A low, wrought-iron fence enclosed the cluster of grave-stones. Knee-high weeds and saplings choked away the grass and whatever flowers had once been planted there, but at least half of the stones remained upright. A thick canopy of old growth trees blocked the sun from much of the plot. Many of their leaves had fallen over the years, forming a thick, moldering carpet over the earth and weeds. A cold breath passed over my face and slipped beneath the neck of my sweatshirt. Goosebumps chased across my skin.

"What are those?" I drew Matt's attention to two lonely crosses, one of stone, one of iron, set outside the fence's boundary. Liza had paused beside the stone cross and was running her fingers over its top.

"They have no markings, or at least none we ever found as kids. I always assumed they were family members who for some reason or other couldn't be buried in consecrated ground."

Eternity separate from their families. It was the cruelest thing I could imagine.

Hailey walked through the small gate and brushed leaves from a stone cherub perched on a low granite platform. "This is my favorite," she called. "Come see!"

Before I could move, however, Rocky let out a yelp, broke free of Hailey's hold, and darted out the open gate and into the woods. Was it my imagination, or were his eyes bulging more than usual? The hair along his back had gone up and although I took off after him as soon as I realized what had happened, I doubted he'd let me catch him. I had neither his speed nor his agility over the stony, uneven ground. What would happen if he escaped entirely? I cursed Matt under my breath as I ran. He'd brought the dog to two children with no experience in taking care of a pet.

"Rocky!" Around me, I heard my own shout from the others like a perverse echo. Deeper, higher, fainter, sharper. "Rocky!"

How would we find one small, mostly black dog in the massive, tangled, treacherous woods? And what would happen if we could not? Fear struck, cold and sharp—could either Liza or Hailey handle another loss just now?

"Rocky!" Something skittered through the leaves nearby, but when I peered in that direction, nothing moved. "Come here, Rocky. I have cookies for you. Who's a good boy? Who wants a treat? Come on, Rocky!"

Minutes dragged, time crawling like one of the slugs I crushed underfoot as I forced my way deeper into the wild, but at last I heard Matt shout in triumph.

"I have him!"

I leaned against the vine-ribboned trunk of an ancient oak for a minute, the sweet weakness of relief leaving me lightheaded and faintly nauseous, before heading back the way I'd come. When I emerged into the light, the others were waiting. Matt held Rocky in his arms while both girls fussed over him.

"I think this little guy has had enough adventure for one day," Matt said when I reached them. "He seems fine, but we should probably go inside."

"I've certainly had enough excitement," I agreed.

"I know I shouldn't have let go of him." Hailey blinked

away a tear. "But I didn't expect him to pull so hard. I wonder what he was chasing."

Had Rocky been chasing something? Certainly, that made the most sense. But with the fur along his spine raised and his stubby tail flat to his rear, he'd appeared to be running for his life.

CHAPTER 6

he afternoon passed in a blur of video games, puzzles, and an illicit game of gin rummy played for pennies. Matt was a good companion and a far better match for Hailey's skills than either Liza or I were. I would be sorry when it came time for him to leave.

Hailey monopolized dinner with a dramatic recounting of Rocky's escape and the ensuing search. Jenn tutted and shook her head, practically shaking her finger at her brother when the tale wound down.

"Who knows what manner of parasite that dog could pick up running loose in the woods? Did you check him for ticks when he came in?"

"He's on a monthly preventative, Jenn. But I suppose I could check Hailey…" Matt grabbed his niece and knuckled her head while she shrieked in protest. Even Jennifer cracked a smile.

"So I take it you didn't see much of the property, then," Prescott said. "It's hardly at its best just now, but even so I am sure you'll find it appealing."

I thought about the dilapidated pool house and what a harsh reminder it must be for him. With his resources, I might have sold the place off and moved out of the area altogether. But maybe he felt Liza needed the connection. My original imaginings of English country estates had long disappeared, but surely there was more to the land than that decaying structure and the grim little cemetery.

"I'll go out again tomorrow. I saw a mailbox at the bottom of the drive when I arrived and I have to write to my family. If I walk down there and stick them in, will the postman pick them up?"

"He will. It's about a half a mile down to the end of the private road, though."

"That's fine. I like to walk."

"She did see the graveyard," Hailey put in.

Prescott choked out a laugh. "That place. Your uncle was terrified of it at your age, you know."

"Hey! No ruining my tough guy image!"

Jennifer shook her head. "You were all impossible." She rested a fine-boned hand on her brother's larger one and leaned around him to speak to her daughter.

"They'd take sleeping bags out there in the summer and spend the night. The next day, Danny and Thane would come back all shaky and frightened and refuse to tell me what happened. When I would finally pry the stories out of Matthew, they gave me nightmares."

"None of it was real," Prescott broken in when Jennifer took a breath. "Danny and I would make scary noises and toss pebbles and stuff. We even rigged sheets and ropes and twigs in the trees. One of us would grab Matt and run away while the other would take it all down, then pretend to have been scared off, too. It didn't occur to us that Matt would tell Jenn and she'd tell her parents. We got in more trouble for that than for anything else we ever did. I couldn't sit down for a week."

"Only fair," Matt said.

"So it was all fake?" Hailey wrinkled her nose. "You never saw anything?"

"Of course they didn't," Jennifer scoffed. "There's nothing to see. Just some moldy old graves."

"We should get sleeping bags and stay out there! Wouldn't that be cool, Liza?"

"You most certainly will not." Prescott's tone would have stopped me dead, but Hailey opened her mouth to argue.

"It's the wrong time of year for that," I put in. "Plus, there's no comfortable spot for a sleeping bag. It's totally overgrown. In the spring, we can weed an area, cut back the overgrowth. Put in a bit of work and you'll have a place to lie down once the weather warms up."

With an exaggerated sigh, Hailey agreed. I glanced over and found Prescott's dark eyes studying me. I hoped I hadn't overstepped, but denying a teenager would only make her plan more appealing. Forcing her to wait and work for what she wanted was both easier and, in most cases, a more effective deterrent.

AFTER DINNER, I returned to my room while the others played their board game. Liza had not pressed me about the book, but I knew it was only a matter of time and I wanted to read as far ahead as possible before plunging in with her. Having made the case for the "openness" of children to hauntings with the Fox family, the author moved into the meat of her topic: how to contact the dead.

Several methods of communicating with the spirits have developed since the days of the Fox family's rudimentary knocking alphabet. The most commonly used of these is the Ouija board. While many consider these to be harmless toys, they are descended from the original "talking boards" or "spirit boards" and not to be used by the inexperienced.

A memory struck, so strong and sudden that I had to close my eyes and remind myself to breathe. It was a soupy, sweaty day not long after we'd moved to Hartford. My aunt had sprained her ankle, so she was home with Ali while mama and I went out for a day on our own. We'd gone to the park and ridden the carousel, mama side by side with me. I wanted to go faster, faster, but my mount bobbed slowly up and down while my legs stuck to the sides. The carousel stopped and I peeled myself off the horse. We wandered by an artist doing caricatures and a man making balloon animals, then stopped for an ice cream. Near the big white ice cream truck sat a woman with a red scarf tied over her hair. Tinkling golden bells hung from the scarf and long, sparkling earrings dangled from her ears. A flowing skirt and embroidered peasant blouse completed the outfit. She sat on a tall stool, with two more stools in front of her. One held a deck of cards and a board with writing on it, the other was empty. Waiting for a customer.

I knew what she was. We'd seen women like that in New York. This was the kind of woman my father referred to as a "carnival queen," a fake Roma. One lived on our block, a woman I'd heard speaking in a lilting, melodic cadence when clients arrived at her door, but who shooed me away in a harsh, discordant accent when I approached her. The sign in her window said *Psychic Readings by Sultana.*

The woman noticed me watching her and winked as a

man walked up. She smiled up at him for a second, then her head snapped back sharply, as if she'd been slapped. The man sat on the empty stool and laid a hand on the little wooden pointer that sat atop the board. I was watching, fascinated, when my mother grabbed my shoulder, spun me toward her, and thrust the swirl of chocolate and vanilla into my hands.

"Let's go."

"What's she doing?" I asked.

"Calling the spirits," said my mother.

"She can't really do that, can she? She's just a carnival queen, isn't she?" Besides, no one called ghosts under the sun's bright heat, with joggers passing by and bums begging for change. That couldn't be right.

"The board is not a toy." My mother leaned down and stared into my eyes. The day disappeared and my ice cream dripped unheeded down my hand. The scent of her apple shampoo tickled my nose. "You never, ever use the board. Do you understand me? Never. When you call out to the other side, you don't know what may come."

Unable to speak, I nodded. If the spirits could be called, right out in public without ceremony or magic, could I talk to my father? Could I ask him how to cope with this strange life we had assumed in Connecticut? Would he advise me?

But I never found out. Long after the summer's heat had died and winter's snow prevented trips to the park, long after the ice cream trucks went into hibernation, my mother's warning had stayed with me.

I forced my attention away from the memories and back to the book. Ms. Holt discussed the history of the talking board—a mercifully dry topic—and the ways one might be used. She advocated a minimum of two people with their fingers on the planchette because a single user was too apt to be fooled by her own subconscious. She also recommended having an independent observer ask control questions to which only she knew the answers in order to test efficacy.

The recommendation seemed sensible, making science out of the magic of my childhood. Quickly, however, the author descended back into what Prescott had characterized as New Age tripe.

> *For those who are truly open to the spirit world, a simple sheet of paper with letters and numbers will suffice. Any token can be used as a planchette, especially an object of particular significance to the one who has passed. A barrette, a favorite photograph carried near the heart, a wedding ring, or even a money clip can serve as a pointer. The important thing with a talking board, as with any form of spiritual communication, is that the caller be open and willing. The ritual use of the formal board and planchette merely oils the hinges of the door to the other side, making it easier to open. With practice, the sensation of the planchette beneath the medium's fingers becomes a trigger, a way of inducing a trance without effort.*

A floorboard creaked in the hall. I snapped the book shut and stuffed it under my pillow. Neither of the girls were likely to drop in without knocking, but I was not prepared to answer Hailey's questions should she ask about my choice of reading material. I counted to five, then ten, but heard nothing more. The house was old. Almost every stair, every square foot of the second floor creaked or squeaked or moaned when pressed. How could anyone, even a slight, skinny child like Liza, traverse the hallway without making a sound?

And yet, the longer I lay there, the more convinced I became that someone stood outside my door. It had to be Hailey, taking revenge for being frightened in her dream and, more seriously, for having admitted that fright to me. If I hoped to maintain my authority, I could not let her get over on me, even in her own head. I could not hope to make it to the door unheard, but neither could Hailey escape undetected. I eased my legs over the side of the bed and darted to the door as quickly and quietly as possible, all the time composing the confrontation in my head.

No one was there.

A shudder shook me and goosebumps crawled over my skin like an army of spiders. I'd been so sure I'd heard a footfall. Old houses made noises—it had taken me months to get used to the way Mrs. Sutter's house settled at night when I'd worked the night shift—but the sound that had pulled me from my reading had been sharp and distinct. And then there was the clutch in my heart, the certainty that a listener waited on the other side of my door.

"Get over it," I said aloud, letting the familiar sound of my own voice fill the space

I HEARD the girls come upstairs and prepare for bed, followed by the adults, but that strange, single footfall was not repeated. Working in care, you learn to sleep anywhere, anytime you can—I suppose it's a bit like the military. One week you might be working days, the next nights. A nap here and there can save your sanity.

Still, despite the darkness of the room, the comfort of the thick mattress and fluffy duvet, sleep proved elusive. Every tiny noise startled me from my restless doze, but at least I was not visited by the specter of my cancer-riddled mother.

At six, I gave up trying to sleep. I scribbled postcards to my sister and my aunt, dressed, and went downstairs. I roused Rocky from his crate, snapped on his leash and headed out for the mailbox.

I'd hoped to see the property but was frustrated yet again. A thick mist rose from the earth. It clung to my clothes and skin and curtained off the road mere feet in front of me. As long as I could see the path beneath my feet, however, I would claim this time for myself.

Rocky whined and pulled at his leash, trying to turn back for the house the minute he'd finished his business. *Too bad, buster. We're out and we're staying out.* Once I made my intentions clear, he resigned himself to his fate and trotted beside me, stopping occasionally to bury his flat face in the wet grass.

By the time I clipped my postcards into the mailbox door and raised the flag, the heavy fog had soaked through my sweatshirt and jeans. The sun struggled to rise, a pale ball strangled by thick haze, but it did nothing to reduce the biting chill. If I intended to make this walk on a regular basis —as I would have to do after weather cut off the cell access and my ability to text my sister—I would have to get more winter layers. Maybe I'd make myself some leg warmers while teaching the girls knitting and crochet.

As I approached the house, a woman's voice floated out of the mist. I couldn't tell precisely where it was coming from, so I stopped short.

"I told you she's just balking temporarily. There won't be a problem."

A deep voice murmured indistinctly.

"Don't be ridiculous. It's just a phase. She'll get over it."

I was almost certain the woman was Jennifer Prescott. Who else could it be? Mrs. Vogel's voice was raspier. We had no guests and no one had driven past me as I trudged back toward the house.

The man mumbled again and the woman laughed. Definitely Jennifer. Why was she standing outside in the foul weather? And who was she talking to?

"You worry about your own part," she said, "I'll handle mine."

I had already deduced that she would be the most obstructive part of this particular job. If she believed I'd overheard something I shouldn't have, she'd find a way to get rid of me before I could complete my contract. She had Prescott's ear. All she had to do was say that I was being inappropriate with the girls or not teaching them what I should and I'd be gone, all my dreams of providing for myself and Ali up in smoke.

If I could hear her, however, she could also hear me. Pitching my voice slightly louder than necessary, I praised Rocky effusively. Since he'd done nothing to merit such acclaim, he looked up at me with confusion in his bulging eyes. I counted to fifty, then moved forward far more slowly than my normal pace, giving Jennifer plenty of time to get out of my path. Apparently she did, for I saw no sign of her or her mysterious companion as I approached the house.

I was feeding Rocky in his crate when Mrs. Vogel arrived.

"You're up early." For the first time, I heard approval in her voice.

"He's had a walk and food. He should be okay for a couple of hours. But I got rather wetter than I expected, so I am going to run up and change."

"Bring your things down and I'll put them in the dryer. They don't need a wash, do they?"

"No. Thank you." What a luxury. In most of my jobs I was responsible for everyone's laundry.

Upstairs, I peeled off my jeans, socks, and sweatshirt and changed into a virtually identical outfit. In eldercare, the uniform was simple: scrubs. I had nine pairs. Most of my clients liked the scrubs because they created a clear class division. Working with children was different. The parents wanted you to look neat but not uniformed. The strange, liminal position of being below the children in status but above them in authority was reflected in choosing appropriate outfits. When I expressed my concerns to Sandy about how to dress for living in, she'd assured me jeans would be fine so long as my shirts and sweaters did not have slogans on them or holes in the elbows.

I stepped into the hall, wet bundle in hand, and the door to Prescott's room opened.

"Miss Allworth. Good morning. Have you been out already?"

I touched my wet hair. I hadn't bothered to take it down and re-braid it when I returned from the walk. "I took Rocky to the mailbox."

"How very industrious of you."

Was he making fun of me? His dry tone gave no clue.

"Have you and Jenn come up with a suitable plan of study for the girls?"

Involuntarily, I glanced down the hall toward Jennifer's room before answering. Did Prescott know that she didn't believe his daughter would ever go back to a normal school? I couldn't imagine he agreed—he was far too focused on getting Liza to speak to have given up hope.

"Pretty much. I won't know how the schedule works until we actually get into the process, and Jennifer doesn't think they need to start until after Matt leaves. As long as that's okay with you?"

His foot hesitated on the stair for just a moment. "Far be it from me to contradict Jenn," he said with a touch of bitterness, "or to inconvenience Matt."

I couldn't help myself. As we reached the bottom stair, I laid my hand on his sleeve. His forearm radiated warmth through fingers still chilled from my walk. "I am here for Liza. Jennifer and Matt are not my concern. If you want Liza to start work this morning after breakfast, that's what will happen."

He stared down at my hand resting on his arm and I snatched it away. An expression I could not interpret flitted across his face and he blew out a breath.

"No. When Matt leaves will be fine."

CHAPTER 7

Since Matt was leaving on Sunday, on Saturday night we all went out to dinner in Portland. This saved me from having to make dinner, since Mrs. Vogel had weekends off and those were my designated cooking days. She'd left a casserole for Sunday and I'd managed tuna salad and egg salad with fruit and cheese for lunch, but I wasn't up to preparing a real meal for Matt.

Not that he would ever have said anything negative. He'd been flirting lightly all week. He didn't mean anything by it— I'd caught him flirting occasionally with Mrs. Vogel, though not as intently as he did with me. He never pressured me, and it was impossible to know what he'd do if I took him up on his implicit offers, but the admiration warmed me and I'd have hated to lose it by showcasing my lack of cooking skills.

The restaurant we went to was basically a pizza joint, which suited both my taste and my wardrobe, but with a farm-to-table atmosphere that brought it above the norm. With a view right out over the bay and a big wood-fired oven, it was clearly a favorite of both girls. Liza smiled like a perfectly normal child as she studied the menu.

At home, Prescott and Jennifer usually sat at the head and foot of the dining table, but here we were at a round table with Liza between me and her father and Matt on my other side.

"So I guess on Monday you become the evil teacher," Matt said. He leaned around me and waved a piece of pizza in Liza's face. "Now you, young lady, you be nice to your teacher."

She grinned and opened her mouth to snap off a bite of the pizza. I was not actually worried about Liza. Aside from her disinclination to speak, I expected her to be a hard worker and an above-average student.

"You, too, Hailey," Matt said. "Do your best."

"Have you talked about what you'll do for visual arts?" Jennifer asked.

I hadn't. I'd been having a good time, taking Rocky out for walks, flirting with Matt, feeling almost like one of the family. Even the ghost book had gotten short shrift; I'd managed only a few pages a night once I'd read what I'd assigned myself to be ready for the girls' classes to begin. But Liza, similarly exhausted by all Matt's games, hadn't requested that we begin it yet. I was definitely slacking in my duties. Luckily, I'd decided for Hailey the day I took Liza to the bookstore.

"Fashion and fiber arts," I said with more confidence than I felt.

"Fashion?" A laugh lurked beneath Matt's question.

At the same time, Hailey crowed. "Fashion—that's so cool! That counts as school?"

"The *history* of fashion. The fiber arts will be handwork—knitting and crocheting. Liza and I already picked out yarn."

"Knitting is very practical." Jennifer chuckled. "Hailey, I think your uncle would love a handmade present for Christmas."

His eyes widened. "No, no. I don't need anything."

I'd figured the woman was bloodthirsty, but sticking her brother with a beginner's scarf or hat that he'd have to wear cheerfully any time he saw his niece was truly devilish. "That's a great idea," I said.

MATT HAD LEFT IMMEDIATELY after breakfast. Although he promised to write to all of us, even me, once he got back to New York, I knew before Jennifer's "you always say that and you never do" that it was an empty vow. He was, after all, a lawyer, and likely very busy. He might spare a phone call to his sister or the occasional email, but sitting down and writing a letter by hand to the hired help? Not likely, even after the flirtation.

A sharp drop in temperature reflected the drop in spirits, and a cold gray rain forestalled any plans to trek the grounds. The air tasted like snow, sharp and bitter, and the radiators along the walls burped and rumbled louder than usual.

Jennifer suggested hide and seek. "We played all the time growing up. There are great nooks and crannies on the third floor. Thane has a service in once a month to clean and they were here two weeks ago, so it shouldn't be terribly dusty."

I'd given up hide and seek after about seven years old. Liza and Hailey were twelve and fourteen.

"The third floor is creepy cool," Hailey said in response to my dubious expression. "One of Uncle Thane's relatives was into hunting and there's a ton of taxidermied dead stuff."

We mounted the steps and Hailey explained their rules to me. The game was as much tag as anything, which explained not only why it was more fun for older children, but also why they had to play on the third floor, not the second. I could only imagine how the thunder of running footsteps overhead would affect Prescott's work.

At the end of the hall, above the master suite, a library with glass-fronted shelves housed a massive pool table that had to have been constructed inside the room. The rest of the furniture—a grouping of chairs around the granite-faced fireplace and a leather-topped desk with matching chair by the far window—was equally substantial. Heavy green curtains, matching the baize of the pool table and the shade of the banker's lamp on the desk, closed the room off from the world outside. An enormous oriental rug in shades of bark and jade completed the picture of gentlemanly privilege.

The room above mine and Liza's was the feminine equivalent to the library and its sheer size explained the phenomenon of attached rooms I'd noticed on my arrival. My room and Liza's would likely have been a single room like this one, divided at some point in the house's history. The furnishings here were lighter, both in weight and color, with pale, buttery yellow and rich gold dominating. Age-stained creamy wallpaper above the wainscoting was printed with faded tea roses and twining vines.

In the final room, a mahogany embroidery frame with a padded stool took up one corner,. A number of chairs and a loveseat, less dainty than the ones in the rose room, surrounded a cotton rug. A small blue wooden chest and an ancient rocking horse sat beneath the window that faced the front yard. If the main floor was what guests saw, the formal entertainment space, and this floor was for family, this must have been the nursery. From my history of education classes, as well as the books I'd read in English, I knew that parents of a certain class—and there was no doubt that the owners of this home had belonged to that class—did not spend much time with their children. It cheered me to see the toy chest and rocking horse sharing space with the embroidery frame.

The taxidermy, on the other hand…A fox mid-jump greeted us at the top of the stairs, and he was far from alone. Where the walls of the first two stories held art of all kinds, up here dead things floated overhead and peered from pedestals in corners. Fish gleamed dully, raccoons held up meticulously articulated fingers, glass eyes in mounted deer heads followed our every move. And in the library, a giant moose head menaced from his superior position above the fireplace.

"Isn't it awesome?" Hailey spun around, her flying arms taking in the gruesome display.

No, I could think of many, many words to describe the taxidermy, from appalling to wretched, but in no way awe-inspiring. "I plead the fifth."

She laughed. "Okay, why don't you and Liza hide first and I'll find you?" Taking our assent for granted, she plopped down on the floor and hid her face in the corner next to a stuffed wildcat to start counting.

Liza shrugged and made for the library, so I took the room with the rose wallpaper. The spindly-legged desk offered no cover, but I could squeeze in between the miniature overstuffed sofa and the wall.

The maid service had done a decent job, but a musty odor arose nonetheless from the flocked fabric of the sofa and I had to suppress a sneeze.

"Ready or not, here I come!" Hailey sang out. Her footsteps thundered down the hall and directly into the room where I hid. I hadn't been particularly stealthy. The space was too cramped for me to move without giving myself away, so I could not see where she was searching.

Another sneeze snuck up on me and as it seized me,

Hailey pounced. I squeezed out the other side of the sofa and ran halfheartedly for the door, but she grabbed me.

"Gotcha! Now we can look for Liza. Next time, you're it."

We found Liza hidden behind the thick velvet drapes in the library. It wasn't the most imaginative spot, but she'd scrunched herself into such a small corner, behind the chair for the desk, that if we hadn't pulled the curtains all the way back we might have missed her. Of course, the problem with wedging herself in so tightly was that there was no escape when Hailey reached out to tag her.

I took my turn hiding my eyes and counting to twenty. I tried to listen to which direction they went, but the creaks came from everywhere. They must have split up. I checked the room where I had hidden first—it would be the easiest to eliminate. A stand with a few delicate vases on it stood in the corner—I knew what it was called, but the word wouldn't come to me—and it butted up against a chair with a quilt draped over it. I didn't think Liza was small enough to fit beneath the chair, but I wasn't taking any chances.

I had no luck finding either girl in the rose room, so I switched over to what I had come to think of as the "family" room. I tipped the rocking horse and watched it sway smoothly back and forth. Up close, I could see it had been hand carved and hand painted and again I was warmed by its presence. My eye fell on the chest. The hasp was shut, but not locked, and I popped the lid open. Liza lay curled up inside and I reared back. I'd half expected her, but her pale face staring up at me out of that wooden box— A picture of that unadorned iron cross standing over just such a wooden box flashed into my imagination but my mind shied from the comparison. I tagged her and then helped her climb out.

She led me back to the library. Together we opened the bottom cabinets beneath the glass-fronted bookshelves. I almost laughed when I saw an ancient cut crystal decanter of brown liquor and a set of glasses in one cabinet. How many years had it stood there waiting for the return of a lifestyle long out of date? On the desk, a stuffed rat had been turned into a pen holder. Unlike the decanter, that had *never* been in fashion. I twitched away from it and Liza grinned. She was accustomed to the grim displays and I was willing to endure them to see her smile. She pointed downwards and gestured that we should take the desk from opposite sides in case Hailey was in the kneehole.

She was, but not alone. I peeked under the desk and found myself confronted by a blotch-bodied serpent winding around a heavy branch.

I screamed.

Hailey laughed and took off and Liza and I chased her down the hall.

WE PLAYED a few more rounds before the rumbling of Hailey's stomach gave away her hiding spot and we broke for lunch. The weather called for grilled cheese, and the girls and I were in the kitchen slathering butter on bread and layering it with cheese when Jennifer joined us, followed closely by Prescott.

"Grilled cheese?" I plopped two sandwiches into the pan and began putting a third together. "Liza, wash those carrots before you put them on the table. I don't care what the bag says, they need it."

"No, thank you," Jennifer said. "I just came to be certain you had everything you needed to start classes tomorrow. I'm going into town this afternoon if you don't."

"I had a thought about that when we were on the third floor." I addressed both of them. The lessons might be Jennifer's purview, but the house was Prescott's. "Can we move the desks up to the room with the rose wallpaper? It's not that the playroom isn't adequate, because it absolutely is, but studies show that people learn better in dedicated educational environments. We are all creatures of habit, and getting in the habit of working a particular space is helpful. Plus, if we wanted to have a more comfortable spot for crocheting, there's the old nursery across the hall. It has sofas. That way we could keep all the schoolwork contained to the third floor."

"That's not a bad idea. The playroom is full of distractions. Thane?"

"First and most importantly," he said, "those sandwiches smell amazing. Do you mind making me one?"

"Not at all." I was being paid to serve them on the weekends, but I appreciated his kindness in asking rather than ordering. I laid a plate in front of each of the girls and then started a new pan with food for Prescott and me.

"I'll move the desks after lunch," he said. "I have to do a few other things around here anyway. There are three dead bulbs in the front hall chandelier, which means it's time to change them all. I've been putting it off because it means dragging the big ladder in from the shed, but Mrs. V has been making noises about having Henry do it." He shuddered. "Henry Vogel on a ladder—my insurance would cancel me if they knew I allowed such recklessness."

Having driven with the wizened little man, I had to agree.

"Mom, can I come to town with you? I want to go to the stationery store and look at school supplies."

"Of course, sweetie. Liza, would you like to come?"

Liza shook her head.

"You're okay on fountain pen ink?" Prescott asked.

A flush stained Liza's cheeks as she nodded. Embarrassment over using such an old fashioned instrument in the age of computers, or something else?

~

THE PLAYROOM DESKS did not suit the rest of the house's decor and if I'd needed further proof that Nathaniel Prescott hoped to send his daughter back to a regular school, the cheap laminate desks would do it. They set the definition for temporary.

Prescott and I each took one side of the desks and carried them upstairs, while Liza grabbed the whiteboard. I would not put holes in the wall to hang the whiteboard as it had been put up in the playroom, but the étagère—that was the word for that shelving unit!—had a central spot that would do nicely to prop it up once I removed the fancy vases to a safer place.

"You choose the one you want," I said to Liza once her father had gone downstairs. "We'll bring in the study materials and put your things where you want them and Hailey's can go on the other desk."

I had decided to use the small writing table with its spindly legs as the teacher's desk. It looked frail, but so did most of the room's pieces, and they'd lasted at least a hundred years, so with a little luck I wouldn't damage it. I moved the vases out of range of clumsy schoolchildren—or their teacher—and brought all the books Jennifer had gathered for Hailey and Liza's schooling up from the playroom. It took a few trips, but with Liza's help it went fairly quickly.

Once I started separating out the subjects in the packet, however, I realized I would need more space than the tiny writing table afforded. I'd seen a metal filing cabinet in the corner of the playroom, so I went down to see whether I could carry it myself.

The file cabinet was rusty and heavy. It was also, I discovered as I looked to see whether I could remove either of the drawers for carrying purposes, filled with papers. Overfilled, even. They were all old, and a film of greasy dust rose from the cabinet as I poked through them. Maybe Prescott would let me throw them out. They'd probably lost all importance long before he was born.

I'd seen him setting up the enormous ladder in the front hall. The chandelier, one of those frivolities my aunt always referred to in disgust as a "dust catcher," had at least a dozen bulbs, but cast relatively little light. It hung from a heavy steel chain in the ceiling and nothing on God's earth could have persuaded me to climb up to clean or change it. My aunt had some kind of contraption she used for lights in the big houses she cleaned with their vaulted ceilings and she still complained about them nonstop. I had no intention of bothering Prescott while he was atop the ladder; the file cabinet could wait.

I went back up to the new schoolroom to finish setting up as best I could and was surprised to find Liza gone. I hadn't heard her while I was in the playroom—had she managed to get down to the second floor to her own room without me noticing? It was possible, she moved like mist.

"Liza?" Of course there was no answer. I ran down the stairs and poked my head into her room. No luck, and the bathroom door stood wide open. A completely irrational fear slid through me, weakening my knees. She could not be in real danger here. And surely whatever psychological block she had against speaking would not prevent her from crying out if she were in pain.

"Liza?"

The door to the family room was closed. Maybe she was playing in there and hadn't heard me? I put my hand on the cut glass knob and a cold shock ripped up my arm and paralyzed my lungs. My feet were bolted in the place by spikes of ice and the muscles in my wrist and arm fused into a single, solid block. Forcing myself to breathe, I gritted my teeth, focused all my strength on breaking that block, and wrenched the door open.

The cold was a living thing, biting and clawing at my skin and scratching at my eyes until they bled tears. Through the haze, I saw Liza sitting on the window seat, her knees drawn up to her chest with one hand on the glass.

"Liza!" The word came out a strangled moan, the sound that wakes you when you scream in a dream. Liza did not turn from the window. I pushed my way into the room, as much swimming as walking, for the freezing air had a thick, viscous quality. Each inch took tremendous effort and Liza seemed farther away with every step I took toward her.

And then a tremendous crash shook the house, Liza's head whipped around, the cold abated, and reality snapped back into place.

CHAPTER 8

It took less than a second for me to realize that the crash had to have been made by Prescott falling from the ladder. Unwilling to leave Liza alone in that strange room, I grabbed her hand and dashed into the hall and down the stairs.

I reached the ground floor slightly ahead of Liza, and considerably more out of breath. Nathaniel lay half under the enormous ladder, which had fallen sideways so that its top rested in the corner next to the front door while the bottom remained in the center of the hall beneath the chandelier.

My heart sank at his pale face and closed eyes, but then he blinked and cursed. When his gaze caught on his daughter, he snapped his mouth closed.

She tried to push past me but I held her back. "Hold on, sweetheart, we don't want to make it worse. Move slowly and don't disturb anything."

"Don't worry," Nathaniel assured her, "nothing's broken. Well, nothing but the ladder, which I probably should have checked out before climbing on it." He hitched himself into a sitting position, back against the wall.

"We should call an ambulance anyway." I peered into his eyes. Hi pupils appeared the same size, so if we were lucky, the fall had just knocked the air out of him for a moment. "You took a hard fall. I'd be more comfortable if they examined you."

"Don't be silly." He tried to stand, sucked in a breath, and sank back down onto the floor. "Okay, let me revise that. Nothing's broken, but I may have cracked a rib."

"I'll call 911."

"No. Seriously. It's not bad, and we can get there faster driving. It takes emergency services ages to get all the way out here."

Liza knelt next to her father and held his hand. He raised her fingers to his face and kissed her knuckles.

"I'm fine, baby. Nothing's going to happen to me. Promise."

My mother had told me the same thing, almost word for word, numerous times after my father's death. And she'd kept her promise for years. I hoped Nathaniel managed the same. But as I glanced at the wreckage of the ladder, my eye caught on the top step. At the sight of the perfectly aligned breaks with barely a splinter from the pressure of his foot, doubt slipped through me.

"If we're going to the hospital," I told Liza, "you should go on upstairs and get a book or whatever you want to keep you busy. You could bring the yarn and hook we bought in town, and I can start teaching you crochet, if you like. You know how emergency rooms are. They take forever to tell you nothing's wrong."

She frowned and studied me for a long minute, as if trying to discern a falsehood in the simple statement, before darting up the steps.

"Look at this," I said the minute she was out of earshot. I pointed to the clean breaks on the top step. The second step had behaved as one might expect, shattering into a thousand splinters from the impact of his weight landing on it when the first one gave way. That top step, however, had separated cleanly from the sides of the ladder. Only about a quarter of an inch at the surface looked broken. The rest had almost certainly been sawn.

"What the—" he broke off when Liza clattered back down the steps, bag in hand. His eyes flicked to mine.

The conversation was not over.

He shoved the ladder away and eased himself to his feet, but when he tried to take a step, he had to bite back another curse. "Sprained ankle," he said. "Molly, can you bring the truck around? I probably shouldn't drive."

"Of course. You're okay, though?"

"Absolutely. I know what a break feels like. Did it once mucking about on a boat. This is just a sprain, and a mild one at that."

I left him with Liza and jogged out to the garage where I found a beat up crew cab pickup with the keys in the ignition. I pulled it around to the front of the house and followed Nathaniel's directions to the hospital.

Once the nurse heard what had happened, she called for someone to whisk Nathaniel away almost immediately, leaving me in the waiting room with the silent Liza. Under the fluorescent lights, her face was even paler than usual and my heart squeezed. She was so alone. Even when mama was dying, Ali and I had each other. And though at times my father's extended family—Nadya and Bo, Milosh and Walther—felt oppressive, they provided a safety net I didn't see in Jennifer Prescott.

"He'll be fine." Unable to resist, I touched her hair in sympathy. "A little banged up, but broken bones mend." Her forehead was cool and clammy. Might she be in shock? I was ashamed not to have considered it. "Are you feeling okay? You're not sick or feeling faint or weak or dizzy? You don't want a nurse to examine you?"

She shook her head and dug the yarn and hook she'd brought out of her satchel and handed them to me. As I showed her the steps of chainless foundation single crochet, her brow wrinkled and she bit her lip. On the pretext of correcting her yarn tension, I laid my hands over hers. Her bony fingers stiffened and she narrowed those dark eyes at me, unfooled. But that was okay. I didn't mind if she knew I cared about her.

Liza was a quick study had put six rows onto the scarf she was making by the time a nurse came out to speak with us. Liza stilled at her appearance and drew even further into herself. The woman smiled as she approached, seeming completely oblivious to the child's fear.

"You must be Liza." She took the chair next to Liza's. "You look just like your daddy. He's going to be absolutely fine. I don't want you to worry. Just a few bumps and bruises. Nothing worse than you might do to yourself in gymnastics class or playing on a trampoline."

I asked for details.

"Sprained ankle. He's being measured for crutches right now. And a bruised rib. It's not fractured, so no need to worry about a lung puncture or anything, but it will hurt nonetheless. They're icing it right now to take down some of the swelling and they'll send him home with pain medication."

A sprained ankle and a bruised rib. I could almost be annoyed at how perfectly he'd diagnosed himself were I not so relieved for Liza's sake.

~

THE EMERGENCY ROOM staff had been efficient, but nonetheless the setting sun had draped the land in a charcoal shroud by the time I dropped Prescott and Liza in front of the house. I pulled the truck into the garage and then sat in the front seat for a long moment, trying to expel the tension from my body. In that silent darkness, my mind returned to the sabotaged ladder. Could I have been mistaken? Everything had happened so fast. We'd been upstairs, then there was the crash, and… but that line of thought reminded me of the peculiar incident on the third floor. With distance, it had taken on the patina of a dream or fairy tale. Yet I could not dismiss it so easily. I could not discuss it with Prescott or Jennifer, either, or I'd certainly lose my place. No one wanted a crazy woman taking care of their children, especially when those children faced psychological problems of their own.

I could call Nadya or Ali. Out here, there was a single bar of cell service. I tapped the phone against my hand several times, considering. I could not burden Ali with this, however. Besides, she retained enough of my mother's superstitious nature to insist I leave immediately, regardless of the benefit to both of us if I stayed on. Nadya, on the other hand, would scoff and tell me I was imagining things. I did not need to call her to hear her opinion; it lived, homunculus-like, in the back of my head. I tucked the phone back into my pocket and forced myself to leave the peace and safety of the truck.

The thick darkness of night, so much deeper than evening in the city, weighed on me as I trudged from the garage to the house. Even the door seemed heavier than usual. But once inside, the scent of Mrs. Vogel's excellent casserole greeted me. A fire crackled cheerfully in the library grate, chasing away the chill.

"Thanks for starting dinner," I said to Jennifer, who stood in the kitchen slicing scallions for salad. "And the fire's a lovely touch for a gloomy day."

"That was Hailey's idea. We used the broken bits of the ladder for kindling. Knowing Thane, he'd insist on fixing the damned thing if we didn't burn it before he got home. It's high time he bought a new one. Aluminum or the like. Something wood boring bugs won't get into."

She'd burned the ladder. All the evidence that Prescott's fall was not an accident was gone. Not that I harbored any illusions about miraculously finding fingerprints or DNA or a big red arrow pointing at who'd tampered with it, but I felt its loss, as must Prescott.

"Thane seems fine, thank goodness." Jennifer scraped the scallions into the salad bowl. "He said the doctors found nothing serious. Is that right? He's not hiding a concussion or torn tendon to be macho, is he?"

"No, he was very lucky."

She laughed, and a bitter edge sharpened the sound to steel. "He always has been."

The man had lost his wife and brother and was unable to communicate with the daughter he clearly loved. He didn't seem particularly lucky to me, but I kept my mouth shut.

Dinner was a subdued affair. Even Hailey, after a short burst of chatter about the cool notebook she'd found, slid into silence.

"I'm sorry." Prescott ran a hand through his hair. "I don't think I'm up for game night. I have a client coming in the morning. I need to be in better shape than I am at the moment."

"Of course," said Jennifer.

Liza patted her father's hand, but then she flicked her eyes at me and I repressed a shudder. The time had come to open the book of spirits.

Hailey announced her plan to take advantage of the lack of board game time to catch up on recorded episodes of General Hospital with her mother.

"I'm a little embarrassed to admit to watching it," Jennifer admitted while she helped me clear the dishes. "I became addicted when I was her age. My mother and I used to sit down every day when I got home from school and have a snack while we tuned into the goings-on in Port Charles. Hailey and I took up the tradition when she was in sixth grade. Her school day ended later than mine did, so we got in the habit of recording it and binging several episodes at a time whenever we had time."

"That sounds lovely. Why be embarrassed?"

"It's hardly highbrow."

I shrugged. "She'll miss that time with you when she goes off to boarding school. You can worry about highbrow then."

For once, I appeared to have struck the perfect note, because she smiled at me. "I never thought of that."

Hailey and Jennifer would be watching television in the playroom, so I suggested Liza ready herself for bed and promised to meet her in her room once I'd tidied the kitchen. My original idea to use the old nursery for reading and handwork lessons had flown like a bat in the night after the strange event preceding Prescott's fall. No way was I discussing communicating with the dead in that room. Had I the right to board up the door entirely, I would have done so without hesitation. As it was, I resolved simply to ignore it, never to enter there again.

Once I heard the shower running, I ran upstairs and retrieved the book from beneath my mattress before returning to my work in the kitchen. I had the uncomfortable belief that Liza saw—and heard—more than she ought, and with only the flimsy connecting door between rooms she could easily discern the hiding spot. It was not that I didn't trust her, but youth imparted heightened importance to everyday occurrences, and the book might prove irresistible.

Liza made a great clatter leaving the bathroom, which I took as a summons. I wiped my hands on the dishcloth, gave the counter a final swipe, and gathered my things to go join her.

"Shall I read to you or will you read to me?" I held the book out as I settled into the wide wingback chair beside her bed. I knew the answer, of course, but I intended to treat her as if eventual speech was a foregone conclusion. She pointed at me and then sat cross-legged, tilting slightly toward me, avid interest animating her face. I began with the introduction.

We like to believe that tales of haunting were the product of gullible and overwrought Victorian imaginations, that we are too sensible, too intelligent for such fancies. And it is certainly true that stories of visitations from the dead have decreased in the Information Age. But it is equally true that the noise of culture has increased.

The dead are not loud. Our ancestors noticed the sudden, minute changes in temperature, the small objects out of place, the shifting play of impossible shadows. We, occupied with earbuds and smartphones and two jobs before dinner, ignore such clues. We are consumed by busyness.

The dead are not busy. And we ignore them at our peril.

As I read, the room closed in, shadows clustering and reaching for us until it seemed the walls themselves leaned forward, listening. So clear, so sure was the sense of presence that I could not help sneaking glances toward the dusky, darkened corners, searching for whoever might stand there. But we were alone.

I stopped at the end of the chapter about the Fox sisters

and their rapping, knocking, alphabetic communication with the spirit of the murdered peddler. Liza's big eyes implored me to continue, but I closed the book, resolute.

"No more tonight. We can continue tomorrow or the next day, whenever we get the time."

Her mouth set, but I ignored the expression. If she wanted to protest, she would need to use words.

"You don't have to go to sleep yet if you don't want to. You can join your aunt and cousin in the playroom or read to yourself or you and I can play a game."

She shrugged, retreating into sullenness.

"Okay, then. I'm going to shower, but if you want me later I'll be right next door."

CHAPTER 9

I slept surprisingly well and resented the ring of my alarm all too early in the morning. The radiator was popping and cracking, but the room still held a chill and I curled under the heavy duvet for several minutes before forcing myself up. Dragging myself down the stairs in search of coffee, I found Prescott alone, his crutches propped against the table. His dark face had a gray cast and tiny lines spread around his mouth and eyes. He was not taking the pain medication the doctor had sent home.

"Can I pour you some coffee?" I offered.

"No, thanks. And please don't hover. Mrs. Vogel's done entirely enough of that this morning. I had to send her to take Rocky out just to get her to leave me be."

"How are you feeling?"

"I'm fine." The emphasis on the last word made it clear that he was tired of answering the question.

I lowered my voice. "I'm sorry Hailey and Jennifer burned the ladder."

He pressed two fingers to the center of his forehead. "Rotten luck. I didn't expect to get anything particular from it, but I'd have liked to have it to show the police in case anything else happens."

"You still have no idea who might have done it?"

He shook his head. "I did send Henry to buy a lock for the shed, though. Told him I thought some things had gone missing. We've never had cause to lock it in the past but if someone's sneaking onto the property, there's a tremendous amount of damage they could do in there. It's been months since I used the ladder, though, so I have no idea when it was tampered with. And I do wonder in the light of day whether we didn't imagine it. Maybe it was rot or beetles and not deliberate mischief."

I didn't believe it, but I had no proof. Before I could voice my suspicions, however, distinctive squeak and thump of Jennifer's tread on the steps put an end to the conversation.

"Are you ready to start lessons?" she asked as we both made up plates. I had let her go ahead of me. Even after a week, I hadn't gotten used to the amount of food available to me as a member of the Prescott household. My elderly clients mostly nibbled and drank nutrition shakes rather than having actual meals. I brought my own food for those jobs, and when I worked with children I was generally expected to eat what they did. Not wanting to appear greedy, I took my cues from Jennifer. It wasn't easy—she ate barely enough to keep a bird alive—but better a bit of hunger than to be thought a pig.

"I am. We'll see whether the girls are."

"It's up to you to be certain they do their work." She wrinkled her upper lip and a bit of her delicate nose. Jennifer, I was coming to understand, was the type of person who needed to remind people of their place in the world. All of us who worked for Sandy had run across her type before. Sandy claimed that they didn't mean anything by the sniping, that having people in their homes who didn't fit neatly into the "staff" versus "family" categories was as upsetting to them as it was to us, but I found that hard to believe. Jennifer had the natural authority of one born to privilege. It would take more than a hard-to-classify member of the household to upset her.

She turned her attention to Prescott. "Is Mr. Simmons coming today?"

"He is." Prescott glanced at his watch. "In about forty minutes. He'll keep me talking forever before he gets around to going over the plans."

I listened intently. I had no idea what went into boat building. I had always assumed buying a boat was similar to buying a car—you went to a dealership and found something you liked or you looked in classifieds for used ones.

"What's he looking for?" Jennifer asked.

"A picnic boat, near as I can tell from what he's said about his lifestyle." Prescott glanced over at me. "You have no idea what I'm talking about, do you?"

I shook my head. "Sorry."

"No reason to apologize. Jenn has worked in the business ever since she and Danny got married, so she knows all the lingo. A picnic boat's like a small yacht, set up for nice weather, calm seas, hanging out with friends and family. You might drop a line into the water from it, but it's not a fishing boat. We call it a Downeast picnic boat because it's a bit more sturdy than the typical lake-water day boat and is modeled after a traditional lobster boat. Not designed for open ocean, you understand, but it can manage a bay or cove or sound just fine."

"Has he mentioned his budget?" Jennifer asked.

"Nope. But he owned a Hinkley a few years ago, and he's well aware that custom is going to cost him more."

"A boat like the one Thane is talking about costs between a million and two million depending on size, configuration, and materials," Jennifer said. "So sometimes you can tell by a person's budget what they're expecting you to build."

Two million dollars for a boat. What kind of person spent that? That figure succeeded in reminding me that I was nothing more than staff far better than any comment of Jennifer's.

THE GIRLS ARRIVED in the new schoolroom at nine-thirty. We started the morning with math. Geometry had been far from my best subject in school, but now the figures and formulas provided welcome stability. No matter that my senses failed, that warm was cold and footsteps sounded where no one walked, the surface area of a sphere would always be equal to its radius squared times four times pi. Was that what Ali found so appealing about medicine? She'd told me once that the body was a machine and she planned to be the world's greatest mechanic. We could not be more different, my sister and I, and my aunt had remarked more than once that our career choices should have been reversed; the fey doctor made no more sense than the pragmatic psychologist.

"Molly," said Hailey, yanking me out of my memories, "what's the point of this? When am I going to need to know how to calculate what the diameter of a circle is if I know the circumference?"

"What do you want to do for a living?" I asked in return. Liza looked up from her workbook, her eyes following the conversation as if it were a tennis match.

"I'm fourteen. How should I know?"

"Exactly. What if you want to go into architecture or engineering or even fashion design? All of those rely on an understanding of two- and three-dimensional shapes."

"Fashion design? How's that geometry?"

"If you have three yards of fabric fifty-two inches wide, how many A-line skirts can you make if each skirt is twenty inches long with a fifteen degree slope on the A and a one-inch hem?"

She stared at me, mouth slightly agape. "Fashion design is math?"

"It's one of the sad truths of life for those of us not great with numbers that almost everything is math. You want to redecorate and figure out how many gallons of paint you'll need? Math. Out to dinner and need to calculate the tip or divide up the check? Math. Managing your household budget so you don't go into debt? Math."

She wrinkled her nose, looking exactly like her mother. "I don't like math."

I forged ahead. "The nice thing about math, though, is that it never changes. Once you understand how it works, really understand it, you can apply it in any realm from figuring out how many skeins of yarn you need for a sweater to programming computers. And doing proofs, like we do in geometry, teaches you how to create an argument, how to speak with authority."

"Huh." Hailey didn't look happy, but she settled back to her work without further complaint.

BY THE TIME three o'clock rolled around and the girls went to put on hiking clothes so we could take Rocky out and get in our scheduled exercise, I wanted to crawl back into bed. I had two girls. How did teachers who had full classrooms hour after hour manage?

The sky had gone gray on gray, a flat dusty silver with heavy, low-hanging charcoal clouds scuttling over the trees. Rain was coming. Still, my fear of the old nursery shored up my determination to take the girls outside. I slipped on my sweatshirt and jacket and went down to get Rocky ready for his run.

I yawned widely as I put his collar on, then started when Nathaniel's voice sounded behind me. "They wore you out, did they?"

"Oh! No, no. They were fine."

He smiled and the wrinkles beside his eyes tilted upward, softening the sharp lines of his face. "By the way, Mrs. Vogel has gone home. Her son has the flu, so she's gone to take care of her grandchildren for a few days. She left a few meals in the fridge so you wouldn't be too put out, but I didn't realize how much the energy the girls would take or I'd have asked her to leave more."

"They're fine, honestly. I'm adjusting to the schedule, same as they are. It will work out."

"If you say so. I wouldn't want to attempt to teach two tween girls. I'd rather spend the day listening to Simmons drone on about his wonderful girlfriend and how he's simply dying to take her out for afternoon cruises so they can be absolutely private ."

I'd seen Simmons. I'd also smelled his thick miasma of pine cleaner-scented cologne. Teaching Hailey and Liza had been exhausting, but drowning in Simmons's odor might have killed me.

Hailey got to the kitchen first, so I allowed her to take the leash. Liza, arriving a minute later, merely bent down and scratched Rocky's ears.

"Let's go to the pond," Hailey suggested as we stepped outside. "You haven't been there yet, have you?"

I had not. In fact, I'd almost forgotten its existence. During Matt's visited, we had regularly traipsed all across the cleared part of the yard, playing soccer and tag and capture the flag, but I had seen no sign of water.

Hailey, holding tight to Rocky's leash, headed in the direction of the family cemetery, which I'd managed to avoid after our first visit. "We have to go through the woods a little ways."

Rocky followed eagerly until we got to the two crosses. Then he planted his feet, sitting so sharply that Hailey almost tripped, and growled low in his throat.

"Come on." Hailey yanked on the leash.

"Stop that. Pick him up. He must not care for this part of the yard. Remember last time? I don't want a repeat of the great escape."

She scooped him up and he settled somewhat, though his eyes still bulged even more than usual, and his expression set my shoulders to twitching.

The girls stepped confidently into the woods although no path indicated the way. Denuded trees clustered thickly enough to block the weak light. In full leaf, they would create a green darkness; now they whispered hoarsely among themselves of the coming winter. We wove our way through the trees for several minutes, until I began to wonder whether Hailey might be playing me for a fool. She would not be the first of my charges who'd tried such a thing. (Nor was "test the newbie" a game limited to young clients—I'd once had an elderly woman attempt to convince me she was allowed to go to the hairdresser on her own.) And then, just as I got ready to call a halt, the woods thinned, the light strengthened, and we popped out on the verge of an enormous body of water.

"Here we are." Hailey placed Rocky on the ground. "Wilton Pond."

"Seriously? Shouldn't that be Wilton Lake?" The green-black water reflected the sky as far as I could see.

"Nope. Not deep enough. That's why it freezes so well for skating."

And why, I supposed, a pool had been built on the Prescott property.

The wind gusted toward us over the surface of the pond, carrying with it the sharp scent of algae. The tips of my ears tingled with the chill, which was harsher here. Rocky, who'd crept forward to investigate the water's edge, barked twice and pawed at the wavelets. Hailey lay down on the narrow strip of dry grass between woods and water and tried to coax him to jump on her chest. Liza wandered over to the edge and began to pluck stones from the water and skip them over the top.

"Liza! That's far too cold to be playing in!"

She rolled her eyes and I could practically hear the *I'm not in it*. She shifted position slightly, turning her head away from me, and continued sliding her fingers through the water.

"Liza!" But her head was tilted in the peculiar manner that suggested she was listening to voices I could not hear. I stepped forward, intending to put myself back into her field of vision. Something tangled around my legs and I felt a push against my back and then I was flying, falling, until I landed with an ignominious splash with my head and chest in the pond and my feet on the grass.

The whole incident lasted less than a second. One moment, I had the situation under control and the next I was scrambling back to my feet, soaking, dazed, and choking on the foul liquid I'd inadvertently breathed into my lungs. Slimy water dripped down my face and the gusting wind sliced through my wet clothes.

"Oh my God, Molly, what happened?" Hailey hovered over me, her eyes round, tearing in the wind.

Someone pushed me. I'd been looking right at both of the girls and no one else had approached us, but I could not shake the impression of hands on my back. I could not mention such a thing to the girls, however. Liza, in particular, needed a mundane answer, no matter what I might believe privately.

"I tripped." I needed to swallow, but the idea of swallowing the pond water disgusted me and I spat instead. "We're going to have to pick up the pace on the way back to the house or I'll turn into an icicle."

Even jogging and running, the trip took close to ten minutes. I had hoped to slip into the house and upstairs without seeing either Jennifer or Prescott, but they were both standing in the front hall when we arrived. For a split second, before they registered my bedraggled appearance, I had the distinct impression that we'd interrupted an argument. But the tension broke and Prescott stepped toward us, Jennifer in his wake.

"What happened?" Concern lit his dark eyes and they swept over Liza before coming back to me. His hand came up halfway, as if to touch my dripping hair, then dropped again. A wave of heat washed through me, half unexpected—and unwanted—desire, half embarrassment.

"I'm clumsy. We went to the pond and I managed to fall in." Despite the warmth in my cheeks, my teeth chattered.

"You should go up and take a shower," Jennifer said.

"No, she should take a *bath*." Hailey spoke with absolute authority. "Uncle Thane has the most awesome bathtub."

A bath sounded like heaven, but not in Prescott's private domain. "A shower will be fine. I need to wash my hair anyway. It's got pond slime in it."

"No," Prescott said. "Hailey is absolutely right. Let's get you warmed up. There's a hand shower in the tub for your hair, and it really will warm you up better than the little shower. Hailey, take Rocky into the kitchen and wipe his paws so he doesn't track mud all over the place."

On the way out of the kitchen, he nodded to Jennifer,

whose pretty, bow-shaped lips had compressed into a thin, flat line. Whatever we'd interrupted, she had more to say and the dismissal rankled.

In any household arguments, you are Switzerland. It was one of Sandy's first commandments. I kept my head down, pretending not to notice Jennifer's anger, and followed Prescott up the stairs. I had never seen the inside of his room and when he opened the door a spurt of interest nearly distracted me from my physical misery. Heavy mahogany furniture filled the space, its muted gleam a testament to decades of use and polish. Deep, forest green drapes with thin blood-red stripes hung at the windows and a burgundy duvet covered the massive bed. It was an entirely masculine space and I wondered whether it had looked the same when Liza's mother had shared it.

And then we moved into the bathroom and my entire world narrowed to the sight of the tub. Long, deep, with jets set on the inside and a hand shower next to the faucet, I could practically hear it singing a siren's song to me.

Prescott coughed. "Let me get it started while you collect a towel and some fresh clothes. I'm afraid I don't have anything exciting to put in it—it's rarely been used since Marianne's death. Occasionally, as you heard, the girls like to turn on the jets."

"Not a problem. Just the idea of a bath is enough. I don't need bubbles."

He studied me for a long moment through dark, inscrutable eyes, then nodded. What conclusion he'd drawn, I had no idea, but I ducked out of the room the minute his gaze released me.

When I returned with my towel, clothes, and a bottle of shampoo, he had gone.

～

THE BATH WAS LOVELY, but despite the heat of the water, my muscles refused to relax and my mind ran in circles. How had I landed in the pond? I closed my eyes and tried to play the moments back. It had all happened too fast in the moment, and the freezing dash for the house had allowed no room for reflection. But even now, with the gentle steam of the tub rising around me, the memories made no sense. The stiff wind had been blowing toward me. I could still feel the sting of it in my eyes. Which meant that whatever had knocked me down from behind had not been carried by the wind.

And then there was the fact that my fall should not have landed me in the pond. No matter what angle I pictured, I was not close enough to the water's edge when I fell.

I shivered in the warm water, then submerged to soak my hair. When I came up, the water had turned to rust. How much mud had I picked up? I turned on the hand shower and more came free, followed by a long stream of pinkish red. Blood? How had I managed to cut myself without knowing it? I ran my fingers over my head until I found the spot, just above the hairline in the front. Gritting my teeth, I focused the pulse of the shower on the wound. Who knew what kind of bacteria called that pond home?

Only when the water ran completely clear did I climb from the tub and force my mind away from the pond and back to the present situation. I had the sneaking suspicion that the argument the girls and I had walked in on concerned my status in the house. My aunt would call it egotism—I had no identifiable reason for my suspicions—but the immediate silence when we'd entered, the difficulty Jennifer and Nathaniel had changing directions, triggered my paranoia.

Whatever the issue, I did not have to face it when I went downstairs. Jennifer was reading a magazine in the kitchen while the girls sat on the floor trying to teach Rocky to roll over, but Nathaniel was nowhere to be seen.

"Feeling better?" Jennifer asked.

"Much." I gave her my best smile. "What a fabulous bath."

"Oh, yes. Marianne did like her luxuries."

I suppressed a gasp. What a thing to say in front of Liza. "Well, in this case, I agree with her. Worth every penny."

Liza slipped from the room. I debated following her, but thought she might prefer to be alone, so I slid to the floor to take her place with Hailey and the dog.

By the time I got the girls into bed, I'd settled back into normalcy, convincing myself that I'd misremembered the afternoon's events. And yet, strange dreams of misty, malevolent figures disturbed my sleep. Three times I woke, choking, a sour taste in the back of my throat. The cut on my head throbbed and seemed to send out invisible battalions that, each time I woke, had colonized another region. My head, my face, my throat, all succumbed to the invading force.

When my alarm pieced my skull all too early the following morning, I shut it off with fumbling fingers and took inventory: I had puffy eyes, a throat like sandpaper and an itch deep down inside my right ear—the one that had landed in the water—that I could not scratch. But Mrs. Vogel had taken the day off. I had to get breakfast for the girls. They fended for themselves on the weekends, but on school days I could not let them sit forever making decisions about which cereal to eat or we would never start on time.

Dizziness assaulted me when I stood, and black spots vignetted my vision. Far away, I heard a callous laugh I recognized immediately as the mother-thing that had appeared to me in my dream. I closed my eyes and waited, breathing deeply, until stability and sense returned. My soft cotton T-shirt chafed my skin and once I'd made my bed I had to sit for a moment to regain my strength.

Food and coffee, that's all you need. It's just a cold.

Leaning heavily on the handrail, I made it down the stairs. As I passed the dining room door to go to the kitchen, however, Prescott stepped out and stopped me. He'd given up the crutches already, though I'd distinctly heard the doctor tell him he should use them for a week.

"I've made coffee," he said. "If you—" He stopped and stared at me. "My God, what are you doing out of bed?"

"I have to get breakfast for the girls." It sounded ridiculous. How could I possibly set a table and fry eggs when the kitchen was so very far away?

"You'll do no such thing. You look like death."

A slender shaft of pain like a paper cut across my heart brought water to my sinuses. *Stop it. Vanity has no place here.* And vanity was all I could allow such a moment to wound.

"No." I shook my head, and my brain rattled back and forth in my skull. "It's just a cold. From falling in the pond."

"Mrs. Vogel's son has a nasty bug that's going around in town. Undoubtedly, your little adventure yesterday weakened you enough for the virus to take hold. Go upstairs and get back in bed."

I wanted to argue, but could not summon the strength. In fact, I could not imagine how I would make it back up to my room.

"I'm so sorry." For some reason, my eyes filled with tears.

"Molly," he said, more gently than I'd ever heard him speak, "illness is a physical failing, not a moral one. You have nothing to apologize for. Yet. If you refuse to take care of yourself and die of sheer stubbornness, that will be a moral failing, and one I will not forgive. My daughter has had enough tragedy in her life. Do you understand?"

"Yes. Thank you."

He muttered something that sounded very much like a curse under his breath, then picked me up as easily has Hailey had lifted Rocky. My paper-cut heart bled a little more at the easy strength.

"Oh, please don't. Your rib. Your ankle. I can manage."

"Shut. Up."

I shut up. In fact, despite the hopping, uneven movement Prescott used to get me up the stairs on his sprained ankle, I was three-quarters asleep when he sat me on my bed, removed my shoes, and tucked me back in under the covers that had taken me so much energy to put to rights. And I was fully asleep by the time he left the room.

I SPENT much of the day in a fevered haze. Liza and Hailey took turns bringing me juice, water, aspirin, and tea liberally laced with some form of alcohol. My curtains remained drawn, allowing little sense of passing time.

When at last my mind felt clear, the room was dark and I had no idea how long I'd slept. Minutes? Hours? I reached for my phone and sent the glass of water on my nightstand crashing to the floor. Pure luck and the rug prevented it from shattering, but it cracked in two nonetheless. I eased out of bed and picked up the halves. At least it didn't look to be an expensive glass.

I took the pieces into the bathroom to wrap in paper towel before throwing them away and when I came out, Matt stood in the hall, leaning against the wall next to my bedroom door.

"Matt? What are you doing here?" *Nice, Molls, really nice.* "I mean, I thought you had gone back to New York."

"I know what you meant. I've had my office phone transferred to the phone up in the guest apartment and I can work from here for a couple of days as long as the service doesn't go down. I have a ton of research and drafting to do, and none of that requires me to be physically present in the office." He grinned. "I'd rather be here, and if I can call in and tell the office that it's because my sister needs me, so much the better."

And if not for the Prescotts, I'd rather be anywhere *but* here. Not that I could very well say such a thing to Matt.

He tucked a stray hair behind my ear. "If it makes you more comfortable, I'm not putting anything on hold but returning to a boring suit-and-tie life. I prefer to do drafting from my apartment even when I can be in my office. My sister knows that. She also knew I was going to Boston to meet with a mediator when I left the other day and thought if I was still there instead of all the way in New York, I'd want to know you were ill."

"It's just a bug. Honestly." I shoved away the memory of distant laughter. A bug complete with hallucinations. "But it was kind of her to call you."

And odd. Because Jennifer didn't strike me as the kind of woman who'd encourage a flirtation between her brother and the hired help. Nor did it fit with her insistence that Hailey's education remain on track. Clearly, my psychology classes had not prepared me adequately to deal with the likes of Jennifer Prescott.

"Come on, let me help you back to bed," He slipped a hand under my elbow. I could have managed on my own, but did not complain. My sister and I were huggers, touchers—the whole Allworth family was—and since my arrival in Maine I'd missed personal contact. I'd worried about fitting in, being strong enough to discipline two teenagers, smart enough to help an emotionally damaged girl, sensitive enough to handle a child who'd lost her mother, but it had never occurred to me that something as simple as a lack of physical contact would throw me off-balance.

"What time is it?"

"Four-thirty. I finished up in Boston at lunch and got here about an hour ago. I checked, but you were out like a light. Jenn said you hadn't even woken up to eat lunch. You must be starving. Let me get you a bite."

"That's not necessary. What I really need is a shower." In his presence I was supremely conscious of the state of my hair and the sickroom smell of my body. "Then I can go down and fix myself a sandwich. I can't believe I slept so long. The girls should have woken me so we could study."

"Like that was going to happen. It doesn't matter. Jenn insisted they read a few chapters of The Scarlet Letter." He shuddered. "I hated that book. In fact, I hated most of the classics of American lit. Give me English lit or even French."

"Please don't say that to Hailey. The first half of the year's reading is American lit and I suspect it's going to be hard enough to convince her to finish the required reading without anyone telling her ahead of time the books are terrible."

He laughed. "I promise. Now, you go shower and I'll scrounge you up a meal."

∼

THE FOLLOWING MORNING, I woke in the sweat-soaked cocoon of my sheets to find both Hailey and Liza next to my bed, American History textbooks open in their laps. Hailey had pulled over the chair that had been by the window and someone had carried in the chair that usually sat next to Liza's bed for her.

"You shouldn't be in here," I croaked. "You'll get sick."

"Nah. We've both been vaccinated for flu. Besides, Uncle Thane called his doctor, who said we'd be fine as long as we took our vitamins and stayed out of the pond. He said it's a forty-eight hour bug and it's all over Portland. Half the kids are out of school with it, and Mrs. Vogel's family has it, too. Mom sent us in here so they could argue about what to do."

Liza tossed a glance at her cousin.

"What? You know it's true." Hailey lifted a glass of orange juice from the nightstand, along with two white pills. "Uncle Thane said you're supposed to take these aspirins and drink this juice and send us down if you want anything else, like soup or eggs or tea or whatever."

"You need to study and your uncle has work to do. If I need something, I'll get it myself."

"But he wants to take care of you. He likes you." She imbued the words with a depth of meaning available only to a teenager. My fever-hot cheeks warmed further and Liza's eyes narrowed.

"That's ridiculous. Now, tell me what you're reading."

"The settling of America. Boring." The final word stretched to a good four syllables. "How am I supposed to remember who's who and where they're from? There are like eight million of them."

"You don't have to remember them all, just the big ones."

"How can we tell which ones we need to know?"

"Get your notebooks and I'll show you how to pick out important information when you're reading."

Both girls left and I swallowed the pills and gulped down the juice. I stood slowly, waited for the inevitable dizziness to pass, and made my way across the hall into the bathroom. Despite the acidity of the orange juice, my mouth felt cottony and tasted foul, so I took the time to brush my teeth as well as to change into a clean pair of scrubs. When I returned to my bedroom, however, only Liza was there.

"Where's Hailey?"

Liza's mouth compressed into an expression of mulish displeasure.

"Will you please go get her, Liza? I can't very well run around looking for her and her mother wants her to study."

Liza crossed her arms and rolled her eyes.

"I don't know what that means." I took a deep breath and began to push myself back out of bed, but then I heard footsteps on the stairs. "She's coming back?"

If a child could snarl silently, Liza did so, and when Hailey appeared I understood why. Prescott filled the door behind her, a tray in his hands with a pitcher of ice water, a traditional porcelain tea pot, a mug, and a glass on it. Guilt rippled through me, followed closely by fear. I was supposed to take care of the children, to take a burden off the Prescotts' shoulders, not to create an additional one. And if Liza turned against me, I'd be out on my ear in no time.

"Hailey told me you were awake."

"I asked them not to bother you."

"Give us a minute, will you, girls?" Prescott brushed a hand over Liza's head as the children retreated, but none of the stiffness left her body. When Hailey shut the door behind them, he sighed deeply before settling into her vacated chair.

"How are you feeling?"

"Much better. Really." I touched the tray, which he'd laid on the nightstand. "You don't need to wait on me. I can take care of myself."

"Considering your current situation, I beg to differ with that assessment."

I opened my mouth to argue, exhaustion having depleted my normal filters, and he laughed and held up a hand. "Joking. I wanted to see whether you had it in you to get angry on your own behalf."

"What do you mean?"

"Nothing. Never mind. The girls aren't too tiring for you in your current condition, are they? I was against sending them in, but they promised to be quiet and to let you sleep. They worried about you so I thought it would be better to let them play nursemaid. You don't need to be the teacher, just let them fuss over you."

"Honestly, it's fine. They were reading quietly when I woke up."

"Good. Jenn doesn't want their studies interrupted, so when I said they could sit with you she said they had to study." He winced. "You can imagine how well that went over."

I could, and a laugh welled up, surprising me. "We'll manage. They're good kids."

"They are. Just be careful not to tire yourself out. Doctor Sanderson says you need rest and fluids, and the more of both you get the faster you'll be back to normal and able to work full time again."

Ah, there it was, the cold wave of reality that doused the warm glow generated by his apparent concern. "I'll do my best."

"Excellent." He rose and opened the door to summon the girls. "I'll be back later on."

We spent the next hour on history until Jennifer interrupted the lesson to fetch Hailey and Liza for lunch.

"Are you doing all right?" she asked.

"Much better, thanks. Sorry to be such a bother, though."

"No bother. I'll have Hailey bring you a bite when they come up after they eat if that's okay. I'm giving them leftover casserole from last night. Does that work for you?"

"Of course. That's very thoughtful."

"Not at all. I can take over Hailey's French lessons while you're resting. I know history isn't on the usual Tuesday schedule, but I couldn't imagine you wanted to teach biology without a whiteboard at the very least."

"No, you're absolutely right." I pulled the schedule out of my fuzzy head. "But the afternoon classes can stick to their normal rotation because today is history of fashion and handwork."

"Perfect." She ushered the girls out and I closed my eyes, intending to rest for but a minute, and fell right back to sleep.

CHAPTER 11

*E*veryone, even Jennifer, came to wish me goodnight after dinner. Matt promised he'd be over in the morning to check on me before his conference call at ten. I heard the girls running up and down the hall as they prepared for bed, then Prescott in Liza's room, his deep voice a quiet rumble as he read to her before she shut off her light.

I tried to relax, begged sleep to come. But the more I courted sleep, the more firmly it turned its back.

I could read. I had yet to explore the library downstairs, though Nathaniel had told me to feel free to read anything at any time. I could not help but remember the morning's embarrassment, however. What if I got down to the library and then could not get back upstairs? I felt stronger than I had, but the idea of having to call out for help…no, I would not browse the library tonight.

And I had no stomach for the one book I could easily reach.

I punched my pillow into shape, rolled onto my side, and tried to force my eyes to shut. They popped open. Beneath the heavy duvet I began to sweat, so I threw it off. The cool air felt good on my skin, but after a minute I shivered. I pulled it back up, flipped to the other side and tried again. In the darkened room, my eyes still refused to close, searching out the room's contours in the scant light slipping around the edges of the curtains.

I could go upstairs, get a textbook. If I wore out too soon, I could turn around because coming down used up less energy. I eased out of the bed, tested my standing strength. No problem. I pulled on the canvas shoes that doubled as slippers and padded out into the hallway. No lamp showed under any of the doorways, but a glow reached into the hall from the large window in the playroom and another filtered up the stairs from the sidelights by the front door.

My eyes adjusted, found the outlines of doors and stairs. The silence of the sleeping house magnified my rasping breath and the squeak of the stairs beneath my feet, naming me an intruder. Eight steps. Twelve. Twenty. My heart raced, but I made it to the top of the staircase without pause.

I plucked the American History textbook from the shelf in the schoolroom along with the accompanying teacher's manual. In the light from the window, I glanced through the advice on teaching the section the girls had brought to my room. Dry. Full of memorization exercises. I would find my own way to interest the girls in the topic.

A noise infringed on my consciousness at the same moment a tendril of frigid air snaked around my ankle. A rhythmic combination of creak and moan, it sounded as if someone were shifting their weight from foot to foot. Screeeeeetch, grooooooan. Screeeeeetch, grooooooan. Screeeeeetch, grooooooan.

My mouth dried and my muscles froze.

The family room. It was coming from the family room.

Close the door. Keep it out.

But my knees locked. The chill slid around and up both

my legs like the long, slimy fingers of some dread sea creature.

My stomach heaved, throwing bile up my throat, and I choked.

Get it together. And suddenly, the answer came to me. It was Hailey or Liza. Probably Hailey, angry about Matt's attentions. She'd followed me up and climbed on the rocking horse, hoping to terrify me. Anger burned away fear and I marched over to the door to the family room, now open a crack though it had been closed when I'd entered the schoolroom. With each step, the sound grew louder and the air grew colder. She'd opened the window. I shoved the door open and sucked in a breath to tell her off.

The rocking horse was perfectly still. The moon's cold light illuminated the room, throwing strange shadows. A column of greasy black smoke swayed impossibly in the corner behind the horse, each twisting movement in time with a creak or groan. I watched in helpless fascination as long ropes separated from the column, two of them, arms that reached for me to pull me to the vortex.

I hit the stairs at full speed and crashed down them, uncaring of the racket until a tall form halted me two steps from the bottom. Shadows exaggerated his features and turned his eyes to pits in his dark face and for a single, gasping breath, I almost flung myself back toward the smoky threat of the third floor.

"Molly?" Nathaniel leaned toward me. "Are you all right? I thought I heard you scream."

Had I? I replayed the scene in my mind, but it was a silent movie with only the morbid music of the house accompanying it. "I was startled. Sorry to wake you."

"You didn't. What startled you?"

The million dollar question. Even if I'd wanted to answer, I could not. A noise. A noise and a draft. An impossible apparition of smoke and soot. "A…mouse, maybe?" Still fairly ditzy, but not completely psycho.

"A mouse."

"Maybe? It was dark. I couldn't sleep, so I went up to get a book from the classroom. I didn't expect anything to move." I took a deep breath. "Are you sure this is the right place for Liza?"

He drew back. "You don't think my daughter belongs here?"

I threw away years of advice from Sandy and Nadya and forged ahead. "You have to admit that this house is a bit creepy for a child who sees ghosts. Whether you believe in them or not, she does. And this environment…isolation from others her own age allows her imagination to run unchecked by the effective, if sometimes brutal, rein of her peers."

"A normal school? That's your recommendation?"

"I haven't worked with her enough to make a recommendation like that. But there's no reason you couldn't continue to homeschool her if that's your choice. Just in a more normal environment where she could practice socializing as well."

"So we should retain your services as her tutor, but move to a more congenial location. Perhaps into Portland proper, where you'd be more comfortable. Is that it?"

"No!"

"Really?" He leaned forward and I did my best not to shrink away. "Let me explain something to you. I brought Liza here specifically to get her away from those peers whose influence you so admire and I took a substantial financial hit to do so. I couldn't move Liza right now even if I believed you. Which I do not. Here we stay. If you can't handle it, you can take off like your predecessors."

Except not all of them had taken off. Even in the dark, he read my face.

"I suppose I have Hailey to thank for telling you that story?"

"You can't expect a teenager to ignore such juicy gossip."

He rubbed his forehead in a way I was beginning to recognize. "I suppose you want to know what happened."

Of course I did. But I'd irked him enough for one evening. "It's none of my business."

He sighed. "Get in bed. I'll fix us both some hot chocolate."

WITH NATHANIEL GONE, I flipped on the lamp, sat on the edge of my bed, pulled off my shoes, and examined my feet and calves. I could still feel the gelid tentacles that had sucked the strength from them, but no marks remained as evidence and when I touched them the skin beneath my fingers felt entirely normal. I shoved them beneath the welcoming duvet, rubbing them together to increase the circulation.

What had happened upstairs?

What was that thing in the corner of the room?

You were in the corner. Kind of...swaying. Hailey's nightmare. But that was in her bedroom, not upstairs. I pictured the house's layout, but the corners did not match. It was not some structural flaw that created a dusty whirlwind in one sector.

I drew my knees up beneath my chin, shivering despite the duvet. I should go home. But if Prescott could not afford to move, neither could I afford to quit. Sandy took a twenty percent cut of our annual salary. If I stuck out the job without earning my bonus, it would be worth $30,000. If I left, I would owe Sandy $6000. Quite aside from the money, I could not abandon Liza. I was the only person who actually believed her. If she was crazy, so was I. And I was not crazy, which meant she needed protection. I whimpered, then pressed my lips together to prevent another from slipping out. *Oh, Mama, you were right about never living in.*

Nathaniel's footsteps on the stairs pulled me from my wallow. If I planned to stay, I needed every weapon and every ally. Including the man my predecessor had tried to murder.

When he settled into the chair next to me and handed me the steaming mug, I gave him my best smile. He gave me back one so tired I almost told him to forget telling me what happened. Almost. But my room had four corners, and I couldn't stop checking them for smoke. I needed to hear his story.

Nathaniel wanted mine first. "You're certain it was a mouse you saw?"

"I'm not certain of anything." On that I could be honest. "Why?"

He sipped at his chocolate and focused on Liza's door. "Before we moved here, Liza went to a private school. We had a housekeeper five days a week, and then an au pair once Liza left school. I knew when that first au pair quit at the very idea of moving up her that finding one for such a remote location would take some time, but the service assured me they'd matched more difficult cases.

"I interviewed four or five candidates in their Boston office before settling on a young woman who swore that Liza's delusions did not faze her, that her own granny had seen spirits for years and everyone in the family simply dealt with it. At first, she seemed a good fit. When Jenn and Hailey arrived I gave her a raise because of the extra work and locked myself into the office. The business took all my time and energy.

"After a few weeks, Jenn tried to tell me that the girl was

getting odd. She had, apparently, gone into town and bought herself a large crucifix which she hung on the wall in her room. And she'd taken to muttering to herself. But Liza liked her, so I let it go.

"And then one night she packed up all her things, and when we got up in the morning she'd already called a taxi to take her to the train. I asked her why, but she refused to say. In fact, she would barely look at me."

If any of the women I worked with pulled a stunt like that, Sandy would drop them so hard they'd never get back up. And yet, when I thought about the family room, it was hard to fault the girl's actions. She must have known she'd never work in care again, but it hadn't mattered a bit.

"Did you ask the service whether she gave a reason?"

"They had no answers. At least none they'd share. They found me a new set of possibilities. This time, Jenn went with me when I did the interviews. The third candidate seemed perfect. Born and raised in rural Vermont, she understood both winter and isolation. She'd moved down to Boston because her husband's job transferred him, but they'd divorced, leaving her with no social circle. Liza and Hailey weren't thrilled—Aimee was older and stricter than the first au pair had been—but they adjusted."

He sucked in a breath, let it out. "I did nothing to that woman. I barely even noticed she was here. After Danny's death, the company consumed me."

"Your brother worked with you before he died?"

"We were partners. He owned half the company. All the marketing, setting up shows, publicity…anything that wasn't actually designing and building the boats, he managed. Jenn does her best, but I'm buying out her half over time."

He shook his head, clearing it. "But regardless, I should have paid more attention to Aimee, especially after what happened to her predecessor. Jenn complained that she was focusing too much on Liza and ignoring Hailey. More, she insisted that Aimee's attention to Liza was a way of getting to me. That Aimee was trying to seduce me into replacing her husband. I blew off her concerns, told her she was imagining things."

"But she wasn't."

"No." He fell silent, sipping his chocolate. I could not make myself drink my own despite its sweet, soothing warmth; my stomach had clenched in anticipation of the finale.

"It happened on a Sunday morning. Aimee was making French toast. She liked to cook. I've tried to reconstruct the scene a dozen times and I still don't remember exactly what I said that set her off. It had to do with the fact that Jenn and I were going to Boston for a boat show the following weekend. She started screaming that I couldn't lead her on and then turn my back on her. Though that was not how she put it. The things she accused me of…I swear to you, I didn't do them. I never touched her. I was so shocked I sat there gaping like a hooked fish. She snatched a butcher knife out of the block and came at me."

The bald, emotionless tone lent extra force to the words and the images hit like blows. The kitchen, bright and clean, the intimacy of the morning as she cooked and he drank his coffee. The shock of violence in the easy domesticity. "What did you do?"

"She wasn't a big woman. I took her down, but she slashed me a few times in the process." He let his gaze wander around the room, avoiding mine. "Maybe you're right. Maybe this is the wrong place for Liza. Maybe it's cursed. But neither Marianne's death nor Danny's occurred here. It's far more likely me who is damned. And selfish as I am, I'm not giving my daughter up, even if she'd be better off without me."

"Now you're being melodramatic. Of course you shouldn't give her up."

"I screwed up. Twice." Now he did focus on me, and so intently I felt like the subject of a stop-and-frisk. "I won't fail her again. So be honest with me. What happened upstairs? Because I don't believe for a minute that you saw a mouse. Or that you even *thought* you did."

"No. I didn't." He deserved the truth. But I deserved to keep my job, and Ali deserved to go to medical school. No way could we all win. I'd settle for two out of three and give him as much of the third as I could. "I went upstairs, which probably exhausted me, and felt a chill. Then I saw something move in the shadows. Not a mouse, but not anything else I can explain, either. You know how strange it is up there with all the taxidermy—I'm putting the incident down to a fever dream brought on by sickness and staring glass eyes. Not worth worrying about. I swear to you, I am not losing my mind. I won't desert Liza or try to seduce or attack you."

His jaw clenched so hard I thought he'd crack a tooth, but then he nodded. "Fair enough."

NATHANIEL LEFT with the command to get some sleep, but I could not bring myself to shut off the light. Indeed, once I finished the last, cold dregs of my chocolate, I pushed out of bed and thrust open the heavy drapes, letting the harsh moonlight illuminate the corners the glow from the bedside lamp could not touch. Nothing stirred; I was alone.

Of course you are.

But I could not shake the memory of that frigid grasp on my legs and the outstretched cables of greasy smoke reaching for me. I snatched my bag from its spot near the wardrobe and launched myself into bed once more, avoiding the shadowy space beneath. Propping the pillows behind my back, I noted everything Nathaniel had told me about Liza's previous tutors.

I had sworn to Nathaniel that he had nothing to fear from me. Despite the growing evidence to the contrary, I believed in my own sanity, which meant more than childish fears and emotional trauma haunted Liza. But the phenomena that terrified me and annoyed Hailey seemed to comfort Liza. The way she tilted her head and sometimes looked beyond us seemed as if she were listening to a presence the rest of us could not see. And she never reacted with fear. On the contrary, she seemed to trust the invisible speaker. I carefully listed every instance I remembered of her attending to that voice and the events surrounding it.

I'd witnessed the behavior the moment I arrived. Liza's invisible companion had whispered in her ear as she watched me from her shadowy perch at the top of the stairs. And it had warned her of Jenn and Hailey's return. She'd ignored me in favor of that voice at the pond, too. Again I remembered the feeling of a push at my back. If that had been a malevolent spirit, might it also have engineered Nathaniel's fall from the ladder? I had never heard of a ghost sawing wood, but perhaps it had convinced someone in the house to do so. Like Aimee and her butcher knife. Had it come to her in the night, wearing Nathaniel's form as it had worn my mother's? Was that why she thought he had made her promises?

I shivered and pulled the covers more tightly around me. The stories about both women terrified me. But if indeed some spirit haunted the house, what was its end game? What might an otherworldly presence hope to accomplish? Did they even function through logic and ambition? The ones our neighbor Sultana conjured came across as pure emotion: love, loss, regret, anger. The messages she passed to her clients did occasionally carry commands—"don't let your father drink away your fortune," "be careful, your new girlfriend is a gold-digger," "your husband still loves you and he wants you to remarry so you can be happy"—but the tone of the messages indicated that personal ambition lived and died in the physical body. The body discarded, ambition focused outward, on the happiness of others.

Not that I believed Sultana. After all, she was nothing more than a carnival queen. My mother's warnings about the other side, on the other hand, echoed through my unquiet mind with the distinct edge of truth. Nothing frightened Em Allworth. Even cancer had merely saddened her. The spirit realm, however, was unpredictable and therefore daunting. No bargaining or reasoning would shut that door once opened and so it must remain barricaded with all possible force.

But here, the door was open. Whatever lived at Rook's Rest—if such a creature could be said to have life—had already passed through. Having seen it as both a cancerous mother and a roiling whirlwind of ash, I could not believe its intentions kind or its ambitions outwardly focused. What it wanted, it wanted for itself, though I had no idea what that might be. Nor what it might do to achieve its goals. Was Liza in danger? So far the thing had made no move to hurt her. But it had moved against her father, and losing him would devastate her. It was no longer safe to ignore the malignant spirit. We had to confront it. Or I did. Preferably without convincing Nathaniel Prescott that I had lost my mind.

CHAPTER 12

I finally managed to fall asleep as the sun's first rays crept through my window, eliminating the last shadowy hiding places in my bedroom. In dreams, I found myself near the little graveyard, standing over the two exiled markers. I ran my fingers across the carving concealed beneath a century or more of dirt and deadfall. I dug and scratched until my nails cracked and my fingers bled, but the stone refused to reveal its secrets.

My own sob of frustration woke me. Reflexively, I checked my hands. Though my fingers tingled and itched, my nails remained whole, mocking the sensation. Psychosomatic reaction. Could happen to anyone after a scary dream.

A faint noise drew my attention to the door. The knob turned slowly, stealthily, and my heart jumped. I was reaching for the heavy American History textbook, the only handy weapon, when Hailey poked her head inside. I swallowed hard and tried to smile.

"You're up! Uncle Thane said I couldn't bother you if you were still sleeping." She shifted to the side and Rocky muscled his way by to sniff and snuffle his way around.

I reached for my phone. Only eight o'clock.

"You're up early."

"I've been up for ages. Uncle Matt wanted me to watch the sunrise with him. She scrunched her features into a disdainful scowl. "I don't know why people make such a big deal over sunrises. Sunsets are just as pretty and they're at a way more reasonable hour."

"I suspect in this case it has less to do with the sun than with the company. Your uncle loves you. He probably wanted to spend time with you alone."

She squinted. "He did ask me a bunch of questions."

"See? He's interested in *you*, not the scenery."

"Maybe. Though we mostly talked about mom. And Uncle Thane. And you."

Me? What had Matt told his niece about me? My own thoughts and emotions with regards to Matthew Brahms were a conflicted mess, however, and I could not go down that road with Hailey.

"Those are all big pieces of your life. You've gone through a lot of changes and he probably wants to be sure you're okay."

"I suppose. No one really worries about my mental health, though. Because of Liza, you know. If my mother killed herself, it would be different. Liza needs the help, not me."

"Still, you must miss…coming here must have been hard for you." I had no idea what Hailey's relationship with Daniel Prescott had been. He'd been her father for most of her life.

She shrugged. "Danny was a nice guy, but he wasn't my real father. And it's not like he meant to leave us, not like Aunt Marianne. She totally ditched Liza."

"That's…not how suicide works. When people get to the point where they are so sad they can't see any way to make things better except by dying, the people they leave behind have faded from their minds. The only thing in a suicidal person's life is intolerable pain; they can't feel the love others have for them any longer."

She cocked her head, a remarkably chilling imitation of Liza's posture when listening to the indistinguishable voice, and studied me. "Is that what happened to your mother?"

The question was like a sword, quick and sharp and twisting. All the blood drained out of my head and my skin went hot, then cold, then hot again.

"No! No, my mother died of cancer."

"Oh. Okay. Sorry. But you sounded like you knew about suicide and pain and stuff."

Oh, yes. I understood pain. My mother had been raving with it at the end. No matter what she took, the pain simply laughed and came back stronger. It ate her alive from the inside. Even when the hospice workers gave her enough to knock her out, the lines around her mouth never eased. I was with her the night she died, and it was the relaxing of those muscles, the final respite from the unceasing agony that let me know she had gone.

The relief I felt in that moment was a shame I would carry the rest of my life. I chased it away, focusing on the present.

"You never told Liza her mother left her, did you?"

She rolled her eyes. "As if. My mother would shoot me. But it's not like she doesn't say it herself."

"She says it? As in, with words?"

"Get real. No, just, like…you know."

"I don't, actually. You'll have to be a bit more specific than that."

"Well, the whole 'the ghost of my mother is hanging out in the studio talking to me but no one else can see her' thing. Because that's like saying her mother left everyone else but not her."

I heard Jennifer in that explanation and gritted my teeth. "I see."

"You don't have to believe me. It's just that whole poor, pitiful me thing gets on my nerves. It's not like Aunt Marianne had a whole lot of time for Liza when she was alive. Why would she suddenly be hanging out with her now? Unless the afterlife is really boring."

So Liza's relationship with her mother hadn't been all roses and sunshine? What kind of guilt might that produce? I'd read somewhere that poltergeists were physical manifestations of emotional turmoil, not spirits at all. I'd be a lot happier with an incarnation of misery than with an actual ghost. Still, I could get more—and better—information from the girl herself if I could crack her shell than what I might filtered through Jennifer and Hailey. This conversation encouraged the unhealthy competition between the girls, so I changed the subject. "Have you had breakfast yet?"

"Yeah. But Uncle Matt said I should tell him when you were awake and he'd bring you yours. He really wants to help because it's going to snow later on so he has to go home soon." The previous day's jealousy had evidently dissipated a bit, and I was not anxious to revive it.

"Well, okay. I don't need much."

MATT ARRIVED in his typical good humor, apologizing almost the moment he set down the tray for the fact that he wouldn't be able to stay.

"A nor'easter off the coast changed direction. It wasn't supposed to land here at all. If I were wrong half as often as the weathermen, I'd lose my job. The house itself is perfectly safe, but a good blow shuts everything off. No phone, no internet—much as I would love to be shut in here with you, I can't lose touch with the office right now. I'll have to take off right after lunch."

"I understand." I glanced at the pale gray light seeping around the edges of the curtains. "Are you sure you should wait until afternoon to go?"

"Trying to get rid of me?"

The teasing and the blush I felt rising in response only exacerbated my confusion and discomfort. Matt was handsome, caring, easy to talk to. So why could I not encourage the flirtation? Why did I dream of a far darker, more somber face when I slept at all?

"I don't want you to get caught in a nor'easter is all."

Still, I had a purpose beyond food or flirtation for allowing him to bring me breakfast and over a plate of soft-boiled eggs and toast, I asked whether the third floor of the house had been open when he had visited as a child.

"Open? Like, in use?"

"Yes. We've changed one of the rooms into the school-room—I don't know whether Hailey mentioned it—and I wondered what they'd been in their heyday. Obviously, someone loved billiards, but that table could be ten years old or fifty or a hundred. And the other rooms don't give many clues."

"That pool table." He shook his head. "It sorely tempted us. But we were never allowed to use it. In fact, the whole room was off limits because Thane's father used it as his office. In the summers, when we spent the most time here, he locked himself into that room and wrote, and woe betide the child who interrupted him!"

"He wrote? He didn't build boats?"

"Oh, no. The boat business came from Thane's mother's side of the family. As did this house, come to think of it. His father is a professor of American history at a university in Connecticut, but you know what they say about 'publish or perish' for professors, so he was forever scribbling away in the billiards room. In fact, one summer he put a giant piece of plywood over the table to create a second desk. Thane and I snuck in there one day and were horrified to see stacks of paper from one end of the thing to the other. Old paper. Dusty, greasy, yellowing, with indecipherable handwriting. That's not the appropriate use of a pool table. Still gives me nightmares." He winked.

"I bet. What about the other rooms?"

"They didn't particularly interest us. I can't say anyone told us to stay out, but we really didn't have a reason to go in, either. We spent most of our time outside."

Had they subconsciously avoided the family room? If I owned a house this size, I'd put another bedroom up there, make a space for guests. Instead, the Prescotts had built an apartment over their garage. And then Thane had considered adding yet another new dwelling by the pool. Why not simply open up the upstairs?

"Sorry I couldn't help more," Matt said.

"Hmm?"

"With the original purpose of those rooms."

"Oh, that's fine. Idle curiosity. You know, being stuck in here all day."

"You could ask Thane. That summer of the ancient papers, Jim was writing a book on Maine history and he had found a lot of stuff about the Wilton family, Linda's ancestors, who originally built Rook's Rest. I never read it—not my thing—but if there's a copy in the house anywhere, it might say."

By lunchtime I'd screwed up the courage to insist the girls take afternoon classes on the third floor. The schedule called for history of fashion and then handwork, either of which I could easily have taught from the comfort of my bed, but I needed to prove—to myself as much as to Nathaniel—that I'd recovered from my night terrors.

The wind howled around the house as we waved good-bye to both Matt and Mrs. Vogel, who was leaving early because of the storm. The gusts set the lights to flickering, but the girls paid no mind, pounding up the stairs with Rocky hot on their heels. I followed at a more sedate pace. Before joining them in the schoolroom, I took a deep breath and laid my hand on the knob to the family room door. The brass warmed against my palm, inanimate. I twisted it sharply and shoved the door open. The rocking horse sat peacefully in its corner, dust motes disturbed by my entrance floating gently over its head.

"Whatcha looking at?" Hailey came up behind me.

"Nothing. Making sure the window is closed for when the snow arrives." I turned away from the view, but did not shut the door behind me. Wood and brass had proved no protection the night before; at least this way I could see any threat take form.

Our morning conversation, however, had alerted me to another, completely mundane threat to Liza's well-being. I paid close attention to her interactions with Hailey.

"Since you're reading about the settling of America," I said, "let's have a look at what the earliest settlers wore."

Predictably, Hailey grimaced. "Eww. Pilgrim clothes. Boring."

"Not at all. Certainly, some chose to keep to a plain, religious garb, but many early travelers brought with them extensive wardrobes. The ability to pay for imported fashions marked you as a member of a certain class in society then, even as it does today.

"And just as in the modern era, people who didn't fit the

mold were scorned. You can imagine how the ladies who powdered their hair and perfumed their bodies looked upon the Native American population. Fashion called for the palest skin, the most ruffled dresses. Even the men wore colorful, tailored outfits."

"With ruffles?" asked Hailey.

"Let's look." I opened the book, and we paged through several outfits that might have been brought to America from Europe.

"Remember, this was before the industrial revolution. Every stitch on these dresses, on these pants, was sewn by hand. They were hugely expensive, so a person might own only three or four outfits. And washing weakened the fabric, could tear seams. So they didn't launder their clothes very often, either. History was a pretty smelly place."

"Gross."

I laughed as Hailey's horror at my statement chased away my own fears. For the moment, these were merely two normal girls in a normal house. Even their competition had vanished in the face of such a repulsive idea. Once the American History section was complete, we took a break and switched over to the handwork portion of the lessons.

"The first thing each of you needs to decide," I said, "is whether you'd prefer learning to knit or to crochet. Liza wants to crochet—we discussed it at the yarn store—but you can do either. Knitting is more versatile, I think, but there's a Japanese style of crochet that allows you to make stuffed animals called amigurumi that are just adorable."

"Which one is easier?"

"I'm not sure either is actually easier, but in my experience, crochet is more forgiving. It's easier to fix a mistake, and a mistake is less likely to unravel your project. That said, most of the yarn work you see around is knit because it makes a flatter, more flexible fabric."

"Can I see both?"

"Sure."

We looked through the beginner's pattern books I'd picked up at the yarn shop, and Hailey agreed that she wanted to learn crochet like Liza. Because I had worked with Liza at the hospital, she was ahead of the game, allowing me to focus on Hailey and we spent the rest of the afternoon learning the basics of yarn tension and single and double crochet stitches as the first flakes spattered and crackled against the windows, flung at the house by the angry hand of the wind.

CHAPTER 13

*A*t dinner, Jenn quizzed Hailey about what she'd learned. I held my breath—she was testing me as much as her daughter—but Hailey answered enthusiastically about the historical clothes and the relations between fashion and industry. Her mother smiled at me and I relaxed.

Until the lights went out, dropping a thick shroud of silence and darkness over the table.

"Give it a minute," came Nathaniel's disembodied voice. "The generator will kick in after a few seconds." Sure enough, a wheezing thump sounded outside and the room flickered back to life.

"Oooh, spooky," said Hailey. "We should tell ghost stories."

"We most certainly will not." Prescott gentled his tone. "But if you've finished eating, we can make s'mores."

"That sounds lovely," said Jennifer. "We haven't made s'mores in years. Liza, why don't you show Molly where the ingredients are."

A catty voice in the back of my head laid odds Jennifer

hadn't eaten a s'more since discovering the meaning of calo-ries as I followed Liza into the kitchen.

When we returned, hands filled with sweets, the others had formed a semi-circle in front of the fireplace. Hailey bounced slightly as she reached for the marshmallows. "Uncle Thane said we could tell stories." She gave him a disgusted look. "Not ghost stories, just campfire tales. Did you ever go to camp?"

"No, I'm afraid not."

"Well, that's okay. Uncle Thane can start. He tells good ones." She shifted closer to her mother and patted the spot between herself and her uncle. So she hadn't given up on her ambition keep me away from Matt, she'd just turned her ambitions to matchmaking. I took my place, careful to avoid touching Prescott as I sat. If he saw through her invitation, he did not let it show.

The firelight played over all of us, and I felt I sat in a circle of intimate strangers. No one looks the same in uncer-tain light. Who were these people under the faces they wore during the day?

"Tell the one about the Indian princess," demanded Hailey.

"Native American," her mother corrected.

"Right. Tell the one about the Native American princess."

Nathaniel took a deep drink from the wine glass in his hand before speaking.

"All good stories begin with once upon a time," he said, and his deep voice sent a shiver up my spine. "As, indeed, do the bad ones. Once upon a time not very far from here, lived on a secluded and heavily forested piece of land a royal family. Now, they did not think of themselves as royal, you understand, for what does 'royal' mean when everyone you know shares your blood, your beliefs, your heritage? But among those who resided in that part of the forest, this was the most respected family.

"The people of the forest, the people of the dawn, lived peacefully. So the daughter of the family, Alawa, grew accustomed to walking where she would without fear, though she was but a child of eight.

"Beyond the reach of the forest, however, away from the peaceable enclave, many men fought over land and water. Alawa's three older brothers understood that their sister's naive joy protected their way of life. Should she learn of the horrors outside the woods, a great part of the beauty of their lives would be lost. So each day, when she set out into the forest, one of her brothers shadowed her.

"Now, one day Alawa's brother Machk saw how near to the strangers she wandered and he raced to spirit her away. But one of the men shot him through the heart. Alawa, hearing the noise, turned just in time to see her brother die.

"All her happiness shattered in an instant and with a great cry she fell upon Machk's body, weeping and moaning. The outsiders pulled her away and tried to convince her to tell them where they might find her family. But Alawa refused to tell. So the men sent her away to a school that she might learn to be more like them.

"Every night in her bed at the school, Alawa cried bitter tears, and the salt scorched the earth the outsiders had won in their wars so that the plants withered and the men began to starve. Only in the heart of the woods, in Alawa's grove, did the earth still nourish those who walked upon it.

"Many times, Alawa tried to escape. But for all her bravery, she was only eight. Then nine. Then ten.

"At last, on the eve of her twelfth birthday, Alawa managed to slip away. During the next seven nights, she ran like a cheetah. During the day, she hid wherever she could.

Finally, as the sun began to steal the sky from the moon on the eighth night, she arrived back at her grove.

"Alawa had grown much in her years away but her brother Keme, the new leader, knew her immediately, and much rejoicing ensued.

"Despite all her precautions, however, Alawa had been spotted by outsiders as she entered the forest. Soon they surrounded the grove, yelling in their strange language and waving guns. Alawa's family readied their own weapons, but she begged to be allowed to speak with the intruders, for she had learned their tongue in her years away from her own people. Flanked by her brothers, she approached the leader of the outsiders. He eyed her with distrust, but he refused to admit fear of a child, and a girl at that.

"'Tell your people to surrender,' he commanded.

"'My people will never surrender' she replied. 'And for every drop of our blood you spill, another patch of earth will grow barren. Have you not seen this yourselves? Every man you murder here will strangle the life from dozens of your own as they slowly starve.'

"The men, hearing this, whispered among themselves of witchcraft and curses, for they were a superstitious lot. And though they wanted to believe their God protected them, evidence had of late been scarce. This, too, Alawa had learned at her boarding school, and she used it when she continued.

"'You think to commit murder in this green place, but murder is never rewarded. My people know how to make the land fertile again, as you see from the growth around you. If you leave us to live in peace, we will teach you how to treat the land so it will provide for you and your children.'

"The leader of the outsiders looked around the grove and his mouth watered and his stomach rumbled. 'You will show us your secrets?' he asked.

"'I will. But we will need your word that our people—all our people—will remain undisturbed.'

"So they came to an agreement. But Alawa got the better side of the bargain, because once her tears ceased, the land began to heal itself and coaxing new life from it became easy. And because of the prejudices of the outsiders, when she insisted on protection for her people, they believed she meant those who lived well beyond her sphere of influence. Fearful of a return of the famines, the outsiders left those people alone as well.

"And so for many years, Alawa's family grew and prospered, and eventually she became their ruler, the wisest woman in the grove."

"And she got married," Hailey added, "And they lived happily ever after."

Nathaniel's lips twitched. "Of course. I always forget that part."

Hailey shook her head. "The happily ever after is the most important part." She tapped me on the leg. "Now you go."

"Oh, no. I don't know any stories." I did, of course. Dozens, even hundreds. But I consumed them, I did not create them.

"It's easy," she assured me. "You just start with 'once upon a time,' and end with 'happily ever after.'"

After a break for another round of s'mores, I stumbled my way through an abbreviated, fantasy-set version of Pride and Prejudice in which I cast Wickham as a troll possessed of a magical token which made him irresistible. It sounded ridiculous to my ears, but satisfied Hailey. Jennifer told a modern version of Cinderella, complete with a texting billionaire in place of a prince, and then it was time for bed.

THE NIGHT'S darkness might have whispered as I climbed the stairs, but Hailey kept up a steady commentary on schoolwork, storms, and stories that blocked out any disturbing noises. Malignant spirits could not overcome the ego of a teenager.

Later, as I lay in bed listening to the low murmur of Nathaniel's voice next door reading *Little Women* to his daughter, my mind returned to Matt's revelations that morning. Jim Prescott taught history. How much of Nathaniel's tale had come from him? I'd learned very little about Native American culture or history in school, but I knew children had been taken from their parents and put in white boarding schools until relatively recently. And there had been no protective treaties negotiated by girls whose tears destroyed the earth, despite the fairy tale.

But if Jim Prescott had run across the story of Alawa while researching his history of New England, might he also have discovered a tale or two about the property on which his house was set? I longed to ask Nathaniel for a copy of his father's book, but I did not dare. Such a request so soon after last night's horrors would give away my purpose and he'd fire me in an instant if he thought I believed the house haunted by some past occupant. Perhaps I could find a copy myself. Both the library and Jim Prescott's former office in the billiards room seemed likely spots. Not at night—I had no intention of leaving my bedroom in the dark—but maybe after breakfast.

As predicted, the virus had run its course in two days, but between illness and lack of sleep, the fluffy bed wove its seductive spell even more quickly than usual, and moments after I curled onto my side and shut my eyes, exhaustion sucked me under.

A child's cries woke me. It was still dark. Darker, in fact, than it had been when I'd climbed into bed. I groped for the nightstand, found the lamp, and pulled the chain, but it did not come on. Had the generator broken down? I listened for the wheezy rattle I'd heard as it worked earlier, but the child's sobbing drowned out everything else. I could not determine from which direction the sound originated. It echoed peculiarly.

I sat up and tried to feel around on the floor for my canvas shoes with my toes. I had to get to Liza. But now, more than the crying registered. The house smelled wrong. The familiar wax and polish, dust and age hung on, but the scent of brine overlaid it all as if the sea had crept infinitely closer as we slept.

A woman shouted in a strange language and a babble of men's voices—in English, but with words I could not quite catch—responded. Why could I understand nothing, no matter how I tried? And then it came to me and the building fear and frustration slipped from my body in a rush of relief. I had not woken at all. I had never recognized a dream for what it was, but Ali regularly did and she had told me she could force herself to wake from them when it happened.

"Wake up," I ordered myself.

The men's voices dimmed slightly, but multiple sets of footsteps sounded in the hallway. Too many.

"Wake up," I said again. The footsteps thundered down the stairs. Voices rose again and the front door slammed.

The crack of the door woke me. Really, this time. The room glowed in the surreal, almost fluorescent light of the moon shining on snow. No child cried, no men shouted, no steps pounded down the hall. Only my heart raced, refusing to let go the fear that drove it into an unnatural rhythm.

I took deep, slow breaths, letting the normalcy of the surroundings seep in and replace the stress. I needed no supernatural cause to explain this dream: I'd merely blended Nathaniel's tale with my own loneliness and need for family.

Alawa's tears had created the strange odor, the voices belonged to the men who had taken her away from her happy grove.

~

BY MORNING, the storm had blown over and the sun shone painfully bright on the icy white landscape. In the kitchen, I found Jennifer pouring herself a cup of coffee.

"That's brave," she said as I buckled on my snow boots. "Are you sure you're ready for the mailbox hike yet?"

"Oh, yes. I feel fine." And I did. After the dream, I'd slept like the dead, and the last vestiges of the virus had fled. Even my mind felt sharper and I realized that Jennifer might prove a valuable resource if approached correctly. As Nathaniel had not appeared, I could safely ask about his father's work.

"The girls aren't terribly excited about American history," I said. "Unless, of course, it's related to fashion. I've been trying to come up with other ways to connect them to the material and I thought I might find something in the book Liza's grandfather wrote. Have you ever read it?"

"Jim Prescott's magnum opus?" She laughed. "No, I'm afraid I'm not that scholarly. I glanced through it once thinking it could be interesting, but dry does not begin to describe it. The girls would hate it."

"Oh, dear. I hoped Liza might find it compelling since her grandfather wrote it. Matt mentioned that he'd researched this land and if anything historically significant happened here they might at least enjoy hearing about that."

She scrunched up her nose. "Matthew said that?"

I nodded.

"I didn't realize he'd gotten through it, though God knows Jim gave our parents a copy."

"I don't suppose it matters. If you haven't seen one around here, the whole question's irrelevant."

"Well, I can't say I've looked for one. He was ridiculously proud of that book. I'm sure he had a stash of them here to pull out when anyone visited. We could hunt them up if you really think there might be anything in it for the girls."

"I need to motivate Hailey any way I can. She'll be going into a new school with children who are used to studying together. If she had personal stories about what they study, it could give her an in with the other students."

"I suppose it could."

Yeah, it sounded thin to me, too, but I wanted Jennifer's help.

"I'll have a look around."

"I'd really appreciate that." I pulled on my jacket and Rocky leaped to his feet and rushed over. "I don't think you can come with me today, little man. The snow's taller than you are."

"Thane plowed the driveway," Jennifer said. "You don't have to take the dog, of course, but you certainly can."

My shoulder blades twitched. I'd assumed Nathaniel was still asleep, though I should have known better. I couldn't help myself, I checked over my shoulder to see whether he'd come in while we chatted.

"The agency told me plowing wasn't possible, that we'd be stuck here when it snowed."

Her laugh tinkled, ice cubes in a cocktail. "In a real snow, that's true. All we have is a portable plow Thane attaches to the front of the Rover. It can handle ten to twelve inches, especially if the snow is fluffy, but not much more and not even that if it's heavy and wet. We'll have plenty of the nasty stuff as the winter goes on, I promise."

"Then I suppose this little guy ought to get his exercise in while he can." I hooked Rocky's leash to his collar, swallowed the last of my coffee, and waved goodbye to Jennifer as I pushed out the door.

A few flakes drifted through the air, chips off the pale china bowl of the sky overhead. Rocky bit at the walls of snow on either side of him and I had to drag him along, ruining his fun, until he finally gave up and darted ahead of me. Nathaniel was nowhere to be seen, and the thick coat of snow muffled all sound but the occasional crack of a branch breaking beneath its weight. Rocky and I might have been the last two creatures on earth. Winter had come upon us in all her glory and soon enough the pond would freeze.

I secured my letters into the outgoing mail clip and raised the flag. Ali would reply immediately. Nadya would take longer. I wished I could correspond with Mama the same way. Send a letter off into the great beyond and simply check a box every day until a response arrived. *You could try the Ouija board,* a traitorous voice whispered. But I wanted to talk to Mama, not to that strange, haggard creature who had stalked my dreams my second night at Rook's Rest. No, I would stick to the plan and search Jim Prescott's book for clues.

Footsteps crunched behind me and I whirled, nearly slipping on the icy ground. I steadied myself on the mailbox and clutched at Rocky's leash, but it was only Nathaniel. He carried a near empty sack of clay and sand mix, and I could see that he'd been sprinkling it along the path as he walked.

"I didn't expect you to be out this morning," he said.

"I had letters." I glanced up and down the road. The plows had been by overnight and less than an inch of snow coated the tarmac. "There will be pickup today, won't there?"

"Absolutely. We're a hardy lot. Something important in your mail?"

"Not at all." Why did I always, always feel gauche, awkward, and faintly guilty around him? "Just letting my family know I'm doing okay. They will have seen the weather reports."

"The roads are slick but safe. If you want, I can drive you into town and you can text or email. And I believe the house phone is still working, too, if you don't mind using that."

"Oh. No. Don't worry about that. It's fine. I don't want them to get used to hearing from me every time there's a storm. My little sister will start to rely on it and then freak out when I don't call."

"You must miss them. Sandy said you don't usually live in with families."

"I don't. But my sister's away at school, so we don't see each other all that much, anyway. I imagine living here is hard for you. Do you see your brother everywhere?"

"It's not so much that—he'd moved away long before he died—but my life would be a whole lot easier if I could chat with him the way Liza did with Marianne before she stopped talking altogether. What if I could just pick up one of the old Ouija boards Danny and I used to muck about with in the playroom and ask him what he wanted me to do for his family?"

His words, so similar to my own thoughts, gave me a jolt and I stumbled slightly. His hand grabbed my elbow, holding me upright.

"I didn't meant to startle you. I have no intention of actually playing with the board. I'm not my daughter."

"No." I tried to laugh. "Of course not."

CHAPTER 14

"I don't want to go outside," Hailey whined when, schoolwork finished, I told the girls to put on their coats. "It's cold. It's nasty. Can't we just skip that part today?"

I looked out at the snow-covered yard. The sun still shone, but an icy draft slipped through the gaps in the old window frame. I could not claim any enthusiasm myself for heading back out, but phys ed was on the program.

"I don't want you to spend all your time parked in front of the television," I said. "So if you don't want to run around this afternoon, we have to plan some kind of activity for the weekend."

"Sledding! There are sleds in the shed, but we have to ask Uncle Thane to get them out for us because they're behind a bunch of stuff. And the best hill is across the street, so it's too far to go today anyway."

"All right. Sledding it is. Tomorrow. Which means you are done for today."

It did not occur to me until she had run from the room and I heard her footsteps on the stairs to wonder how Hailey might know about the sleds if they were hidden away. Had she explored the shed on her own? And if so, might she have seen someone else while she did? Nathaniel's fall weighed on me. I would rest easier if I could attribute the sabotage to a completely mundane enemy.

I had hoped, with another hour or so until sunset, to be able to search through the pool room for Jim Prescott's book. But Liza had another activity in mind. Her steady gaze never left me as I tidied the classroom, and when I lifted my bag from beside my desk, she jerked her head to the side in a distinct "follow me."

My heart sank. The ghost book attracted her as surely as it repulsed me. I'd avoided it as long as possible, however, so I nodded. "Where shall we go?"

She aimed her thumb at herself.

"Your room it is."

We walked out together, but I made her go into her room while I removed the book from beneath the mattress. In her room, I found Liza perched on her bed, writing in a small notebook that she hurriedly stuffed under her pillow when I entered. A diary? I'd kept one at her age.

I ignored the notebook, though I could not ignore my curiosity. Liza kept herself completely closed off, utterly hidden away. Not merely through her lack of speech but through a deliberate dampening of affect. The journal could provide a key to everything she endured. But I could not invade her privacy. Not if I expected her to learn to trust me.

I opened the book and flipped to the spot where we'd left off. The chapter title—The History of the Talking Board— ambushed me and I had to take several deep breaths before I could begin. Three times in a matter of hours the Ouija had come up. Even I could feel the weight of the number.

Liza listened intently as I read the chapter, and when I closed the book she leaped from the bed and gestured for me to follow her. Down the hall we went, and into the playroom. There we found Hailey engrossed in a video game, and Liza's expression blackened. A sick weakness washed through me as I realized what she'd intended: Nathaniel had mentioned that he and Daniel had Ouija boards. She must want to try to communicate with whatever spirit she felt inhabited the house.

But not in front of her cousin. I broke out into a cold sweat. Could I find and remove the boards while the girls were out sledding and then play dumb? Perhaps Nathaniel knew where to lay hands on them. I could ask him to do it— surely he would understand why such a game, while harmless for him and his brother, could be detrimental to his daughter even if the board's answers were only reflections of the subconscious wishes of the questioners. I would ask him after dinner. All I had to do was keep the girls together until then.

LUCK WAS with me for the remainder of the afternoon. Hailey stubbornly refused to leave the video game, thwarting Liza's evident desire to be alone in the playroom. Meanwhile, Liza squirmed and fidgeted for a good half hour, then grabbed a book and plopped herself in the corner of the playroom where she could watch in case her cousin got up for even an instant. And as for me, I collected my crochet and settled in to oversee the situation, hoping to ward off any untimely searches.

Stalemate.

Mrs. Vogel had to call up the stairs twice to get Hailey away from the television for dinner, by which time I had pried Liza loose and herded her downstairs. Safe, at least for the moment.

At dinner, I brought up the topic of sledding.

"Oh, absolutely," Nathaniel said when I suggested it. "We have a couple of blue plastic sleds and one of those red flexible flyer ones in the shed. I'll dig them out in the morning." He grinned at Hailey. "I suppose your uncle Matt told you the story about how Danny and I almost got him run over sledding down the big hill across the road?"

"Yup."

"It wasn't true, you know. That hill's not steep enough to land you in the middle of the street. He stopped with at least three feet to spare. I think the whole thing scared the driver far more than it scared Matt."

Jennifer shook her head. "It scared my parents most of all, even though they didn't hear about it until later. I thought for sure we'd never come back for Christmas vacation."

"Will you sled with us tomorrow?" asked Hailey.

"Oh, I don't think that's really my thing."

"Come on, mom. Please?"

"You used to love it, Jenn. Why not?"

"I suppose I could," Jennifer agreed. "But if I slide out into the middle of the street, someone is going to pay."

The hours after dinner before the girls went to bed seemed interminable, and every time Liza stood or stretched or shifted, I jumped. But she stuck it out with the rest of the family downstairs until it was time for bed.

I waited by my door until I heard Nathaniel finish his nightly reading session in her room, then ambushed him in the hallway.

"We need to talk," I whispered.

He raised his eyebrows, gesturing to my room, but I shook my head. I could not chance Liza listening in. Nor did I particularly want to draw Jennifer's attention. She had yet to come upstairs, so I had a few minutes in private. It wouldn't be long. Nathaniel usually went back down after reading to Liza; if he did not return soon Jennifer would become curious.

Playroom, I mouthed, and he nodded.

Once we were there, I told him about Liza's preoccupation with the Ouija boards and asked whether he knew where they were.

"Oh, hell. I should never have agreed to let you read that book with her."

"I know. But it's done."

"I have no idea where those things are. Probably tucked away with the Snakes and Ladders or the Monopoly set that's missing most of its pieces. Or maybe up in the attic."

"She was really anxious to look in here—as if she'd already seen one. Can you take them sledding tomorrow first thing and I'll try to find it and get rid of it? I know you have to go back downstairs now, and I don't want to make much noise anyway. Neither of the girls is sleeping and I don't want them to get curious and find us looking."

"And when she asks—and she'll find a way to ask, even without words—what happened to the board?"

"I don't know! I'll think of something. Maybe she's only seen the box and never thought of using the board itself. What if I remove the board from the box? Or the planchette?"

"I dislike deceiving my daughter."

"It's not at the top of my list, either. But I can't believe that allowing her to try to contact a ghost—even if the ghost isn't really there to be contacted—is a good idea."

He sighed. "No. Not that she needs the board. She used to just talk. Like Marianne could hear her. And like Marianne was answering her. Freaked me right out, I don't mind telling you, but she didn't need pseudo-spiritual help."

"But she's not talking now. So that avenue's been cut off."

"I suppose." He rubbed his forehead. "I don't want to lie to her. Did she seem to want your help with the board?"

"Yes. Maybe, as you say, because she's stopped talking. The book said questions needed to be spoken aloud. So she'll need a voice to work the board."

"Then let her find it. When she does, tell her you won't use it without me. We'll get her through it together."

Everything in me rebelled at the idea, but I nodded. I would find a way to put him off. To put them both off. I would not open that door.

WORRY WORE ON ME, but every time my eyes drifted shut, the crack of a branch, the call of an owl, the creak of a board would send a spurt of adrenaline into my blood. Impossible currents swirled, brushing across my nose and ruffling my hair, raising goosebumps over my skin. Fantasy? Reality? I could no longer trust the evidence of my own senses. The faint scent of dirty smoke filtered into the room. I choked, blinked, sat up.

What on earth? I flicked on the lamp, but the room appeared normal. I sniffed again and the odor tickled the back of my throat. Where was it coming from?

A muffled noise from Liza's room had me shoving myself from the bed. I crept toward the connecting door. If the girl was up, I did not want her to find me spying. A draft slipped from beneath her door, icy on my toes as I pressed an ear to the wood.

Nothing. I laid my hand on the knob and turned it, the clicking whine loud in the sleeping house.

"Liza?" I whispered. I poked my head around the door, and every drop of blood in my body froze.

The gaunt, haggard image of my mother's cancer-riddled

figure, ribboned in fine threads of ashes and dust, hovered beside Liza's bed, stroking her head with a bony claw. I tried to draw breath, but managed only a rasping wheeze. The corpse thing turned to look at me and smiled. Almost, I could hear her speaking to me, telling me to come to her, to love her, to be with her. To be warm in the bitter cold of the world.

I launched myself at it without thought. It shifted, no more my mother, but that strange, pulsing cloud of smoke I'd seen upstairs. I snatched up the chair next to Liza's bed and struck out with the chair, screaming as I waved it over the bed.

"Get away from her! Get away!"

The chair slammed into something solid and nearly ripped from my grasp. I fought to hold on though I felt it slipping and about to fall onto the bed. Then, in a rush of freezing wind, the smoke disappeared.

Before I could recover, Liza's door slammed open. Nathaniel stood there, expression black as widow's weeds and radiating both fear and fury.

"What is going on in here?"

I could not answer. I set down the chair, catching Liza's watchful, wakeful eyes as I did so. Her face was moon-pale in the darkness and suddenly I realized that I should not have been able to see the creature at all. And yet, its features were etched deeply into my brain. My legs gave out, so I sank into the chair without a word.

"Liza, are you okay?"

She nodded.

"Miss Allworth, I think it's clear that this is not the right place for you. We are expecting more snow next week. I suggest you pack tomorrow—today—and leave while you can."

Shame and relief washed over me in combination. I had

failed. Failed Liza, failed myself. But if Nathaniel sent me away, I had to go.

"No." Liza's whisper was so thin I should not even have heard it, but I did. We did.

I whipped around to stare at her, hearing Nathaniel gasp. When I looked back at him, he was steadying himself against the doorjamb, his face nearly as pale as his daughter's.

Footsteps in the hall signaled Hailey's entrance, then Jennifer's, but Nathaniel never took his eyes from Liza. He groped his way to her bed like a drunk and settled on the edge.

"Please let Molly stay." Again that thin, hoarse thread of sound, unnaturally loud in the silence of the room.

Jennifer choked and clapped her hand over her mouth.

"At long last, it speaks." Hailey was unimpressed as only a teen can be.

"Hailey!"

"Oh, come on, mom. Get over it. She was going to talk sometime." She looked at me. "Was that you screaming? What happened?"

Nathaniel swung his head round to pin me in that uncomfortable way he had, waiting for an answer.

"I'm not sure." Too many eyes watched me. Too many ears listened. I had to work through the events on my own before I could begin to talk them over with anyone. "Maybe a bad dream."

"There was something in here," Liza's voice was still small and she frowned as if it physically hurt her to speak, but she was steady. "Molly chased it away."

"Something like what?" asked Hailey.

"I think," Nathaniel interrupted, "that it's entirely too late to make sense of any of this tonight. Hailey, pack yourself back off to bed."

"I want to know what Liza thinks she saw."

Liza glared at her cousin. "A wasp," she muttered. "Maybe there's a whole nest in your room."

"There's no wasp nest in my room! And no one screams like a banshee to get rid of a wasp."

"Depends on whether or not you've ever been stung by a particularly nasty wasp," said Nathaniel. "But regardless, I don't see any wasp now, so I think it's safe for everyone to go back to bed."

He stayed put, however, and there was a warning in his eyes that kept me in place, too. After a long moment, both Hailey and her mother left. Only then did he rise and check to be sure that the hallway was empty before shutting the door and returning.

"Now, let's have the truth."

I looked away.

"You saw her," Liza demanded. "Tell him."

"I don't know what I saw."

Nathaniel's mouth flattened and his eyes narrowed. "Are we back to this ghost nonsense again? Liza, I'm sorry, but your mom is dead. That's not going to change. I would do anything on earth to fix it, but I can't. And neither can you. You need to remember your mom and love her without pretending her spirit is hanging around."

"I'm not making it up. Molly saw her."

He glared at me, jaw working.

"I saw *something*," I said. "I can't tell you exactly what it was, but I can say fairly surely that it was not your wife. Your mother."

"Another mouse?" Sarcasm lay thick and heavy on the words.

"No."

"It was mom. It was."

"No, honey, it wasn't."

"How do you know? You never met her, so you wouldn't recognize her."

"That's exactly the problem. I wouldn't recognize your mother. But the thing I saw in your room, that I did recognize."

Her eyes widened. "Who was it?"

"It looked like my mother. Not yours. And something that appears in different forms to different people, well, that's not apt to actually be any of the forms it takes, now is it? Can you trust something like that?"

Nathaniel pressed two long fingers into the front of his forehead where a vein pulsed. "So you saw your mother? What was she doing?"

"No. It wasn't her. That's what I'm trying to tell you. It's...only vaguely human. It looks like the worst memories of my mom, the things I've tried to forget, the shell she was at the very end of her life, when all her vibrancy and vitality had been sucked away. Like a poor artist had tried to create my mother out of dust and dirt and smoke and mirrors and came up with this simulacrum."

"Is that what you see?" he asked Liza. "Your mom the way she was that day?"

She swallowed, then swallowed again. "Not exactly."

"Can you tell us exactly?" I started to reach out, but then withdrew my hand. I missed my own family, but I could not make the mistake of believing myself part of this one. It had been less than ten minutes since Nathaniel had attempted to fire me. It would not do to forget my position.

"She's pretty. I mean, she was pretty...that day...you know. Like, pale and pretty. Her eyes are wrong, though. When she talks to me, when she invites me to come with her, it's like she has a secret. Mom had secrets, too, but they never scared me. Sometimes, now, I get scared."

"Does she look the same as she did at your old house?"

"What is that supposed to mean?" Nathaniel barked.

"Does she, Liza?"

The girl thought for a minute, then shook her head. "She's more solid. At home, she was kind of fading. And she didn't want me to come with her. She asked me about school and stuff, and told me everything would be okay. Since we moved here, she's gotten...angrier, I think."

"This is the most ridiculous thing I've ever heard. Ghosts. And not just one, but I imagine you interpret this to mean that two separate ghosts have latched on to my daughter?"

"Do you take me for an expert? Because I assure you, I'm not. Not all Gypsies read fortunes and talk to the dead, you know. Most of that's fake."

"Good to know," he said dryly. "Because I thought you'd be calling in a few of your relatives to clear the place of evil spirits next."

That cut deep, but I wrapped the wound and soldiered on.

"Liza is the expert here, not me. Liza has been talking to whoever, whatever this thing is ever since you moved here."

"I don't really talk to her. Not like I did at home. She mostly talks to me."

"What does she say?"

Nathaniel gritted his teeth at the question, but let his daughter answer.

"She tells me how lonely she is, and how sad she is that we're not together."

I remembered the seductive call of the mother-thing. "What does she want you to do about that?"

"I'm not sure." But she didn't meet my eyes.

I would have pressed, but Nathaniel had other ideas. He stroked Liza's hair. "It doesn't matter. We can worry about it tomorrow. Right now, I am just happy to hear your voice, sweetheart. I'm so glad you decided to come back to us."

"I didn't go anywhere."

"I know. But I missed you anyway." He smiled sadly and my wounded heart bled a little more. I'd seen that same fading, the distance that made me want to grab Liza and hang on for dear life. Unlike her father, I wasn't at all certain that her speech indicated a return but at least it gave us a way to reach her.

Nathaniel kissed her forehead. "Can you sleep now? You're not afraid?"

She shook her head. But then, the spirit had never frightened her.

"Good. Miss Allworth, would you mind continuing this conversation downstairs?"

"No, of course not."

"You're going to talk about me, aren't you?"

He hesitated, frowning, and I remembered that he tried not to lie to her. "I promise to tell you anything we discuss that will affect you. How's that?"

Her frown perfectly mirrored his. "Why can't you just stay here to talk?"

"Because Miss Allworth and I have grown-up things to work out."

"But you won't make her go away?"

"I won't make Miss Allworth do anything she does not wish to do. Will that do?"

She turned her dark eyes on me. "You don't want to leave, do you, Molly?"

Yes, I did. Desperately. But leaving meant relinquishing Liza to the thing that wanted her to join it in the land of the dead. Even if Nathaniel survived that, I doubted he'd come out with much of a life. I could not abandon either of them.

"I'm not going anywhere," I assured her

I was shivering, so I stopped in my room and pulled on a sweatshirt over my pajamas. Hardly the most elegant outfit I'd ever worn for a conversation with an employer, but Nathaniel wore only sweatpants and a tee shirt himself. And in part because of intimacy of our situation, I could not retreat from thinking of him as Nathaniel although he'd returned to the formal Miss Allworth.

I found him in the library pouring himself a drink. He held up his glass in question, but I shook my head.

"I don't drink."

"You're a better person than I am, then."

"It's not a moral thing. I like to stay in control."

"And a glass of wine will make you lose control?"

"You're not drinking wine."

He barked a hoarse laugh. "No. No, I am not. That scene upstairs calls for scotch. But if you want wine, I'll get it for you."

"No." I sat down in a chair opposite his spot the couch. He looked at the space between us and raised one black eyebrow.

"I don't bite, Miss Allworth."

"You're angry."

The other eyebrow went up as well. "What gave you that idea?"

I waited and eventually he put the glass down on the coffee table and sighed. "Angry doesn't begin to describe it."

"I'm sorry." I couldn't even say what I was apologizing for.

"How long have you been seeing...things...in this house?"

"The first time was the day you fell. That was just a second or two, though. And I can't honestly say that I saw anything specific. It was more a sense of wrongness."

"And you didn't consider that I deserved to hear about it?"

"I didn't plan to let it affect my job."

"Oh, yes, the job. Mrs. Martin spoke very highly of you. She swore you were level-headed, one of her best employees. You wouldn't take off, or develop peculiar ideas, or succumb to religious mania." That brutal, biting sarcasm was back. I absorbed it, kept all defensiveness from my tone when I replied.

"My mother worked for Sandy as well. Her recommendation came from two generations' experience with my family."

"She told me that. You don't have to stay. I release you from your obligation. I'll pay her fee if you leave."

"I promised Liza I'd stay."

He sipped his scotch. "My daughter is too smart. She knew I would try to convince you to go, and spiked my guns before I could get a word in."

"She sees me as an ally. The first adult who's taken her claims seriously. If you gave her the benefit of the doubt, she'd desert me soon enough."

"The benefit of the doubt. Let's talk about what that might look like. I pretend to think that there's a ghostly presence in this house?"

"You don't pretend. You just told me that Liza was smart.

If you pretend, she'll know. You have to accept that your own beliefs could be wrong. That another realm might actually exist."

"Fine. For a minute, we'll say it does. So a creature from that other realm has come to this one to...what? Hang around a teenaged girl who's lost her mother? For what possible reason?"

"I told you, I have no idea. I'm not a medium, or even a carnival queen."

"Carnival queen?"

"A faker. A fortune teller. One of those women who wears jingling bracelets and earrings and hypes her Romani heritage even if she doesn't have one and pretends to commune with the spirit world."

"Ah."

"But..."

"But?"

"Liza said the ghost is lonely. I don't imagine occasional contact with a living child could alleviate that."

He glanced up from the drink he'd been studying. "Spit it out, Miss Allworth."

"If you accept that we're dealing with a ghost, then it can likely only have a real relationship with another ghost."

"You're telling me this thing is trying to kill her?" The question sounded almost academic. He didn't believe his daughter was in jeopardy. And why should he? They'd been living in the house for months without incident. At least without any harm coming to his daughter. The incidents with the other tutors and the ladder he blamed on completely mundane causes.

"It hasn't yet, so perhaps that's not the goal."

"But you ascribe some malicious intent to this thing, or you wouldn't have run into Liza's room to chase it away."

"If you could see it, feel it, you'd understand. It's cold. Nasty. There's no love in it. No joy. Nothing, for want of a better word, *human*."

He nodded. "If you say so. Let's continue. Hypothetically, some evil spirit lives in this house and haunts my daughter. What should I do about it? I've already told you I can't afford to move."

"You say that, but this place, the way you live... Before I moved in here, I shared a two-bedroom apartment with more people than live in this whole house. You can't support Liza in the style to which she's accustomed, but isn't poor and safe better than comfortable and threatened?"

Not that there was much safety in poverty, but I had never felt, even when things were at their worst right after Mama's diagnosis, before Nadya and Bo made room for us, the way I did when I'd seen that creature hovering over Liza's bed. Even the memory made me nauseous, and it must have shown on my face.

"You really believe she's in danger." Nathaniel shook his head.

"I do."

"Then I suppose I owe you the truth. I can't leave. We can't leave. I stopped paying attention to the business after Marianne's death. I coasted, left everything to other people to manage. Danny said it was under control, but his accident forced me to wise up, to focus. The finances are a mess. I have an accountant and a tax attorney trying to untangle it now. Marianne and I set up a trust years ago, when things were good, to pay for Liza's tuition. That's where your salary is coming from, so it's safe. Eventually, perhaps as early as spring or summer, we'll be back on our feet. But right now, abandoning ship is simply not feasible."

"What about your parents? They can't help?"

"If I landed on their doorstep with this story, both my daughter and I would be institutionalized faster than you can say Ghostbusters. They're firm believers in reality, my parents. And in standing on your own two feet. And every other good, New England Puritan value. They never warmed up to Marianne. The fact that I'd married an artist appalled them. She was too moody, too emotional, too flighty. They weren't even surprised by her suicide. I never told them about Liza's ghost stories. I knew they'd say she'd inherited her mother's instability." He grimaced. "But you don't have to stay. As I said earlier, I'll settle up with Mrs. Martin. We'll find a suitable excuse for her."

But if I went home, Sandy wouldn't give me the good jobs. She'd sniff out whatever lie Nathaniel came up with. And I couldn't maintain my self-respect, my desire to become a school counselor, if I abandoned Liza. One way or another, my future was tied to the Prescotts.

"No. I'm here for the duration." With the concession, exhaustion swamped me and I felt myself listing to one side. For better or worse, I'd made my decision. And even if Nathaniel never called me Molly again, at least I'd told him the truth.

He let out a long breath, and his posture relaxed slightly. "Good. I admit to being glad I won't have to answer to Liza for your absence. But you still haven't told me what you think we should do about her situation."

"No. And I'm not thinking terribly clearly right now."

"No. Of course not. You should get some sleep. Will you be able to?"

"Yes, I think so."

"Then we'll talk more in the morning."

~

Despite my confidence, sleep eluded me until the sun's first bloody rays stained the sky. When a sharp rap at my door woke me, my eyes were filled with grit and my head pounded. Hailey let herself in without waiting for an invitation and sat in the chair next to my bed, drawing her knees up under her chin.

"So. What happened last night?"

This, at least, Nathaniel and I should have discussed. I had no doubt he would get the same question from Jennifer.

"Nothing of importance." I picked up my cell to check the time. Five after eight. Curiosity had a salutary effect on a teenager's sleeping habits, apparently. "It's early. I need another hour of sleep, and then maybe we can convince your uncle to dig out the sleds."

"No way!" Her shriek pierced my throbbing head. "I'm not leaving until you tell me the truth."

"Suit yourself," I said, and rolled over, pulling the duvet over my head.

She yanked it down. "Come on. I heard you go downstairs with uncle Thane."

"If you heard us go downstairs, you know that our discussion was none of your business."

She huffed and narrowed her eyes. "Uncle Thane will tell mom and she'll tell me. We don't keep secrets."

"Great. Then you don't need me." I pulled the duvet back up. Another knock at my door and I gave up on getting more sleep.

Jennifer stuck her head in. "Hailey! I thought I heard you. Go on downstairs and get breakfast. I need to have a conversation with Molly."

She groaned.

"Now, Hailey."

She stormed out, slamming the door behind her and

sending another spike of pain through my skull. Jennifer sighed.

"She has a temper, but she's a good girl." She eyed me up and down, and I resisted the urge to sit up straighter in my bed. She'd invaded my private space; she could deal with the informality.

"Thane is my family," she said at last. "And I care for Liza as my own daughter."

An odd assertion, given her widely disparate ambitions for the two girls, but I said nothing. Zipped lips led to job security.

"I don't know how you managed to get her to speak. Perhaps the whole screaming fit scared her. Perhaps it made her think you believed her ridiculous ghost fantasies. Perhaps the time was simply right. No matter, we are all grateful that she's gotten over of the worst of her issues."

I bit my tongue.

She sat down in the chair Hailey had vacated. "I am sure Thane expressed his appreciation last night. But I need to be frank with you: others before you have gotten the wrong idea about him." She waited, but I didn't say a word. My bedroom, her ballgame. "He had an affair with Liza's last tutor. It did not end well."

Interesting. Nathaniel denied the affair in his story. I was all for female solidarity, but in this case, a case where the female in question had then attacked Jennifer's "family" with a butcher knife, I couldn't quite see how she'd landed on Aimee's side.

"Did you hear about that?"

"I did. First from Hailey, then from Nathaniel."

She waved a hand and her wedding set caught the light, fracturing it into a thousand shards. Too bad Nathaniel couldn't convince her to sell that. It would bring them enough to live on for a while. But I doubted it would even occur to him to ask. He had too much pride.

"Nathaniel probably said there was no affair. And more than likely he didn't think there was. Men and women interpret emotional ties so very differently, don't they?" She didn't wait for an answer. "But I like you, Molly. I don't want you to get caught up in the same trap Aimee did. She thought his casual affection meant more than it did. She thought she was going to marry him."

A trill of laughter at the ridiculousness of such a belief and then she sobered.

"But the attack was partly my fault. I helped select her, you know. Went to the interviews, talked to her. I should have understood how lonely she was, how likely to fixate on Thane. He's always had a magnetic personality. Ever since we were children.

"I did warn him, but I left it too late. And I never spoke to her about it, which in hindsight I should have. I don't want to make that mistake with you."

This was not a question, but she waited for an answer.

"I see," I said at last, although I didn't.

"Do you? Thane adores his daughter. Right now, he's undergoing a wave of euphoria, and for the moment it will focus on you. Don't mistake his gratitude for anything more serious."

Had she missed Nathaniel's decided coldness the night before? Or was she so intent on securing her own position that she feared any challenger, no matter how ill-equipped?

"Of course not," I said.

DESPITE ITS SIZE, the house crowded, suffocated, and

forgoing even coffee, I pulled on my boots and coat to walk down the drive to the mailbox. The itchy frustration running over my nerves intensified when I stopped to pet Rocky, so I ignored his pleading eyes and left on my own. The sky hung dark and low overhead. The massive hawk I'd seen the day I arrived sewed giant circles in the clouds as he searched out his hapless prey. Although I'd taken the trek many times, today the bleak loneliness of the environs enthralled me. Without Rocky's cheerful, snuffling presence, the world seemed infinite, unconquerable, as oppressive in its own fashion as the claustrophobic interior of the house.

To my surprise, two of the pieces in the box were addressed to me. The first, a postcard from Ali, was brief and cheerful. She loved her classes, had found a helpful study group, and the only thing that would make her happier would be to have me with her. She hoped my employers and new charges understood how lucky they were to have me. This last made me laugh out loud—completely out of character, it was clearly intended for Nathaniel to read when he picked up the mail.

The other item for me was a letter addressed in a hand I did not recognize. It had no return address, and a Massachusetts postmark had been smeared across the bright stamp. I peeled off my gloves and slipped a finger beneath the envelope's flap to tear it open and went straight for the signature. A single, boldly scrawled *M*. Matt. He'd actually written.

Dear Molly,

I bet you thought I wouldn't write. I almost didn't. I write all day at work and generally prefer to use the phone to communicate outside of office hours. But I stopped off for lunch on my way home and thought I'd drop you a note from the outside world while I was on the road.

Also, I have to admit the less than admirable desire to prove you wrong. I could see on your face that you didn't expect a letter. You don't hide your feelings well. It's quite endearing, actually. In the legal system, everyone wears a mask. As I imagine your face now, I hope that mixed with the chagrin at having been proving wrong there is at least a little pleasure.

I also hope you'll get in touch with me if there is anything I can do for you. It is probably presumptuous of me to believe there is anything in the world that you cannot handle that I can, but there you are. I am afraid I am presumptuous. It comes with the territory for an attorney—we all think nothing is beyond us.

In any case, I have little to say, having left your side only hours ago. But I realized I had not given you my cell number and I do want you to have it, even if it is only useful when the power is on.

Please do look after yourself as well as you look after the girls,
—M

I folded the letter carefully and slipped it back into the envelope. How odd. I tapped it a couple of times against my chilly lips, considering how I should respond, then shook myself. I had more to worry about than Matthew Brahms. Nonetheless, I tucked the letter deep into my pocket so that it would not get mixed in with the mail I carried in my hand.

I could hear angry voices even before I opened the back door, and almost turned around and set off for the shed to look for the sleds myself rather than entering, until I heard my name.

"Miss Allworth is not the problem," Nathaniel said.

"No? Have you forgotten Aimee? And Shae? You wouldn't listen when I warned you about them, either."

"This is not the same."

"Of course it is. She's helped Liza more than the others did, I'll give her that, but I don't trust her. She's more than a little crazy—whatever you're not saying about last night, that much is clear—and she sees you as her golden ticket."

Fury heated my cold skin. *Snake.* But at least I understood my position, and Jennifer's. The statement made her goal as clear and sharp as the winter air. She planned to replace her dead husband with his brother. I'd have to make her see that I posed no threat to her ambitions. Nathaniel might, indeed, be grateful that his daughter had recovered her speech, but gratitude—at least among my set—did not form the basis of romantic relationships, and my own ambitions touched only obliquely on romance anyway. I was lonely without my family, that much was true. I hoped, someday, once I had my degree and a job that allowed me independence, to start a family of my own. But so many hurdles came before that— Ali's education and my own, finding a job in a shrinking market—that love and marriage had fallen off my radar.

And with his daughter's life on the line, I was fairly sure it hadn't crossed Nathaniel's mind, either. Not to mention his fury at me for, as he saw it, playing along with his daughter's delusions. I blew out a breath, fogging the cold air, and pushed the door open. "I'm back! Alas, I come bearing bills."

"Well, that's no fun," said Jennifer with a determinedly cheerful air. "Nothing good in the mail?"

I riffled through the stack of mail. "Bills and junk. Two catalogs. Is that good?"

Jennifer's eyes narrowed slightly before the lines smoothed out . "Well, I suppose it depends on where they're from!"

Nathaniel's expression closed, but his eyes slipped to her. He could hear the false note as well. What was she hinting at?

Matt's letter. But how could she possibly know about that? Unless... I felt slightly sick. Unless she'd told him to flirt with me in order to keep me out of the way. Would she have revealed her intentions to her brother? Suddenly I remembered her voice in the fog, exhorting an unseen man to do his part. I stuffed the letter deeper into the pocket of my jacket.

"I did get a postcard from my sister in college."

"Where is she?" Jennifer asked.

"St. Louis. She's pre-med, so the classes are hard, but she's loving it."

"Pre-med? That's impressive." Nothing in Jennifer's tone indicated that she was impressed. "But medical school is very expensive."

Nathaniel saluted with a coffee cup and slipped from the room. He hadn't spoken a word since I'd interrupted the argument.

I focused on Jennifer. "We're hoping for a scholarship. But every penny I can earn helps, so you don't need to worry about what we talked about this morning—no foolish ideas will derail me from getting a good reference so I can go on to another job after this one. I know you understand the importance of family. Wherever she's accepted, I'll want to move to be near her. After this job ends, of course."

An out-and-out lie, as I had no intention of leaving Hartford, where I had job security, to hover over my grown sister like a prying nanny, but with any luck it would reassure Jennifer. I needed her to back off. I might have to give up hope of ever having her help with Liza and whatever clung to her, but I could not afford to fight her interference at the same time as I found an unseen force.

"I totally agree." She dropped into a seat and took a sip of the coffee in her hand. "You're a smart woman, Molly."

Yeah. Smart and more than a little crazy.

"My brother was quite taken with you, I think."

"He's very sweet. But as I said, I'm focused on Ali's education."

She nodded. "Like I said, smart. Well, he can wait. He's good at that. You have to be to make it through law school and then all the years of being a peon at a big firm. Don't count him out too soon."

Now that I recognized her motives, my own path became clear. I could not control my emotions, but I could let Jennifer believe her plots were succeeding.

"I won't," I promised.

CHAPTER 16

J managed less than ten minutes alone in the kitchen after Jennifer left. It was barely enough time to shed my outerwear, suck down a cup of coffee with heavy cream, and devour a couple of pieces of toast slathered with jam. As I finished my hasty meal, Liza joined me.

"Shall I make you some breakfast?" She was too thin. When I'd arrived, her slight appearance had seemed part and parcel of her psychological damage. A child who did not speak could hardly be expected to eat properly, after all. Now, it seemed more threatening. I could almost believe the otherworldly force was depleting her from the inside, hoping to bring her across by simple attrition.

She pulled a tea bag out of the tin on the counter, set a the kettle on to boil, then popped open the pantry door and stared in. After a moment, she turned her head slightly, acknowledging me with the barest of glances. "Daddy wants to see you."

Of course he did. I would want to see me, too. But why hadn't he come himself?

"He's in the shed." Her voice was still a raspy whisper.

"Is your throat sore?"

She shook her head. "Just hard to talk."

"It may be swollen or get tired easily since you haven't used it for so long. Try cold drinks if the hot ones don't help."

I poured more coffee into my mug and wished Nathaniel had chosen to meet in the house, rather than have me slog back out through the snow. But he had likely caught on to Jennifer's ambitions long before I had and was trying to avoid making her jealous. How did he feel about her? My mind shied away from the idea of the two of them together.

"Where's your cousin?"

"With Aunt Jenn." Liza carried a box of cereal to the table and I caught a private, wicked smile flickering over her lips before she took a deep breath and spoke in a rush. "I mentioned the pattern books to Aunt Jenn and told her to pick out what she wanted me to make for her. I think she's trying to limit the damage."

I remembered Jennifer's pleasure in inflicting a first-timer's project on her brother and tried not to laugh.

"You're a terrible child." I winked at her.

She preened slightly, finally facing me full-on, and I laughed outright.

"All right. You keep them busy. I'll be back soon."

The shed sat slightly behind and to the right of the garage. Unlike the driveway, which Nathaniel had plowed, the path leading from the garage to the shed had been shoveled out by hand. The icy walls had collapsed in several places overnight and I slipped as I crunched through the clots of snow and ice.

The shed itself resembled a miniature barn, the same style as the garage, only smaller. One of the double doors stood open, wedged into the crust of icy snow to prop it back, but I could see no movement in the dark interior. Cautiously, I stepped inside.

"Nathaniel?"

"Back here." A disembodied voice floated toward me from behind a rack of gardening and woodworking tools. I wove my way past a substantial riding lawnmower, a rack of paint cans and brushes, and an industrial shelving unit holding window air-conditioning units. With each step farther inside the shed, the air became dustier and more chemical. By the time I reached Nathaniel, who had wedged himself behind another set of shelves and was trying to pry loose a red plastic toboggan, my nose was running and my throat tickled.

"What's up?" I sneezed. "It can't be healthy in here."

"Yeah, I know. I plan to clean it out in the spring. Some of this stuff has been here since I took it over from my folks. We hardly ever come in here, so cleaning it out always falls down to the bottom of the to-do list." He handed me the sled. "Put this out there somewhere, will you? I have to get the other one."

"What did you want to talk about?"

He stopped his rummaging. "I should think that would be obvious. We need a plan."

I blinked. "Are you...a plan for what, exactly?"

"I'm not willing to say that any supernatural force is out to harm my daughter, if that's what you're asking. But she believes it is, which is the important thing. I have come around to that. The psychiatrists she saw all told me not to enable her, not to indulge her fantasies. As a result, she stopped talking to me. I like to think I learn from my mistakes, so I mean to go on as if there really were an evil in the house, a curse on me and mine. And I need to fight it. I need Liza to *see* me fighting it."

"Okay."

"The thing is, I have no idea how to vanquish a ghostly foe." He yanked on a piece of plastic and a pile of assorted junk tumbled down as the second sled came loose. "I'm accustomed to more mundane evils. The contractor who doesn't finish his work. The extortionist banker. Which is, by the way, why I checked where the ladder usually sits. The dust is disturbed, but anyone could have done that. The saws are all still here. Still in their correct places. Even if we fingerprinted them all, the chances of finding anything out of place are minimal. And I am not willing to have the cops out here to upset the girls on that kind of chance. Besides, proving that a human is out to get me won't convince Liza that a ghost isn't *also* on the scene. So tell me, what's your recommendation?"

"Ghosts aren't part of my everyday life, either."

He sidled out from behind the pile and gazed intently at me. "I need to apologize to you. I never should have said what I did about your family."

"It's okay."

"No. No it really isn't. But I can't fix it, so all I can do at this point is promise to try to do better." He blew out a breath. "I'll likely upset you again. I still can't believe this ghost story is real. But if you'd asked me a week ago whether such bigoted words would ever come out of my mouth, I'd have said not a chance."

He touched my cheek with one long finger and I felt the shock of it right through the numbing cold of the shed. "It's important to me that you understand that."

I nodded, my throat dry.

He drew slightly away and blew out a breath. "You mentioned 'carnival queens' as fakers. Are there...what would you call them...fortune tellers, seers, mediums...who aren't fakers?"

It cost him, that question, so I considered it carefully. I thought of the woman in the park, the whiteness of her skin and roundness of her eyes as the customer had touched the board, the fear that oozed from her pores despite the bright sun, and my mother's orders never to pull aside the veil. Had she been a carnival queen? Had that been an act? I doubted it. The fear in her eyes had been too real.

"Maybe," I said at last. "I've never tried to find out. But logically, if ghosts exists, surely so do people who can contact them."

"Then that's today's project. To find one."

"How?"

"It's going to snow again soon. We'll be cut off. I'll propose a trip to town for supplies. You say you'll stay home. I'll figure out how to ditch Jenn and come back for you, and we can go meet a couple of local…practitioners. One thing about Maine—if you're looking for something strange, you'll find it here."

I doubted Jennifer would allow herself to be ditched so easily, but that was Nathaniel's problem. Mine was facing up to the fear of what might happen if we managed to find a true sensitive.

NATHANIEL HANDLED JENNIFER MASTERFULLY. He mentioned the snow forecasted for Tuesday and said they ought to lay in supplies. He asked the girls whether they had everything they needed and then tossed off a question to Jennifer about whether she needed to cancel any appointments for the following week, "you know, for the hairdresser or anything."

"Do I need it?" She touched her perfect, shiny locks.

"Oh, not at all. But I know you like to go occasionally, to get it—well, whatever you do to make it look so nice—or to have a massage or spa day instead of spending all your time cooped up here."

"Mom, let's have a girls' day out," said Hailey. "We can go to the spa."

"You should all go," said Nathaniel. "I can do the shopping."

Liza shook her head, that familiar stubborn frown settling over her features. "I'd rather go sledding. I don't want to go a spa."

"I'll tell you what," I offered. "Why don't I take Liza sledding, Jennifer and Hailey can spend the day at the spa, and you can run your errands without any of us?"

Nathaniel shrugged. "Works for me. Jenn?"

She considered for a long moment. I almost held my breath, afraid she suspected the conspiracy, but then she nodded. "Let me call and see if they have appointments."

Half an hour later they were on their way. Liza and I watched the Range Rover pull away, and I offered to take her sledding.

"It will be at least an hour before he can drop them and get back here."

She shook her head. "I don't really want to. What did you guys talk about in the shed? He didn't have time to tell me, just warned me to complain and say I didn't want to go into town."

I explained that he was hoping to find a medium in town and her eyes widened. "He believes me?"

I couldn't lie. "Not entirely. But more than he did. He's opening his mind to it."

"A medium." She hummed in the back of her throat. "So even though you said it's not my mom, you think it's a ghost."

"Maybe. And maybe medium is the wrong word. A sensitive. Someone who knows more about this type of thing of than any of us do."

Her forehead wrinkled and she glanced over my shoulder. A chill went over me. What did she see? Was the thing standing there, invisible to me, speaking words only she could hear? She blinked several times and narrowed her eyes before refocusing on my face.

"Won't she have to come here? "

"They can't visit the house. How on earth would we explain it to your aunt? We'll have to hope for the best."

She glanced over my shoulder again then shook her head. Was she talking to it, or had it left, secure because we were not bringing anyone into its domain? I brushed off the question at Liza's next words.

"What about the book? We should read until Dad gets home."

I'd hoped she would forget about the bloody book once she could communicate with us, but Lady Luck had never been a frequent visitor in my life. "You're sure you wouldn't rather go sledding?"

Her mouth set in its stubborn line and I gave in. I brought the book and my notebook down to the kitchen, but instead of continuing from where we'd left off, I suggested going back to the passage about how to tell a true sensitive from a carnival queen. I copied the questions the author suggested asking into my notebook, taking my time in order to minimize the amount we could read before Nathaniel's return.

Still, my stalling was no match for Liza's determination. After the Ouija chapter came a section on automatic writing and one on mirror scrying.

"But all these things say you have to know who you're trying to contact in order to talk to them, and we don't. And the mirror trick—she says you can see them, but that's probably just wishful thinking. I mean, it's no good if you can't actually have a conversation."

"Why do you want to talk to a ghost?" And hadn't she *been* talking to it? But no she'd said it spoke to her, not that they conversed. And I had never seen any indication that she could initiate contact.

She frowned, and the wings of her eyebrows met over her nose. Not for the first time, I thought life might have been kinder had she slightly less of her father. What looked strong on him seemed dark and sullen on her.

"How can I help her if I don't talk to her?"

Help? Her? But something else occurred to me with Liza's words. "Liza, why did you decide to start speaking again?"

She turned that dark, thin face up to me and blinked. "Because you saw her. And didn't care if anyone knew."

Hysteria bubbled near the surface. Oh, how utterly wrong she was. I had no desire at all for anyone to know what I'd seen. In fact, I'd have hidden it if I possibly could. But now that the truth was out, I could not regret it. So I smiled.

"Why do you want to help the spirit?"

"Because she needs something. Can't you feel that when she visits you?"

It felt more like a craving to me, like an addiction completely out of control. But I supposed that was need of a kind.

"And what will happen if you help her get what she needs?"

She ducked her head and shrugged, suddenly uncertain. "I…are you sure she's not my mom?"

"Sure? Like one hundred percent? No. But pretty sure, yes."

"I always thought she was. And wouldn't you want to help your mom if she came to you? Even now?"

"Of course. But we have to be careful. Will you promise me not to try to contact—whatever this is—without me or your father?"

She rolled her eyes in an expression so typically teenaged

that it lightened my heart. "He already made me promise that."

~

WE DROVE into town and had lunch at the same pizza place we'd eaten at with Matt. The casual flirtation and laughter of that night seemed a hundred years past.

"We need a plan of attack," Nathaniel said around a mouthful of cheesy dough. He'd brought up a list of five psychic businesses around town. Two we discounted right away because they leaned too heavily on New Age mysticism and Celtic mythology. The other three he called. All were by appointment only, but all three had openings and he set us up for appointments at every hour starting at one.

The first meeting was with a man, a Dr. Tom Davidson. "Wonder what his doctorate is in," Nathaniel muttered as we approached the brick storefront with its black wooden door and single window draped in heavy burgundy velvet.

"Shut it," I said and immediately regretted it. What viper had taken over my mind, shutting down the logical woman who kept such comments to herself?

But he just chuckled and rang the bell.

Davidson was a short, chubby man, with little round glasses tinted a dark gray and a bald spot that gave him the appearance of a tonsured monk. He hardly looked the part of a carnival queen.

"Now," he said when he'd seated us at a small round table in his parlor, settling Liza between me and Nathaniel, "what can I do for you?"

"Shouldn't you know that?" Nathaniel raised an eyebrow and the desire to slug him, hard, had me clenching a fist.

Davidson took no offense, however. "A skeptic," he said, delighted. He removed his glasses to reveal nearly colorless eyes. I'd never seen their like and goosebumps rose on my skin. Contact lenses. Had to be. But I could see no lines, no matter how hard I studied them.

"I do prefer to work with at least one skeptic. It keeps me sharp. But usually, skeptics don't bring their children. Only true believers do that."

Those strange eyes moved between the three of us, resting for a long time on Liza. I squirmed, but she did not react in any way.

"How interesting." He blinked twice, as if clearing grit from his vision. "You've tried a psychiatrist, then?"

I jerked. He smiled.

"Oh, no. That's not psychic, I'm afraid. That's simple body reading. The child belongs to you," he told Nathaniel. "Though she looks enough like this lovely lady to be her daughter. You would have taken her to a psychiatrist for whatever problem she has long before you allowed anyone— even your...girlfriend? No, that's not right, but someone you care very much for—well, you wouldn't allow anyone to bring your daughter to me unless all else failed."

Twice in one day people had mistaken Nathaniel's feelings for me. A ripple of guilt slid over me. They had to be reading my cues, not his. How embarrassing for him.

Nathaniel ignored the comment about our relationship nodded in grudging admiration of the rest. "That's your regular evaluation. What about your psychic evaluation?"

Davidson reached across the table and held out a pudgy hand to Liza. "Will you, my dear?"

She hesitated a long, long moment before taking it.

Davidson closed his eyes. "You miss your mother a great deal," he said. When Liza did not answer, he continued. "You don't need to worry about her. Regardless of what some uninformed clergy believe, suicide does not damn one eternally. It's not even the act itself that creates a lingering spirit.

No, that occurs because the person realizes, in the moment of the act, that they have left things incomplete. It's the desire to fix their mistakes, the very same desire that often leads to suicide, the same kind of regret, that creates a restless spirit. She wanted to assuage your pain. Once she realized she wasn't helping, she moved on."

His nose twitched. "This is not your mother, my dear." His eyes opened and he stared into Liza's face. "Do not encourage her."

"What does she want?" Liza whispered.

He shook his head. "That I cannot see. But she doesn't belong here, with you. She should have moved on long ago. I feel only her aura, clinging to you like a cobweb."

Twice, this thing had appeared in female forms—as my mother, and as Liza's. If it had appeared to Hailey as me, that would be three. But that was not to say it could not be masculine just as easily. "Dr. Davidson, you say not to encourage her. What makes you think this is a woman?"

He tilted his head to the side. "I'm not entirely sure. As I said, there's a distinct aura. And it's feminine."

Not terribly helpful. "And how do we make her go away?"

Liza made a wordless noise of protest, but Nathaniel put a hand on her shoulder.

"Unfortunately," said Davidson, "I have no idea."

OUT ON THE SIDEWALK, Nathaniel appeared a good deal grimmer than he had when we entered. "I shouldn't have used my real name to book the appointments. A simple internet search would bring up the facts of Marianne's death."

"He said it wasn't Marianne, though," I pointed out. "And yes, he could have gotten a good deal of that from cold reading, but not all of it. And he didn't ask for more money for further readings. He wasn't faking."

Nathaniel's jaw clenched and I could practically hear his teeth grinding. How difficult it must be for him to discover that there was a whole world he'd never imagined and that something it meant his daughter harm.

"Why did you ask about making her go away?" We'd been walking, but Liza stopped, forcing us to stop with her. "I don't want her to go away."

"Why not?" Nathaniel shook with the effort of keeping his voice calm.

"Because. Even if she's not mom, she cares about me. Why should she have to go away? It was her house before we got there."

I shivered. Without Liza's help, we stood no chance whatsoever of getting rid of the malignant spirit. It wanted her. It spoke to her and only her.

"You said back at the house that you wanted to help her," I offered.

She nodded reluctantly.

"Well, even if she does care about you, you're not her family. She's stuck here, away from the people who knew and loved her. Shouldn't we help her find them? After all, loads of people will love you as you go through life. It's not fair to hold her here, where no one else can talk to her or care about her."

She crossed her thin arms across her chest and frowned. Nathaniel opened his mouth, but I shook my head slightly and he subsided. After a moment, he put one arm over his daughter's shoulders and the other around mine. I glanced up and a quick, gentle grin flickered across his face. It warmed the cold hollow beneath my breastbone created by Liza's question.

The storefront for the second medium, Lady Ivana, could

have been built and decorated by the same designer who put together Dr. Davidson's shop. Perhaps in a remote corner of Maine existed a bulk outlet—*going into business as a psychic? We have it all, from rental space to curtains!* I shook away the thought. Hysteria wouldn't help anyone.

Lady Ivana answered the door before Nathaniel could ring the bell. No great feat given the security camera scanning the street from the second story, but I twitched slightly nonetheless. Behind her, the shop's interior was dim and an odd odor wafted out.

"I am Lady Ivana." She pushed the door wide and the sunlight caught on silver rings that circled every finger. A thick layer of makeup hid her natural skin tone and a waist-length black wig covered her hair. "I hope you don't mind the mess. I didn't have time to clean up after your call and with the weather forecast I wasn't expecting visitors today."

Mess hardly described the shop. Psychics R Us had exploded all over the interior. Swags of herbs hung from the ceiling tied with complicated knots of hemp. Bowls of folded paper packets and tiny, satin-tied scrolls littered the counter that ran along the left side of the shop. The shelves along the right held books, tarot decks, crystal balls, and amulets of all shapes and sizes.

I sneezed.

"So sorry. I had a terrible visitation yesterday so I smudged with sage to cleanse the place before your arrival. It's effective, but the smoke can put people off. Come on through. My reading room is in the back."

She led us to her parlor, almost identical to Dr. Davidson's but for a deck of tarot cards and a silver bowl half-full of water resting in front of one of the seats at the table. The same burgundy velvet that hid the view from the street hung from rods along each wall.

Her movements were sparrow-quick and jerky as she

seated us and then took her own place in front of the cards. "Now, what can I do for you today?"

Nathaniel slid a glance at me and said in a completely flat tone, "I'd like to talk to my dead wife."

"Of course." Lady Ivana put the cards aside, slid the bowl of water to the center of the table, and lit two candles.

"Take a seat, everyone, and let your fingers rest on the edge of the bowl." She fixed an eye on Liza. Just because Liza was a child and apt to be disruptive, or did she see something in the girl? "Lightly."

We obeyed and she closed her eyes and hummed slightly. The table shook slightly and I saw Liza's eyebrows go up. I caught her eyes and rolled my own. If Nathaniel was determined not to believe, Liza was too gullible.

After a moment, Lady Ivana shook her head. "Something is blocking her from coming through. I thought I had her for a moment—did you feel her?—but then it went dark. This will require further exploration."

Seven minutes later and fifty dollars poorer, we were out on the street. "Charlatan," Nathaniel pronounced as the door shut firmly behind us.

I agreed. I'd suspected before she opened her mouth—those who lacked talent relied on an abundance of tools—but her ridiculous performance attempting to contact Marianne clinched it. Especially once she launched into her sales pitch for further sessions.

"The last one's a ways out. Let's pick up groceries first since we have time, then I can drop you home after the appointment and come back for Jenn and Hailey."

I paid no attention to what went into the cart and would not have been at all surprised at checkout to find nothing but tuna and peanut butter. The food was an excuse, a show for Jennifer to mask the real and vital purpose of our trip.

CHAPTER 17

*A*driana Livingston worked out of a converted Colonial a few miles outside Portland proper. Four steps led up to a wide front porch and a hand-carved wooden sign hanging by the buzzer panel indicated that she shared the building with two chiropractors and a nutritionist.

"I'm on the second floor," said a pleasant, neutral voice when I passed the button. "First door on your right."

The place smelled of pine cleaner and an earthy, spicy scent a long-unused part of my mind identified as sandalwood. Perhaps one of the chiropractors practiced aromatherapy as well, for the scents, along with the oaken floors and whitewashed walls, proved calming.

Livingston stood in the doorway to her office. A tall, slender figure with a neat blonde bob wearing tan slacks and a baby blue sweater set, she radiated an easy confidence. She clasped my hand with cool, bare fingers when she introduced herself, but merely nodded at Liza. She led us to a small seating area beneath a window hung with heavy chocolate-colored linen drapes held back on either side by white hooks. Nathaniel and Liza settled on a loveseat while I took a plush chair nearby. Only then did Livingston seat herself in the lone wooden chair.

"I was sorry to hear about your wife." She crossed her legs and laced her fingers in her lap. She switched her focus to Liza. "It must have been very difficult for you."

Liza nodded, wide eyed.

"But I must admit to being surprised to hear from you, Mr. Prescott. Marianne gave me the impression that she hid her visits to me. She told me you were a skeptic right to the bone."

"You knew my wife?"

"She came to see me several times. I recommended she seek help from a more mundane source."

"Help with what?"

Livingston considered the question. Did psychics have an obligation to protect their clients' privacy? Even after death? If death did not constitute an end to life, perhaps the contract continued indefinitely.

"Marianne believed her paintings were haunted, even possessed."

I remembered the cracked earth, oozing neon paint and the discomfort they'd inspired on first sight. Just good art, or something more?

"Oh, for—" Nathaniel clamped his lips shut.

"She brought me several. I still have them. But I felt nothing beyond the emotional connection to the work of a talented artist from most of them. No supernatural force inhabited them. Yes, they disturbed me. In particular one with two crosses. Do you remember that one?"

Nathaniel shook his head.

Livingston frowned. "I have the others at home, but that one I could not keep. Green and gray, a lonely, quiet spot for a grave. It might have been peaceful in the hands of a different artist. But Marianne did not do peaceful. I could almost understand why she thought it was possessed."

"What did you do with it?" Was it still in the house? Could it be that simple? A spirit trapped in a painting?

"We burned it. I admit, I did not think it would do a jot of good—it was just a painting, though an exceptionally good one—but Marianne's state of mind came before her artistic prospects. She did not want to sell it, did not want to keep it, so we burned it to give her peace. I thought that was the end of it. And yet..."

"And yet?"

"And yet, here you are. Her husband, the skeptic. Her daughter, the haunted. And the woman drawn into the web, all sitting in my office."

"You believe my daughter is haunted?"

"Don't you? Isn't that why you are here?" She fixed me with moss green eyes that reflected the snowy scene outside. "You've seen her, haven't you? The unquiet spirit."

I froze, and the whole room waited. Even the dust motes floating through the air paused in their journeys. The muscles in my neck tightened, refusing to move, and when I finally managed to nod, the crack was audible.

"Who are you?" she asked me.

"Liza's tutor."

Perfectly plucked brows rose and she blinked twice. "Really?"

"Should she be someone else?" Nathaniel asked.

Her lips formed a tiny smile. "Not at all. Besides, right now you all have more to worry about."

"And what, precisely, should we be worrying about?"

"She doesn't like you."

Nathaniel recoiled. "Molly?"

"Oh, no." Again that private smile. "Not Miss Allworth.

The spirit. She likes your daughter, but you are another story. I could feel her when I took your hand."

Nathaniel snorted. "And you think it—she—is dangerous."

Adriana aged as I watched, a slight sagging of the skin beneath her eyes, and a downturn of her mouth stealing her vibrancy. "To you, absolutely. Eventually, to all of you. You haven't noticed?"

"Noticed what?"

She picked at one perfect nail. "A spirit fades with time if left alone. It requires energy to maintain a presence in this world, and it acquires that energy from the emotions of the living. As it becomes stronger, it weakens those whose energy it is draining."

I studied Liza's pale skin and hollow eyes and shuddered. She did seem to be fading away. I had hoped that would change when she began speaking, but it had not. Could her father not see it? "You're saying this thing is like a sort of vampire? That it will suck Liza dry?"

"Not just her. Remember, as it gets stronger, it becomes more physical in the world. It will be able to cause more damage to those in its way."

"So what's your suggestion," Nathaniel asked. "A spell? A charm? A candle?"

"Should we leave the house?"

She answered my question first. "If you'd come to me when this first began, I'd have recommended leaving. This spirit was attached to the location, and woke up at the taste of Liza's grief. In the early days, you might have run. In time, she would have faded once more. But now, she has formed a bond with Liza. You might weaken that bond temporarily if you left, but I doubt you could break it."

"She doesn't want to hurt me," Liza said.

Livingston smiled, but it did not reach her eyes. If anything, they turned down further than before. "Have you ever been to the zoo and seen the bears or the wolves and thought how cute they were?"

Liza nodded.

"But you can't play with them, right?"

Another nod.

"And it's not because the bears or the wolves want to hurt you. They don't. But they don't realize that you aren't the same, that what seems like playing to them could kill you."

"How do we make it go away?" Nathaniel cut right to the heart of the matter.

"I don't have an easy answer to that."

"Of course you don't."

"I am a medium," she chided. "I communicate with the dead. But they have to want to talk to me. This one most emphatically does not. I can sense her rage, her sorrow, but they are emotions, not fully formed thoughts that give me a clear picture of how to encourage her to move on."

"Fat lot of good you are," he grumbled.

I ignored him. "What do you recommend?"

"You have no idea who she is? What she wants?" Livingston addressed the question to Liza, who refused to meet anyone's eyes as she shook her head.

"She's lonely," I offered. "We know that."

"Lonely." Livingston drew out the word, tasting it. "No, that's not enough. There has to be more."

"More? It's what I felt, it's what Liza told us she felt, too."

"An unquiet spirit forms when a person dies with regrets, with tasks left unfinished, with needs left unmet. The death is usually violent. When my husband was diagnosed with cancer, we went on vacation. We talked over everything. When he finally passed, I knew I wouldn't be able to reach him beyond the veil because I was the one with regrets, not him. I was the one who had held back, kept things secret. If I'd suddenly had a heart attack before his death, my spirit would not have rested because I wanted to be sure he passed as happily as possible and I wouldn't have gotten a chance to do it. I would have been afraid he might discover the things I'd hidden from him.

"Loneliness is too unspecific a desire to form an unquiet spirit." She slanted a glance at Nathaniel. "And it doesn't explain her fury at you."

"I didn't do anything to any damned ghost."

"No, I don't imagine you did. You're a stand-in. But that doesn't make her any less angry, or any less lethal."

"So we return to the original question," I said. "What do you suggest we do?"

"I can call friends who specialize in hauntings. They may have ideas about how to force her out. That's not my forte."

"Great. Refer us to a few of your friends so they can bleed me dry in hundred-dollar increments."

I kicked him, reminding him of our conversation that morning, but Livingston merely laughed. "Oh, dear, no. A hundred dollars, that's for the initial consult. I usually charge twice that, but when I heard your name I wanted to meet you. You'd have to mortgage that house to afford anyone who could really rid you of the problem, and that's assuming the spirit isn't too deeply dug in."

"It's already mortgaged," he said. "Twice over. So I guess your friends are out of luck."

"It's not my friends who need luck," she said. "Find out what this spirit wants. Convince it that it does not belong here. Sever the connection to your family. Otherwise, I will be attending your funeral as I did Marianne's."

NATHANIEL DROPPED us at the house and went back to get Hailey and Jennifer from the spa. None of us had spoken more than three words the entire drive, and I felt burned out, beaten up, and unready to face the normalcy of the others.

I dragged myself into the kitchen and Liza followed me. But much as I cared for and worried about her, I needed to be alone, apart even from her.

"Take the dog outside for a while, okay? He's been locked up too long."

When she had run outside with Rocky, I collapsed into a chair and tried to make sense of my turbulent emotions. If the spirit derived energy from our fright and grief, she'd have a banquet in my heart. I pulled out my notebook and tried to make notes on what we'd learned. But the words wouldn't come and when Liza returned I was setting coffee on to jump-start my brain.

"Molly? Do you think Miss Livingston was right? That the ghost wants to hurt my dad?"

Standing took too much energy, so I lowered myself into a chair to wait for the coffee to brew.

"It's not so much that she's right, as that we can't afford to discount her beliefs. After all, remember the ladder incident."

"But a ghost didn't do that."

"No, a person did."

"They did?"

Oh, hell. I'd forgotten that Liza hadn't seen the clean break. She still thought Nathaniel's fall a simple accident. How angry would he be if I told her the truth? In my estimation, she was strong enough to handle the information, but I wasn't her mother.

"Molly? What do you mean by a person did it? Was it Aimee? Did she sabotage it? She tried to hurt him before, you know."

"I honestly don't know, Liza. And I shouldn't have said anything until I did know. It looked as if the top step had been tampered with. We couldn't really check because by the time we got home from the hospital it was all cleaned up. But if it was Aimee, she's gone now so your dad's safe."

Her mouth trembled and tears clung to her lashes. "Is it because of me?"

"What do you mean? Of course not!"

"Why would the ghost like me but not Dad?"

"Honey, I don't know. But we'll figure it out." I laid a hand over hers on the table.

"But she only tells me what she wants to—I can't ask her questions and get answers. That's why I wanted to use the Ouija board, but the rules say two or more people, and you have to ask your questions aloud."

"I'm surprised you didn't try to convince your cousin to do it."

She shrugged and looked away.

"Did you try to get Hailey involved?"

She shook her head. "I couldn't ask what I really wanted in front of her. And she would have pushed the indicator around—I'd never trust her not to."

"So, if you wanted to talk to the ghost so much, why did you stop speaking?"

"There wasn't anything left to say."

I touched her hand, felt the chill of her skin. Was the spirit stealing her life even as we sat here in the warm kitchen?

"That's not all there was."

She shook her head. "I wanted to talk about mom, but it made my dad sad. And then we moved up here and he really, really didn't want to hear about the ghost. He thought he'd done the right thing, you know? Taking me away from mom's studio. So I stopped mentioning the ghost, but it got harder to find anything to talk about. It was like the less I said about her, the bigger she got, until she filled me up and I couldn't get words past her space."

"That's what happens with secrets," I said. "You imagine that it's a tiny thing you have to avoid, but the longer the secret goes on, the more it seems that every road leads to it, and you can't go down any of them for fear of revealing it."

She nodded. "But then you came. And you bought the book. And I thought maybe I could tell you about her. But she was still too big. Until the other night, and then the words kind of popped out, like they were greased and slipped past her."

"And it's been easier to talk since then?"

"My throat hurts now, but yeah. You and dad know about her. So she got smaller."

I only wished that were true. I suspected she had backed off to regroup now that Liza had taken a bit of initiative and the rules had changed. We'd been gone most of the day, and twilight shadows reached into the kitchen. I shuddered and got up to flick on the lights. I waited while the coffee finished brewing, hoping inspiration would strike, but when I turned back to Liza, I still had no ready answer. I sipped from my mug, considering.

"Even if we could talk to her," I said at last, "how would we know whether she was telling the truth? People don't always, and I don't imagine ghosts are any different."

CHAPTER 18

After lunch on Monday, we returned to the schoolroom and to American History, which reminded me that I hadn't found the book Nathaniel's father had written about the house. I set the girls to reading a chapter from the text and slipped down the corridor to the billiards room to search for it.

Weak sunlight filtered past the thick drapes, providing only dim illumination, so I flicked on the overhead light. The green lampshades on the chandelier above the pool table tinted the light so the room appeared submerged, drowned in the pond as I had so nearly found myself. A chill draft slipped by and my vision slipped. Superimposed over the billiards room I saw the nursery and I felt myself struggling toward Liza through air as thick as frozen molasses. I shook off the feelings and thrust the curtains open, dispelling the watery illusion.

Jim Prescott had written his book here. Even if he had left no copies of the finished product—this was, after all, merely a summer home at the time—maybe I could unearth the research he'd done on the house and its builders.

196

The unquiet spirit was linked to the property, I was sure of it. She had died here, and from what Adriana Livingston had told us, not well. The death would have left a mark, a scar on the history of the land and with a little luck, Jim Prescott would have discovered it.

The bookshelves held an array of academic works on history, mythology, anthropology, geography and geology. A man of wide ranging interests, Jim Prescott. Had he ever seen anything at Rook's Rest that he could not explain? Nathaniel had called his parents pragmatists, even Puritans, but way at the top of the bookshelf, a number of items disputed the claim. Old pamphlets, books, texts Prescott had printed out or photocopied, then bound with masking tape along the spine on which he had written the titles.

Raymond, or life and death: with examples of the evidence for survival of memory and affection after death. My fingers itched to pull that one down, but it would require climbing onto the bottom cabinets and even then I might not reach the shelf. A moment later, I realized I needed to get up there, because there were more.

Spiritualism. I hadn't learned much about it in school other than that it had flourished in New England among the devout. So perhaps Jim Prescott needed the material for his book, though the sheer number of texts implied a deeper interest than necessary for what would likely be no more than a chapter or two in a textbook.

After Death, or Letters from Julia: A Personal Narrative.

The Other World, or, Glimpses of the Supernatural: Being Facts, Records and Traditions Relating to Dreams, Omens, Miraculous Occurrences, Apparitions, Wraiths, Warnings, Second-sight, Witchcraft, Necromancy, etc.

Spirit-Possession: A Treatise Upon Modern Spiritualism, Comprising the Experiences and Theories of a "Retired" Spirit-Medium.

Communication with the Next World: The Right and Wrong Methods.

For a pragmatic man, Jim Prescott had a wealth of information on communicating with the dead. Had he ever tried it himself? Could a historian resist? I imagined him sitting at the heavy desk late at night, a hand on the planchette of his sons' Ouija board, laughing at his own actions but unable to resist the lure.

I hoisted myself up onto the cabinet top, and found myself facing an entirely different set of texts. Several of these were printed and bound, while a fair number of others appeared to be the standard academic fare. But there were also a number with lurid covers that I could not imagine having been accepted as study material when I was in school. All related to Native American history, religion, culture, language. The classic *Bury my Heart at Wounded Knee*, which I had read in college. *Facing East from Indian Country: A Native History of Early America*, which looked well-thumbed. And one that caught my eye because it brought back so strongly the story Nathaniel had told while we sat by the fire. *Out of the Depths: The Experiences of Mi'Kmaw Children at the Indian Residential School at Shubenacadie, Nova Scotia*. Had the tale of Alawa the Native American "princess" come from here? But no, that had been set in Maine, not Canada.

"What are you doing up there?"

I had not heard Jennifer enter, and her voice startled me into losing my footing on the narrow countertop. I grabbed for the bookshelf to steady myself and almost brought a stack of piled books down on top of me. I managed to remain upright and inched around so I could climb down with a tiny bit of dignity.

"I was looking for Jim Prescott's history book."

"For God's sake. You're supposed to be teaching the girls."

"They're working on a lesson. They know where I am if they have questions."

"This is completely inappropriate."

"I'm sorry." I swallowed my frustration at being unable to reach for those seductive texts on the top shelf. "I can go back to them."

"What's with that book, anyway? And don't give me that nonsense about how it could be useful for Hailey. You don't care about her boarding school experience any more than Aimee did. You're hiding something from me."

I cast about frantically trying to remember what I'd said to her on Friday about the book. The intervening events overshadowed the encounter, however. It might as well have been a year since we'd spoken.

"Don't bother." Jennifer spun around. "I can tell you're just thinking up a lie."

After she left I remained where I was for a long moment trying to decide whether I should continue my search or go back to the girls. In fact, I was still standing there when I heard a short, sharp scream and a loud, prolonged clatter.

I rushed from the billiards room and almost collided with the girls coming from the classroom.

"Mom!" Hailey shrieked and dashed down the steps.

I leaned over the railing and saw Jennifer picking herself up from the floor at the base of the staircase. She glanced up and the virulent hatred in her eyes forced me back a step.

"Mom, are you okay?" Hailey tugged on her hand and she looked away from me.

"I'll be fine." Again, she turned her eyes upward. "Pack your things. This time you've gone too far."

"What are you talking about?"

Nathaniel came out of the ballroom office. "What's going on?"

"Your new tutor pushed me down the stairs."

"I did not!"

"I felt your hand on my back. And don't try to lay this off on the girls. I could see the classroom door and neither of them came out. You were the one behind me."

"You're mistaken. I was still in the pool room." But I knew what had happened. Once again I felt the memory of the pressure of a hand on my back out by the pond.

"Right. Looking for Jim Prescott's history textbook. Don't start with me. I don't know what you hoped to get out of this, but it's over. Now. Tell her, Thane."

He sighed. "Why don't you both come into the library? Liza, Hailey, you go back to work."

"No." Liza stomped down the stairs. She and Hailey took up identical postures, arms crossed, expressions set.

Nathaniel rubbed his forehead. "Okay, then. We'll all do this. Molly?"

My mouth went dry and I descended slowly. I could not read Nathaniel's face at all.

"Are you injured?" He asked Jennifer as we entered the library.

"No, but that's not the issue. The issue is her intent. She has to go, Thane, even you must see that now."

Nathaniel did not answer. We all sat, Jennifer and Hailey on the sofa, Liza and Nathaniel and I all in separate chairs. A moment later, he was up, pouring himself a drink. He raised the glass in our direction, but both Jennifer and I shook our heads.

He returned to his seat and took a long sip.

"It's my word against hers," Jennifer burst out. "You've known me forever. I am not a liar."

"I wish it were that simple. I believe that you felt someone behind you, felt what you thought was a hand on your back."

"What I thought—what are you trying to say?"

"I'm saying that I've come to believe that we're not alone in this house."

That stunned her into silence. Stunned all of us. I hadn't expected him to admit it so baldly. Up until that moment, I hadn't been at all sure he was on board with the whole ghost idea.

"If you want me to leave," Jennifer said stiffly, "you can just say so. There's no need to pretend a sudden belief in ghosts. I've known you all your life, Thane—that won't wash. Do we still have phone service? I'll call Matthew right now and have him come pick us up."

"That might be best."

Her eyes widened and her skin lost its delicate rose color. She'd bluffed and he'd forced her hand. Her eyes flicked quickly around the room as she tried to regroup.

"Thane, please, this isn't necessary."

He shook his head.

"I'm sorry, Jenn. I can't agree."

With a huff, she stalked out into the hall and I could hear her on the phone, though I could not make out the words. The rest of us sat in awkward silence.

"Matthew will be here tonight. Late. It's a long drive."

"I know. I'm sorry, Jenn. If she hadn't tried to hurt you..."

"She. So you admit it."

"The ghost is a she," said Liza.

"Oh for— There is no ghost. Admit that much."

"I can't," said Nathaniel. "You have no idea how much I wish I could. But I was told... A psychic told me that she would get stronger. She's attached herself to Liza, and she's feeding off the emotions of the people around her. I didn't realize she meant that the spirit would attain the ability to do physical harm. I thought, if she existed at all, that she'd continue working though humans. Like when she convinced Aimee to attack me."

"A psychic told you this?" Jennifer focused on me. "One of your relatives helping you out? A little Gypsy fun?"

I kept my mouth shut, wishing I could disappear.

"This has nothing I to do with Molly. I went to see a medium in Portland while you were at the spa."

Jennifer sank back down onto the couch. "That's why you were late picking us up?"

"Yes."

"And what else did this woman tell you?"

"Does it matter?"

"Of course it matters! If there's really a dangerous spirit in this house, we should all leave. Why didn't she recommend that?"

"Because it's no longer attached to the house. It's bound to Liza. Wherever Liza goes, it goes."

"Why would a spirit attached to Liza push me down the stairs? I'm here to help Liza." Jennifer's fingers twisted in agitation and a thick, poisonously sweet disbelief coated her words. I could almost feel sorry for her: she thought we were playing her for a fool. But the memory of her casual dismissal of Liza's chances at a normal life mitigated my sympathy.

Nathaniel, still unaware of his sister-in-law's schemes, shook his head. "For whatever reason it convinced Aimee to attack me? And convinced someone to sabotage the ladder. Which could have killed me."

Hailey twitched and drew her knees up beneath her chin. She'd taken in the whole bizarre conversation without so much as batting an eye, but at the mention of Thane's fall, she flinched.

"Hailey," I said, "do you have something to tell us?"

She shook her head.

"Hailey?" Jennifer touched her daughter's knee. "Did you see anyone mucking about with the ladder?"

"It wasn't a stupid ghost." She squirmed. "It was me, okay? I did it."

Jennifer gasped. The picture of Nathaniel lying caught beneath the ladder flashed in my mind and my stomach heaved. None of us, it seemed, knew how to respond. But Hailey continued.

"I didn't mean to really hurt him, mom. But you always hated when Danny was sick. You said you were a wife, not a nurse. But then you brought us here so you could get married again and ship me off to boarding school. You forgot what being married meant. Waiting on a man hand and foot. I figured if he sprained an ankle or broke a leg or something, you'd remember how much you hated that. I didn't mean anything worse to happen." Her face scrunched up. "I don't even remember how I got the idea. But it seemed so obvious. All you needed was a little reminder that you didn't like taking care of a man and we could go back to being alone. We had such a good time before Danny."

I wanted to scream, to shout at her, to curse her stupidity and selfishness. And I wanted to cry for Nathaniel, forced to listen as she spilled poison about the underside of his brother's marriage.

All the color had fled from Jennifer's face. She swallowed. "That's not true, Hailey. We discussed boarding school long ago. It's about your education, your future, not my marital state."

She gathered herself and I had to admire her self-possession when she turned to Nathaniel. "I apologize. I had no idea. Clearly, moving out is the right thing to do. We'll leave in the morning."

CHAPTER 19

*A*fter Hailey and Jennifer left the room, Nathaniel swallowed the rest of his drink and mumbled a curse under his breath.

"I'm sorry," I said.

"For what? For the fact that my brother's wife wanted to marry me or the fact that my daughter is haunted? Or maybe the fact that my niece tried to kill me."

"She didn't mean to—"

"Don't be naive. It doesn't suit you. Of course she did. She's as selfish as Jenn. If she could put me permanently out of the picture, so much the better. The only security I have that she didn't purposely set a bee loose in Danny's car that morning is that she would have known Jenn was driving with him."

Against my own judgment I reached out and laid a hand on his thigh. I wished I had the right to wrap my arms around him and soothe away some of the tension I felt beneath my fingers. But I didn't, so I blinked back tears and resorted to logic in place of emotions. "But Jenn *was* with him. And children don't always understand adult relationships. I wouldn't put too much stock in what Hailey said about Jenn's attitude toward her marriage. She only heard what she wanted to hear, the times Jenn expressed her frustration or discontent. She didn't pay attention to the good things because they didn't suit the story she told herself about her mother's relationship with Danny."

"I do wonder why the spirit tried to shove her down the stairs, though. And why now."

I swallowed. "I was in the billiards room looking at information your father had about contacting the dead."

"Contacting the dead? My father? I hardly think so."

"Well, maybe the texts have been there since before your parents took the house, before he used it as his office. But there's an extensive collection of information on spiritualism way up on the top shelves. If that poses a threat to the ghost for any reason, she might have considered Jennifer's accusation a way to get rid of me before I could get any further."

"What led you to the billiards room?"

"Your father's book. The one about the history of Maine. Matt said that while researching it, he'd come across information about the people who built this house. I thought it might have a hint as who the spirit is. If she'd come from your family, you'd know about her. Or I assume you would. If your great aunt or someone had died horribly here, you'd have spoken up at Adriana Livingston's."

"True enough."

"Which means that she died before your family took over, or at least long enough ago that your family doesn't talk about her anymore. I hoped your father might tell her story as part of his history."

"You really don't want to attempt to get through that book. I've tried multiple times."

"I don't need to read the whole thing. Just the section about Wilton Pond and the house. I can't help feeling that my fall into the pond wasn't an accident. Which means she's strong out by the water, just like in the house."

"I'll get the book." Nathaniel looked from me to Liza. "I must be losing my mind. But I'll get it. I want this over."

He rose stiffly and left the room, all his usual grace gone. We'd stolen that from him along with his faith in the world and his assurance that he knew real from imaginary. He had seemed superhuman when I'd first seen him standing in the hall of Rook's Rest and now I missed that strength and surety.

He was gone only a moment, and when he returned he handed me a hefty hardcover. The cover had been designed to look as if it had been torn into four pieces, each showing a different person—a Native American, a French soldier, a British soldier, and a man in a dressed as a sailor, though I had no idea whether his clothes indicated a particular nationality. The rather dry title told me why Jenn, Matt, and even Nathaniel had avoided reading the book—*Maine: Seafarers and Settlers through the Civil War*. Still, I thanked Nathaniel for bringing it to me.

"I have to go up and talk to Jenn. We've been friends all our lives and I can't let her leave like this."

"It occurs to me that Hailey saw the ghost, too. We thought it was a dream. But the first night I was here, she saw a woman in her room. It might make Jennifer feel better if she knew that Hailey had been touched by the spirit, that she didn't come up with the ladder sabotage on her own. I suspect that once she takes Hailey home, that corruption will pass since she was never the true object of the spirit's anger."

His dark eyes studied me but I could not read their expression. "You're very generous."

"It's no more than the truth."

He nodded. "I'll be back down when I can. I doubt we'll be having a sit-down dinner tonight. If you get hungry, fix yourself a bite. That goes double for you, Liza. You're getting too skinny."

She flung herself at him and hugged him fiercely. For a second he was too shocked to respond, but then he wrapped his arms around her and rocked her. "I'm sorry I didn't believe you, baby."

She sniffed a little and pulled away. "It's okay, dad. I should have kept trying."

"We'll both do better next time," he said. "Now, you stay here with Molly while I go upstairs."

The room seemed colder when he left, so I built a fire. It took me a few tries to get it right, but soon enough the fatwood starters were popping, their sweet, resinous scent filling the air.

"I'm going to look through here and see if I can find anything about an unnatural death on the property," I told Liza. "Do you want to go upstairs and grab a book or your crochet?"

"Do you really believe she's in there?"

"Do you disagree? Is there something you're not telling me?"

She shrugged, glancing away.

Despite the fire, ice rippled over my skin. "Have you been talking to her?"

"She's waiting for me. I can feel her. It's like she's kind of hanging over my shoulder all the time."

"Don't talk to her, Liza. Please."

"Why not? It would be easier than reading that old thing and hoping you find a clue."

Fear clutched deep and hard and I struggled to articulate my reasons. "The easy way isn't always the right way. Adriana Livingston said that the spirit was attached to you. Talking to it, to her, might gain us information, but at what cost? It might strengthen her attachment to you. We want to sever that if possible, to send her to her own people, so we have to be very careful how we proceed."

She crossed her arms over her chest and for a moment I thought she would argue. But then she turned her back on me and left, returning a few minutes later with her crochet. We had to tease out a few knots that had formed in the yarn and frog back two rows to a mistake, but at last she settled quietly beside me on the couch, leaving me to study Nathaniel's father's book.

The sun sank in the sky and I had to get up to add new logs to the fire twice as I read.

I had no clear idea what I was looking for, so I could not skim nearly as quickly as I would have liked. Despite the wealth of texts in the billiards room, Prescott disposed of the spiritualist movement in a single chapter. He did refer to three of the pieces I'd seen upstairs, but mostly to scoff at them with an academic's superiority.

Although the book spent far more time on Native American history and culture than my own American History textbooks had, the Indian schools were given short shrift as they were not particular features of Maine's history. Instead, Prescott explained, Maine's abuse of the Native population had taken the form of forcing children into the foster care system. This anomaly made me even more curious about the single Canadian book I'd seen upstairs.

I needed to talk to him, to get the details the book merely hinted at, to find out what he'd discovered in all those texts about spiritualism and why he wanted to know about the Native boarding school experience. Nathaniel had called his parents "Puritans," so I couldn't very well tell them our theory, but there had to be a way to get the information because I could almost taste its importance.

~

Nathaniel had not yet returned by the time I went to bed. In the quiet darkness of my room, I drifted off.

And woke with my breath trapped in my lungs, hands of smoke wrapped tightly around my neck, lifting me from my bed. I tried to pry them loose, but my own fingers felt nothing against my skin, though the pressure never ceased. I grabbed for the nearest object, found the lamp on the bedside table. Threw it hard against the wall, where it shattered. At the explosion, the stranglehold eased slightly, dropped me, and in that instant I gasped in a single gulp of air before the invisible grasp choked me once more. More objects followed. The ghost book, the mirror hanging on the wall. With each crash the thing that held me flinched, but I was losing the battle. Each flinch was shorter, each breath I managed smaller, and I was blacking out.

Far away, I could hear Liza screaming, though I could neither see her nor make out the words. And then the thing was gone, and I was on the floor, choking on thick, brackish liquid, and my room was full of people. I sat up and tried to speak. Failed. Spat out more liquid. Tried again.

"How did you get rid of it?" I choked the words past the sore scratch of my throat.

Nathaniel moved to help me up, then shifted me to the bed. "I have no idea."

"Good God," said Matt, visibly trembling and slightly green. "What was that?"

"The reason we called you. The reason Jenn and Hailey shouldn't be here."

Both Jennifer and Hailey, I noticed, stood off to the side. Hailey was crying, her face pressed into her mother's breast. Of all of us, Liza seemed the least shaken.

"What happened?" I asked her.

Matt answered. "I've never seen anything like it outside of a horror movie. And if you put it in a horror movie I'd have called it unrealistic." He picked up a chunk of the mirror I'd thrown and handed it to me, tilting it to show my neck, where a long, coiling, snake-like welt was rising.

"There was nothing there," he said. "But you were…hanging. Swaying like someone was holding you. Your feet were about an inch above the floor and we could see the pressure on your neck. An indentation."

"That's how she died," I croaked. "Our ghost. Has to be. That's what Hailey saw. Isn't it? That nightmare you had, where a woman was in the corner of your room?"

"Stop it!" Jennifer shouted. "Just stop! Leave my daughter alone!"

"I'm sorry," I said. "You're right. She's traumatized enough."

"You can't stay here," Matt said to me. "For God's sake, Thane, none of you can stay."

Nathaniel shook his head. "I told you. It's not tied to the house. It's tied to us."

"To Liza," Jennifer corrected.

In that moment I hated her as I had never hated anyone. More than I hated the faceless thug who'd shot my father or the cancer that had stolen my mother. More, even, than I hated the spirit who'd just attempted my own murder.

She sighed and ran a hand across her face. "I'm sorry. I didn't mean that. I don't understand this. I don't know how to act."

"No one expects you to," said Nathaniel gently. "We're all off kilter here."

"I still don't understand. If I was…as you say…what did you guys do get rid of her?"

"Nothing," Matt said. "And I doubt I'll ever forgive myself for that. Liza kept screaming 'get away from her,' and I half thought she was talking to me, but Thane went over and grabbed you and you fell down on the floor. You weren't breathing. The indentation began to fade, but you didn't wake up. So he gave you mouth to mouth. Then you spat up weird, swampy water and woke up."

I shuddered. I still tasted that water, the unpleasant, dirty flavor with the faint coppery aftertaste of blood. And it made no sense, even in the context of the nightmare landscape we inhabited. I had felt the hanging as clearly as if I were awake when it happened. It had to be how the spirit had been killed. So how was the pond involved?

Nathaniel's next words yanked me back to the present. "Matt's right, though. Molly, you should pack your things. You can leave with them at first light."

"No—"

He overrode me. "No one goes anywhere alone until the sun's up. We'll spend the rest of the night downstairs as a group."

"I have to change," said Jennifer. Her sheer, flowing white gown, combined with her blond hair and pale skin, painted the very picture of a traditional fleeing spirit, utterly unlike the object of terror currently working its will on us.

"I'll go with you." Matt flicked a glance in my direction, then looked quickly away. A shudder passed over him and I realized he feared being alone with me. Feared *me*. "Come on, Hailey, let's help your mom. You should put on a sweat-shirt over your pajamas, too. It's chilly downstairs."

They hurried from the room, leaving me alone with Nathaniel and Liza. I wanted to change, too. Not because my sleeping scrubs were inappropriate, but because sweat had soaked them and now they stuck, clammy and uncomfortable, to my chilly skin.

"Can you stand?" Nathaniel asked.

"Of course." When I slipped from the bed, however, my knees wobbled and tears threatened. I grabbed for the bedpost, but Nathaniel came to my rescue and wrapped a long arm around me. My whole body sagged for a moment and the intensity of my own desire to simply fold up into him scared me nearly as much as the idea of facing a ghost. I pulled away and managed a stiff smile.

"Thanks. I guess I'm a little shakier than I realized."

He crossed his arms and regarded me with that inscrutable expression. "One could hardly expect anything else. Take it slowly."

I plucked at the front of my top, pulling it away from my skin.

"Molly wants to change, Dad," Liza said. "She's all gross."

He looked blank, as if he didn't understand the words.

"I'm fine." How many times had I said those words since my arrival in Maine? Had they ever been true? Even once?

He shook his head, clearing it. "No, of course you need to change. I'll be right outside. Liza, you stay with Molly. If anything happens, holler."

athaniel stepped into the hall and pulled the door shut. Why would he leave her with me? Her dark gaze was as impenetrable as her father's.

"Are you holding up all right?" I waited for her to nod before I drew my top over my head and ran it behind my neck to wipe away the sweat gathered beneath my braid. Liza sucked in a sharp breath and my fingers went to my throat where the thick welt rose. "That bad, huh?"

She nodded, and two tears slipped down her cheeks.

"Oh, honey. It's okay. Really. We'll get through this."

"It's my fault," she whispered. "I wanted her to come. I wished for her to come. I wanted everyone else to go away. She's only doing what I asked for."

I pulled a sweatshirt over my head to give me a chance to collect my thoughts. "You know my mother died a few years ago, right?"

She nodded.

"I was much older than you. But I still had all those same feelings. I love my sister. Adore her. But right after mama died I wished she wasn't around. Not that she'd die, or that she'd never been born, but that I could just be alone with my memories of my mother, without being responsible for anyone else."

"You did?"

"I did. Trust me, I wouldn't lie about something as terrible as that. And then, of course, I felt guilty for those wishes. Which made me angry. Which made me wish she weren't around so that I wouldn't feel guilty. It's absolutely natural, and doesn't make you in any way at fault for what's happening here. You didn't say 'hey, ghost, shove my aunt down the stairs,' did you?"

I meant it as a joke, but she shook her head somberly. "But I didn't tell her not to. Aunt Jenn wanted to send me to an institution. A crazy place. She told Hailey."

"I'm sure that's not true." Actually, I knew Jenn planned to hide Liza away somewhere, but I refused to believe she'd told her daughter so.

"Hailey was right about her mom wanting to marry my dad. And it would have been easier with me out of the way."

"Even if that's the case, your dad would never let it happen. And she's leaving now, so it's irrelevant. You didn't want your father to get married again. That's not the same as hiring a ghostly assassin to push your aunt. We all have feelings we'd rather not. We all think uncharitable thoughts. We're only responsible for how we act, not how we feel."

Those owlish eyes regarded me long enough that Nathaniel knocked on the door and asked whether we were okay.

"Out in a minute," I called. Liza's bony fingers reached up and I let them touch my neck. "Not your fault, honey. And guilt doesn't help. I felt that when my mother died, too. Like if it hadn't been for me, she would have had insurance. Would have gone to a doctor sooner. But you can't fix the past. You can only fix the future. Don't waste your energy on guilt—and I do understand I just told you we can't help how we feel—but don't let it hobble you. If you spend all your time worrying about what you did wrong, you won't be able to help us make things right. And we need your help. Yours above anyone's because without you, we have no way to connect to her."

She straightened from her slump.

"You mean that?"

"I really do."

WHEN I OPENED the bedroom door, everyone had gathered in the hall. Two hefty suitcases sat at the top of the stairs, and Nathaniel was promising to send Jennifer the remainder of her possessions once she and Hailey had found a place to settle.

A bit of color had returned to Matt's cheeks, but he did not meet my eyes when Liza and I joined the group. Instead, he lifted the bags and started down the steps. The rest of us followed.

In the living room, Nathaniel built a fire and Matt poured himself a large glass of bourbon.

"That seems like a great idea," Jenn said. "Get me a vodka tonic, will you?"

"Sure. Anyone else?"

I shook my head. Nathaniel offered to make hot chocolate for the girls, both of whom agreed.

"Not by yourself," I said when he stepped toward the door. "You were the one who insisted we go nowhere alone."

"Right. Of course." He hadn't meant himself. In typical male fashion, he considered himself invulnerable. The rest of us needed his protection, but he did not need ours.

"I'll come with you," I offered.

"Come on, then." He did not stop to see whether I obeyed and I followed those stiff shoulders down the shadowy hallway and into the kitchen. He poured milk into a small saucepan and glanced over at me. "You want a cup?"

I remembered the last time he'd brought me hot chocolate, the thick, sweet comfort of it, and nodded. He poured more milk in and set the heat to low. Rocky whined in his crate, but when no one came to take him out, he settled back to sleep. The book I'd bought said dogs could often sense spirits; either the author lied or Rocky lacked the sensitive gene.

"I'm not leaving with Matt and Jennifer and Hailey. You need me here."

He ignored me for a minute, rummaging in the cupboard for a tin of cocoa, then prying off the lid and scooping several spoonfuls into the pan with the milk.

"She's focused on you," he said at last, though he still did not turn around to face me. "You can't stay here. She's made it clear that she has no compunction about killing you. Your attack was far more brutal than Jenn's."

"I have a theory about that."

"Why does this not surprise me?" He stirred the pot, then faced me. "Let's have it."

"I pose a bigger threat to her. Jennifer has no chance of figuring out who she is and sending her away. I do."

"You're convinced that her identity is the key to her banishment?"

"I am."

"Why?"

The question I'd hoped he wouldn't ask. "A number of reasons. Part of it comes from the book I bought for Liza, part from what my family always said about carnival queens, part from what Adriana Livingston said about earthly regrets.

"An unquiet spirit forms because of a regret. And eventually, that regret becomes all-consuming. It's their ambition, their sole reason for staying on this plane rather than moving on. If we find out who she was, we can find out what she regrets, what her ambition is. That's what's tethering her to Liza. All we have to do is sever the connection."

"That's a great deal of supposition."

"I know, but it feels right. And what other option do we have?"

"Then Liza and I will figure it out. We don't need you. And you can't help anyone if she kills you, which she seems determined to do."

And, oh, that hurt. It ripped right through the warm, rich scent of chocolate clouding the kitchen, a cold blade twisting in my breast. Of course he saw no place for me with his daughter. Placing the blame on me provided a buffer from his own guilt, which must be at least as overwhelming as his daughter's. Despite seeing the defensiveness beneath his words, I had to take two shallow breaths before I could speak.

"I can't." I was too deeply attached to both Nathaniel and his daughter, but I could not very well admit such a thing. He'd just gotten past the unwelcome revelation of his sister-in-law's feelings. "I understand that you'd prefer to be able to save Liza on your own, but isn't it better, in the long run, to have an extra pair of hands?"

"Why are you so determined to stay?" he persisted.

Because I love you. Love you both. Because you're my family as much as Ali. But one did not say such things to one's employer, especially when he'd endured his sister-in-law's wiles and a previous tutor's accusations of seduction.

"Because your daughter's a great kid. She deserves a great life. If there's any possibility that I can help give her one, I can't abandon her."

"And can you help? Did you find anything in my father's book that might give us a clue?"

Out of one battle, straight into another. "Not enough. I need to talk to him. I can't help feeling that he knew more than he wrote down. I noticed a decided lack of information about spiritualism, despite how strongly rooted it was in this part of the country, in the final text. And yet, he has so many books about it."

"What, you think he was performing séances in his office? I assure you, he was not."

"I didn't say that. I assume when researching any book an author gathers more information than he uses. Your father likely found out far more about this property than he wrote down. But they're exactly what we need."

"Okay, but how do you expect me to ask him? Call him up —assuming the phone's still working in a few hours when he gets up—and say 'look, Dad, this house is haunted and I need to know whether you have any idea whether my ancestors murdered anyone here?'"

"I can do it."

"He has no idea who you are."

"And isn't it better for him to think you've hired a lunatic than to think you are one? I promise, I'll find a way to make it sound normal."

He rubbed his forehead. "I must be mad even to consider it."

"We're all a little mad at the moment. Consequence of living with an unquiet spirit, I expect."

The milk spat and he cursed before tending to it. He did not speak to me again before gesturing for me to follow him back to the living room.

As we entered the library, I studied the group around the fire. None of them spoke and Jennifer rocked slightly as she stared down into her drink. *She is drawing our energy away. Not just those she deliberately targets, but all of us. One by one, we'll simply disappear, and no one will remember we ever existed.*

I shook away the thought and picked up Jim Prescott's textbook, which I'd left on the coffee table when Liza and I turned in for the night.

"You think she's in there," Jennifer said. "That's why you wanted it."

"I hoped she might be, but I didn't find her."

Matt frowned. "You can't still be looking. For God's sake, hasn't she done enough damage to you? Give over and come with us when the sun rises. I'll go up right now and watch over you while you pack."

"That's not going to happen."

"Why?" Matt raked a hand through his hair. "Do you have a martyr complex? You have to die for… for what, exactly? So that no one can say you quit a job? I'm well aware of the financial restrictions Thane put on your job. My sister and I discussed them. But I'm sure he won't hold you to them."

"I've already told her that," said Nathaniel.

"Then what? What's the problem? Thane and Liza are tied to this place, but you're not. You have a life. A family. You told me about them. Your sister, the one who's pre-med. It doesn't bother you that you could die here, and leave her all alone?"

That wound had been bleeding since my conversation with Liza. I was as susceptible to guilt as the next person. Maybe more so. But I had to take the advice I'd given her. And if I could not admit my feelings to Nathaniel, I certainly could not speak in front of Matt and Jennifer. I could not tell them that Ali would want me to stay for the simple reason that I wanted to. She'd be so excited that I'd found a place, a new family to love—even if they didn't love me back—that she'd never expect me to leave on her behalf.

"I am all too aware of what might happen. But Ali…" My mouth dried and I could not speak. I sipped at the cocoa, but what I needed was the cleansing bite of ice water. I searched for an answer close enough to the truth to be convincing. "Ali would never want me to abandon anyone to an angry spirit. She's going to be a doctor. Her whole life is about helping people. And when it comes right down to it, that's what my life is about, too. We've always understood that about each other."

"She's not going to be a doctor if you die here and she has to get a job instead of finishing college," Matt said, the knife followed by the sting of acid.

I swallowed the tears clogging my throat and hardened myself. This was the man who'd flirted so charmingly with me. For the first time, I could imagine him in a courtroom. "I survived my mother's death. Ali is the same age now I was when she was diagnosed with cancer. If I die, she'll finish college. She might have to work for a year or two between college and graduate school, but she'll go. She's smarter and stronger than I ever was."

"And you? What did you want to do before that?"

"We don't always get what we want."

"And you're content have your sister answer the same way? In five years, when she's working for the same woman who sent you here because medical school is expensive and she needs to make a living?" He threw up his hands.

Nathaniel coughed. I'd forgotten, in those few heated moments, that Matt and I were not alone.

"It may be the only time anyone ever hears me say this," he said, "but Matt's right. People depend on you."

Other people. Not him. Not Liza. My face hurt and I walked over to the window and peered out into the night rather than answering. My first impression of Rook's Rest had been of a place out of time. How much or little had it changed since the night—and I had no doubt it had been at night, though no evidence supported the idea—a woman had lost her life here?

"I need to write to Ali," I managed at last. "To all of them." I faced Matt, ignoring Nathaniel. "You'll take the letters with you?"

"No. Your sister deserves better than a letter."

"We'll take them," said Jennifer. "There's stationery in the office. Shall I come with you?"

My heart squeezed at the idea of saying goodbye to my family in front of Jennifer.

"I'll go," said Liza. "The ghost doesn't want to hurt me, so Molly will be safe if I'm with her."

Nathaniel started to protest, then subsided. Had he accepted my determination to stay, or was he waiting until the last minute for a final protest? I wouldn't put it past him to knock me out and stuff me in the car with Matt.

The shadows in the hall shifted and stretched with the movement of the trees in the wind outside, reaching for us until we flipped the light switch in the ballroom. I sat at Nathaniel's desk, selected a pen from the chipped mug, and pulled the legal pad sitting in the center of the blotter closer to me. What could I say? Matt was right; Ali did deserve more. But I could not imagine calling her and trying to explain that I might not live to see her graduate, not while listening to her voice.

"Why won't you go with them? Really? Aren't you scared to stay?"

Liza was little more than a dark blot, wavering with the tears in my eyes.

"Because my sister doesn't need me. No matter what your

uncle says. She loves me, and if I don't survive she'll miss me, but this, right here, is life or death."

"So you'd stay no matter what?"

"I'm not sure what you mean."

"With any family who needed you?"

My scant training had given me no tools for this situation. What was the best answer? The truth? I had no idea what it was. Or maybe I was lying to myself. Self-deception had become deeply ingrained in the years since Mama's death. *No, I don't mind giving up my studies. No, I don't mind changing adult diapers. No, I don't miss going out on dates. No, I don't miss staying up late studying with a group of similarly-focused friends. No, I don't need a peer group, my family is enough.*

That last wasn't entirely a lie. My family had been enough. For a long time. Until I'd come to Maine.

"You're special," I told Liza. And that was true, if only part of what kept me at Rook's Rest.

"Because I talk to ghosts?"

"Because you're you."

"And because Dad's Dad?"

A blush crawled up my neck. Leave it to a kid. She'd sussed out her aunt's interest easily enough. I hadn't realized my own had been so plain.

"Let's leave your father out of it, okay?"

She shrugged. "What are you going to tell your sister?"

"I wish I knew."

The words came more easily than I'd imagined once I started, however. As I'd told Matt, Ali would never condone deserting a family in need, so I started there. By the time I'd finished, my scrawl covered three pages of the legal pad and the collar of my sweatshirt was soaked with tears. Nathaniel had checked on us twice. The third time, I had folded the letter and slipped it into an envelope.

"Liza, go back to the library. I need to talk to Molly for a minute."

I braced myself for the next assault. The windows in the ballroom were hung with heavy drapes, but through the open door I could see that the hall had lightened. Dawn was coming, and with it Matt's departure.

But instead of arguing, Nathaniel plucked the envelope from my hand and tucked it into his back pocket. He leaned a hip against the desk and sighed.

"You look like hell."

"Thanks." I glared at him through swollen, gritty eyes.

"Go home, Molly. Be with your family."

"And waste all the work on that letter?"

"You don't understand."

"Then explain it to me. You need me to help Liza. Why are you trying so hard to push me away?"

"Because I can't have your death on my conscience. Upstairs... what I saw... I can't handle that again."

"Check the door. I want to be sure Liza's not listening."

He frowned, but did as I asked, shaking his head to show the coast was clear when he returned.

"You don't need to worry about your conscience. If I don't survive this, chances are you won't either. But if it makes you feel any better, I intend to finish this fight on top." I'd come to an understanding as I'd written to Ali, a recognition of aspects of myself I'd avoided thinking about for years. I stood up so I could look him in the eye.

"My mother told me I could achieve anything. For a while, I forgot that. Forgot that I'm an Allworth, and Allworths are unbeatable. Cancer took my mother, but it didn't beat her. There's a difference. This thing, whatever it is, whoever she was, I've had enough. The whole reason she's succeeded as far as she has is that we've been playing defense. I'm done with that. It's time to take up arms and become the aggressors. I'm not going to hide and wait for her to attack any more. If I let her chase me out of here, I won't be able to look at myself in a mirror for the rest of my life. If being the person my mother raised me to be gets me in trouble, that's on me. It's not on you. I absolve you of any responsibility. You did your best to force me out. Now let it go."

Bravado, pure and simple, but it was what I had left. And maybe he saw the fear lurking beneath the words, but he gave in and straightened to his full height. "Then I suppose we should get started."

CHAPTER 21

An hour later, we stood on the front steps and watched the others drive away, taking Rocky with them. She'd split us in half. Three gone, three remaining. But I couldn't help feeling lighter, as if removing Jennifer, Matt, and Hailey made us stronger, not weaker. And when Liza's hand crept into mine, I squeezed it tightly, a silent promise of solidarity.

"What now?" she asked.

"Now we find her."

"How?"

"We have to go to the billiards room." My stomach lurched. The third floor terrified me. Every inch of it. But the sun was rising, a brighter gray over the dreary landscape, and we had no time to waste. "In another hour or so, we can call your grandfather and I can see if he discovered anything in his research, but until then we're starting from scratch."

Nathaniel led the way. Perhaps it was just as well that he'd never felt the malignant spirit the way Liza and I had. Yes, he'd seen me unconscious in her grip, and the picture Matt had drawn of that was horrifying, but without my memories of the desperate attempt to reach Liza in the nursery and the creature I'd seen standing over her bed, he strode ahead into a battle with confidence I could not muster.

On the third floor landing, he faltered. He reached out to flick on the light, but nothing happened when he hit the switch.

"Huh. The lights are on in the rest of the house."

Yes. And they'd been on here when I was teaching, when I discovered the spiritualism books, when she pushed Jennifer down the stairs.

"She doesn't want us up here," said Liza in a strange, high-pitched voice. The truth of the situation had caught up with her and fear had finally set in. "She's angry."

Nathaniel straightened his shoulders and strode down the hall. "We'll open the curtains. That'll give us plenty of light."

The statement seemed ridiculously bold once we'd entered the billiards room, however. Dust motes floated through the weak sunlight and the atmosphere had thickened overnight.

"Where are these books you're so set on examining?"

I pointed to the top shelf.

"Leave it to my father to put them all the way up there. Okay. I'll climb up and hand them down to you. Are there any that you particularly want, or all of them?"

"The ones with the information on the paranormal and the ones about the Native Americans."

"Why those? Surely you don't think this haunting goes all the way back to when this was tribal land."

"I don't know how far back it goes and neither do you. But your father raised you on the tale of Alawa and he has a book up there about Canadian boarding schools for Native kids. I refuse to believe that's a coincidence. He studied the displaced children. And yet, there's only the slightest mention of it in the book about Maine."

"Because Maine didn't have boarding schools. We have a horrible, shameful history of sending Native kids to foster homes and even having them adopted out of their communities permanently. But those didn't really ratchet up until the 1960s, and it didn't impact this house. My mother was already summering here by then, so we'd know about anything untoward that happened."

A draft slipped by and I felt fingers on my neck. It took all my willpower not to raise my hands to swat her away. It would do no good. But we needed to get off the third floor.

"Please. Just bring them. We can carry them all downstairs to sort through."

"Your wish is my command." He leaped up on the counter, far more gracefully than I had done, and began pulling the bound manuscripts down. Every so often he would stop, read a title aloud, and grimace.

"These can't have been Dad's. Seriously. Maybe they were already here when he started using this room as his office."

"Then we can all thank whoever had it before your father."

"Grandpa Bill." He nodded. "Yeah, that makes a lot more sense. Crazy old man."

"Matt said he was living in Morocco now?"

"Yeah. I hope you don't expect to call him for help. He's unreachable."

WE WERE HEADED DOWNSTAIRS with the first batch of books—even with Liza's help it would take two trips to ferry everything to the library—when I saw her. She did not hover or float as a misty apparition the way ghosts in novels always had. Instead, I was aware of her as a flicker, like the glimpse of a dancer seen in a strobe-lit club. A flash of brown unruly hair, a darker blot on the darkened stair, nothing I could point to and say *there, there she is, let's get her.* And yet, she was. Watching, waiting. I felt her as much as saw her. She had not yet ingested enough of us to completely solidify her form, but hurrying down those steps, my arms filled with books, I knew it was only a matter of time.

Passing that spot on the way back up, I kept my eyes firmly on Nathaniel's back. Mama would have approved of his posture. I could barely see the outlines of his shoulder blades beneath his T-shirt. Liza, who had the center spot behind him and in front of me, tended to slouch. I'd need to address that in the future. If we had a future.

"We should get a Ouija board from the playroom," Liza said on the way down. For a moment, I saw her again, a shadow of a shadow, standing near us on the second floor landing, dark hair whipping in a wind that did not affect the rest of us.

Nathaniel detoured to the playroom, where Liza dug a battered Ouija box out of a pile of well-used board games. The sight of it in her pale hands made me slightly queasy, but a series of thuds from the library was followed by a cracking crash and we all ran for the stairs.

The wind that had whirled around the shadow on the second floor had torn through the library, sending the neat stacks of books we'd laid on the coffee table flying. One had slammed into the window, shattering it, and the cold streamed in along with flakes of snow.

Nathaniel cursed. "What the hell just hit the window? The wind wasn't supposed to pick up like this until later. Maybe we should go into town. Hole up in a hotel for a couple of days until the storm's over. I'll go get the Rover and pick you guys up out front."

"No." I grabbed his arm, unthinking. He studied my hand, resting there on his forearm, and something I could not read passed across his face. "Don't you see? It wasn't the storm. There's no snow inside."

His gaze flew to the shattered window and back to me. "Get your coat. You, too, Liza. I'll meet you out front."

Dread seized me in a grip colder and stronger than the stranglehold of the spirit. "No. Don't. We can't let her split us up. We'll all go."

We all grabbed our coats from the kitchen and headed outside. The wind grew wilder, blowing snow and ice down from the branches and up from the ground in a tornado of stinging spray.

"Can you drive in this?" I had to shout to be heard above the howling gale that stole my breath and threw my words into the trees.

Nathaniel did not answer. He forged ahead to the garage and punched in the door code. Nothing happened. He tried again with the same result.

"We can go around to the side door," he shouted. "The overhead door opens from the inside manually. But the path isn't shoveled. You should really wait here."

I shook my head, more certain than ever that she intended to separate us so she could hurt him. He had been a target long before my arrival. I grabbed hold of his jacket with one hand and reached for Liza with the other and we struggled through the deep drifts in a human chain.

The suffocating darkness inside the three-car garage blinded after the dirty white storm outside. When Nathaniel cursed and pounded on the hood of the Range Rover, it took me a minute to see what had upset him.

All four tires had been flattened, and the two nearest us had screwdrivers sticking out the sides.

"Back to the house. Double time. This storm's getting worse, and we don't want to be stuck out here." Nathaniel scooped up Liza and settled her on his hip despite her size and took my hand with his free one.

Blowing snow had nearly obliterated the path between the house and garage, so we stepped off it several times. Twice I fell, tripped by the deceptively even whiteness of the snowy ground and the corresponding lack of depth perception. The house was a massive, black silhouette against the gray trees, a half-solid form behind the snow's white scrim, and had it not been for its size, we might never have found it.

The fire in the library had gone out. Nathaniel knelt to rebuild it, and I walked over to the broken window to see if the drapes could block the hole. Wedged into the broken glass, with a shard driven straight through it, was the paperback about the Canadian boarding schools. I pulled it out, which broke yet more of the window, and set it to the side. Then I opened the window, stuck the bottom of the drapes outside, and slammed it shut. The drapes billowed and drafts pushed their way around and through them, but it was better than no barrier.

"We can duct tape them to the walls, too. That will help," said Liza.

"Good thought."

I picked up the book and tried to ease the shard of glass out, but it was stuck fast.

"Does it mean something?" Liza asked, observing my actions.

"I'm pretty sure it does, yes." I glanced out to the hall where the phone sat on its stand. "I don't suppose that's going to work in this weather."

"Won't know until we try." Nathaniel headed for the door

and the room seemed to hold its breath. Suddenly, I pictured the door slamming shut, separating us. I grabbed Liza's hand and hurried after him. He dialed and I thanked whatever benevolent spirit looked after the phone.

"Dad?" He paused, and I could hear a man speaking. "I'm okay. But I don't have time to chat. I need you to do me a favor." Sputtering from the other end. "Dad, really, we're in the middle of a storm and we could lose the phone at any second. Please. I need you to listen. Yeah. Okay. I'm going to put you on with Molly—what? Oh. Right. Molly's Liza's new tutor. Dad, I told you, I don't have time to answer questions. Please. Talk to Molly and tell her what she needs to know."

A second later, he handed the phone to me and I found myself wordless. A huge breath, and I mustered the arguments I'd come up with.

"Mr. Prescott? Hi, this is Molly Allworth."

"Do you want to tell me what's going on, Miss Allworth?"

"I don't have time. I promise, we'll clear it all up later. I had some questions about the books you used for research. The ones in the billiards room?"

"What were you looking for in there?"

"Are all those books yours? Because I didn't see much on the history of spiritualism in *Maine: Seafarers and Settlers through the Civil War*."

"You read it?"

"I skimmed. Were those books yours?"

"I looked through them. But in the main, they were my father-in-law's. He's a character."

"And the Native American books?"

"Oh, sure. I did a lot of research on local tribes."

"What about the book on Canadian boarding schools?"

He did not answer and I thought we'd lost the connection. "Mr. Prescott? Are you there?"

"That wasn't part of my project. It was part of Linda's mother's. She was constructing a family history."

"She's Native American?"

"No..." a scuffle took place on the other end of the line and then a woman's voice came on.

"Who is this?"

"Molly Allworth. Liza's tutor."

"Miss Allworth, what can my family history possibly have to do with you?"

"It's not me. It's Liza. I've gotten her to talk, but I am working on bringing her further along. I'd be happy to give you all the details, but not now."

"She's talking again?"

"Yes. Can you please tell me why your mother would have been interested in Native American boarding schools in Canada?"

"Because she had a sister adopted out of one of the residential schools. My grandparents had had no success conceiving, and they were desperate for a child. My grandmother's sister had married a Canadian—a Catholic, so imagine the scandal—and she told my grandparents that if they weren't too picky about their child's skin color, they could adopt. There wasn't the oversight there is now, you understand? This was the 1920s. So they adopted a Native child and brought her home. And then in 1931, they got pregnant with my mother and her twin sister.

"The other girl, they'd named her May, and my mother never did find a record of her real name, she was about ten or eleven when my mother was born. You're welcome to go through mom's papers. They're in the room on the third floor that looks like a ladies' sitting room. She lost enthusiasm for the project and never finished. I bought that book myself, the one you mean, because I considered picking up where she left off, but I never had time."

The schoolroom. That meant climbing those stairs at least one more time.

"May, your mother's sister, she's still alive?"

"No. She died in 1938. Influenza. It took my mother's twin as well."

"Did she—" But my time was up. Dead air buzzed on the other end of the line.

e returned to the living room and I told them what I'd learned.

"Mom's family?" Nathaniel said. "How did I not know this?"

"Why would you? She died decades before you were born. By the time your mother thought about taking up her mother's genealogy project, May was all but forgotten."

"It's interesting, but I don't see how it helps us. May died of influenza. That's not tragic or sudden. And why would a little girl who died right alongside another little girl suddenly start haunting the house after almost eighty years?"

"Maybe it's not her. But she's connected. She has to be."

"Maybe she's not the ghost, just a conduit or something," said Liza.

"What do you mean?"

"Well, maybe she knows what happened. We can call her. Ask her. Maybe she'll tell us."

"Just like that." Hysterics nearly choked me. "We just call her up, same as we did your grandparents, and have a little chat with her."

"We can use the board. We don't have any choice." She pulled the lid off the cardboard box and laid the Ouija board on the table. When she reached for the planchette, a little, involuntary squeak forced itself from my throat.

Nathaniel made a T with his hands. "Okay, time out. Cool off. We are not rushing into anything. My mother said the papers were upstairs?"

"Yes, but I didn't get a chance to ask her where. We've had class in that room every day and I haven't seen them."

The lights flickered and Nathaniel frowned. "This is our first winter with the generator and I'm not sure how it will hold up to this storm. We should go up and look now. We have plenty of wood in the mudroom for the fire, along with flashlights and candles, but I don't want us digging around upstairs if the lights go out."

No joke. I had no desire to go up with the lights on. But once again, I steeled myself, took Liza's hand in my own, and followed Nathaniel up the stairs.

This time, even he felt the difference in the atmosphere. Though nothing compared to the raging wind outside, the draft was too strong to be natural and eddies of cold air curled all around us.

Again I felt those fingers on my neck. Long and strong and too big to belong to a child. They rested cold and clammy against my skin, not squeezing but reminding me that they might at any moment. That my life was, literally, in her hands.

"She's here, isn't she?" Nathaniel asked as he pushed open the classroom door and ushered us in.

I nodded, unable to speak, and he put an arm over my shoulders.

"If you can hear me, ghost, spirit, whatever you are," he said, "we're only trying to help."

The door slammed behind us hard enough to shake the floor and topple the mug of pencils sitting on the desk.

"I don't think she believes you," said Liza.

"Where would your mother have kept her papers?" I wanted out of that room as soon as possible, assuming we could even get the door open.

Nathaniel shook his head. " I never paid attention. You checked inside the writing desk?"

"I put everything from the desk into the cabinet below those shelves." I pointed to the delicate built-in that occupied a corner, where I had stuffed all the fancy glass vases from the etager for safe-keeping, but then I remembered the filing cabinet in the playroom.

"There are more papers in the playroom. Maybe they were moved and your mother forgot. Or didn't realize."

"We can look there next." He yanked on the door of the cabinet and the knob came off in his hand. The temperature dropped and without thinking, I crossed myself. A second later, the vases above his head began to rattle and shake and then one flew off, as if thrown by an invisible hand. I did not even have a chance to duck; it crashed into my forehead and knocked me backward.

The room faded and reality slipped away. A slim figure flitted around the writing desk. She wore a dress with a narrow skirt and puffy-shouldered sleeves that tightened to show off impossibly tiny wrists and hands. Two small children played on the rug. In the background, the shadow of another presence hovered, but I could not see her.

I CAME to on the sofa in the living room. Liza was perched by my waist, while Nathaniel knelt on the carpet next to me. My head throbbed and I raised my hand and felt a lump on the my forehead.

"Look at me," I said to Liza. "I'm a unicorn."

A halfhearted smile lightened her somber face for a moment.

"Did you find the papers?"

"We brought everything that was in the cabinet down. Haven't had a chance to look at it yet," Nathaniel said.

My stomach lurched and the room spun a little as I sat up and I had to take a few deep breaths.

"Easy." Nathaniel sat next to me and put a hand on my back. "You probably have a concussion. Unfortunately, there's not much we can do about it right now."

"Don't worry about it. Let's have a look at the papers." They lay on the coffee table, loose papers piled in a tall stack beside an overflowing three-ring binder.

Liza plucked a few sheets from the pile and handed them to me. They appeared to be copies of newspaper articles about the Fairchild family.

"That was my mother's maiden name," said Nathaniel. "Her grandfather was a Wilton, the last of the family who built this place. His daughter, my grandmother, married William Fairchild. Wild Bill, my father called him."

"I remember Matt telling me about him." It seemed a hundred years ago now. Bill Wilton, boatbuilder and adventurer, now living in Morocco. "So this article is about your grandparents, the family that adopted May."

"I suppose so."

The newspaper article detailed a fire "of mysterious origin" at Rook's Rest that had temporarily forced the family to find lodgings in town.

This is not the first tragedy the Fairchilds have suffered this year. In June, they lost two children, Ellen Elizabeth, age 7, and May Louise, age 18. Last night's fire appears to have started at the north side of the house. An upward draft brought the smoke in the window of their remaining daughter's bedroom, nearly taking her as well. It was sheer luck that Nate Fairchild was still awake and realized what was happening in time to save his wife and daughter. He got them out of the house and put out the fire, but not before it had consumed much of the north wall.

"I guess you were named for your great-grandfather," I said. "The hero."

Nathaniel shrugged. "I never knew him."

"May Louise Fairchild," said Liza. "Now we know her name."

"I wonder how she felt about being May Louise Fairchild," said Nathaniel. "Did they rename her? What was her name at the residential school? Had they called her by her real name, or had they renamed her as well?"

"That's so sad," said Liza. "I wonder whether she's buried in the little cemetery."

"No." I was certain of it. "She's one of the outside graves."

"Why do you say that?"

I tried to apply logic to my gut reaction. "They didn't consider her part of the family. She was Native American, brought to them from a Catholic school in Canada. She was second best. That cemetery is sacred ground, but not sacred Catholic ground and certainly not appropriate for a Native American girl. How long had she lived here? Had she actively accepted their religion? I doubt it. I have to wonder whether she even accepted the name they gave her."

"Which one of the graves?" Liza was frowning.

"Probably the big stone cross. They would have wanted to show some respect for her as a family member, but not as much as they showed for their own daughter, who'd be buried inside the fence."

"That sucks," said Liza.

"It does," I agreed.

"No wonder she's pissed off and haunting us."

"If it's her." I touched my neck. "I can't help thinking the spirit we're dealing had reached full maturity, though. Eighteen would have been a legal adult, but I got the impression of a strength I am having a hard time ascribing to an eighteen-year-old suffering from influenza, however unhappy her life was."

"Whoever the spirit is," said Nathaniel slowly, "she's not Catholic. So it might be the kid, angry at all the people who took her from the life she loved."

"How do you know?"

"Because you were praying when she clocked you."

I pushed my mind back, felt my hand crossing my head, my heart, and heard my own voice murmuring an Our Father in the freezing room.

"I didn't realize you were Catholic," he said.

"Lapsed. A long, long time ago. My mother used to take us to church in New York, but after my dad died, when we moved to Connecticut, we stopped. I didn't realize I was speaking. It just...came out. Habit, I suppose."

"Fear drives us back to the basic comforts of youth," he said. "I remember when Marianne died and Liza got quiet, my instinctive reaction was to turn to my mother. It's ridiculous, and once logic reasserted itself, I knew it was impractical, but my lizard brain turned to the authority figure of my childhood."

A gust of wind blew down the chimney, driving smoke past the heavy wrought-iron fireplace screen and into the room. My eyes watered and I choked, as did both Nathaniel and Liza.

"I'd as soon not relive that night, thanks," he said when the air cleared. "Let's see what else she copied."

Another article lay beneath the first, and the headline

blared such a gruesome message that I instinctively snatched it away to hide it from Liza.

"What does it say?" she asked, pushing at my hand. "I want to see."

I shook my head and handed the paper over her head to Nathaniel. He glanced at it, then got up and walked over to the fireplace to read it. I feared he'd throw it in to protect his daughter, and from the desperate expression that tightened his features, he considered it. But at last he returned and laid the article face up on the coffee table where we could view the horror together.

THAWING WILTON POND GIVES UP DEAD BODY.

CHAPTER 23

"It's her," I said. "It has to be."

"So now we know how she died, and where, but we still don't know who she is."

"Actually, it doesn't say how she died. Just that they found her in the pond. Where she'd obviously been since before it froze over the previous year." The year before the fire. The year before the influenza epidemic.

The article said that the woman's body had been too badly decomposed for them to make an identification. No women had been reported missing within the past year in the community, so she was not local, which reduced any chance they would find her identity. An artist had attempted a pencil sketch to go with the report, but the broad-faced woman with long dark hair might have been anyone. I didn't suppose for a minute that they'd had forensic sketch artists studying bodies in the 1930s, so the picture had probably been included to sensationalize the story and attract more eyes to the paper than to provide actual information about the victim.

Liza curled into herself, making tiny mewling noises, and

Nathaniel gathered her into his lap. "It's okay, honey. It was all a long time ago."

"Do you think they skated on the pond back then?"

My stomach flipped. I could picture it as clearly as she did. Liza's grandmother and her family, which that winter would still have included a twin and an adopted older sister, teasing and laughing and skating atop the body of a murdered woman frozen beneath their feet. Currier and Ives gone horribly wrong. I tasted bile and for a moment was back in the pond, thick, scummy water filling my mouth.

"She was gone," I said as much to myself as to Liza. "It's terrible to imagine, I know, but she was past caring." Because someone had hanged her before they dumped her body in that pond to rot. I could feel the rope's welt around my own neck as surely as it would have shown on hers had she been found before decay had set in.

"What if she wasn't? I mean, not dead, of course she was dead. But she's still here. So what if she wasn't past caring?"

"Speculation on whether she cared or to aside, the important question is still *who was she?*" Nathaniel focused on the salient issue. "What connects her to this house? The article doesn't have her name."

Liza leaned over to the coffee table and picked up the planchette, turning it over in her fingers.

To forestall any more talk about calling spirits, I reached for the papers. "Let's go through the rest of these and see whether there's more about her."

We separated the stack of paper into three sections and each of us took a chunk. It only took about twenty minutes to find that none contained any information on the mysterious woman from the pond.

"We're so close," I moaned. "We're right there. We can't give up now." I picked up the binder and flipped through it. The pages were covered in tight, small, elegant handwriting.

"My mother," said Nathaniel.

Here she had chronicled the family. She had used her own mother's research to weave a narrative history from the bare facts. It started with the earliest American Wiltons, emigres from England who had landed at Plymouth and made their way north, then north again, to settle in Acadia, in lands brutally and bitterly contested between the French and British. They'd been traders, trappers, fishermen, and hunters, and she painted their world with a delicacy I hadn't seen in her husband's drier, academic tome.

"That part doesn't matter," Nathaniel said.

I pulled myself away. If we lived through this, I would go back to Linda Prescott's work.

I flipped forward to the end of the written pages to see how far Linda had gotten. The narrative only made it to the Civil War, but she had continued charts, graphs, and outlines right to the 1950s when her parents had married. The family tree and several of the other papers had notes saying "see photo box" and I asked Nathaniel if he had any idea what it meant.

"We have a hell of a lot of pictures," he said. "Mom's childhood friend Patsy became a professional photographer. She stayed with us when it wasn't wedding season, and took a ton of pictures. Mom has them all in boxes in the master bedroom. I keep telling her she should take them home, that we're not going to look at them, but she and Dad don't really want them, either. The thing is, they're only the latest in probably three or four generations' worth of photographs and she thinks they all need to be kept together. Like they're going to be valuable someday or something."

"I like them," said Liza. "Seeing those people in those cool old-fashioned clothes."

"I know you do." He ruffled her hair. "That's the only reason I haven't thrown them out. Your mom liked them, too. She used to pin them up on a board as inspiration when she was painting."

"I want to see them," I said. "Not the recent ones, but the ones from the 20s and 30s. Can we get them?"

"We can try. I have to admit, I'm not exactly eager to go back upstairs."

My stomach rumbled, embarrassingly loud in the silent room and Nathaniel put down the papers he was holding.

"These are useless. Let's adjourn to the kitchen, have some lunch and regroup."

On the way out of the living room, I stopped and picked up the book on Canadian schools. Using a silicone potholder to protect my hand, I eased out the glass shard and scanned the first few pages. I was still reading, horrified, when Nathaniel placed a bowl of steaming soup in front of me and laid a hand on my shoulder. It was only when I looked up that I realized tears were dripping down my cheeks.

"What's the matter?"

"These poor kids. I had no idea."

"It's not where my grandmother's sister came from, you said."

"No. And this is too late—the stories come from people who attended the school in the 1950s. But I can't believe it would be so different at any of the other institutions. Your great-aunt May must have lived through hell."

He shook his head. "Let's not focus on that. You said May's not our ghost."

"It all starts with May. Can't you feel it?"

"I saw her." Liza's statement came out of the blue.

Nathaniel and I both stared at her.

"You saw May?" he asked.

"The woman. The day you fell off the ladder. I was in the sitting room on the third floor in the window seat and she was on the ground, looking up at me."

I shuddered and laced my fingers around the hot bowl, trying to warm myself. It didn't help. "That day... Liza, did you hear me calling you?"

"Calling me?"

"I had been looking for you. Did you see me in the doorway? Before your father fell?"

Her features screwed up into a thoughtful frown. "No. It was weird. Like everything else was out of focus except her. She was sharp and clear and she called me. And I heard her."

"What did she say?" Nathaniel's harsh tone was born of fear, not criticism, but Liza flinched.

She drew her knees up under her chin, folding herself in half on the chair. Her eyes filled with tears and she took several deep breaths, unable to answer.

He knelt beside her seat and wrapped his arms around her. "Tell me, sweetheart."

"She said I should jump." The words were a whisper, a mere thread of sound winding through the kitchen.

My heart cracked and stopped. I struggled to breathe. I'd felt it that day, the danger Liza was in. I couldn't have named it, but the clawing desperation that had driven me to reach her nearly swallowed me again right there at the kitchen table.

Nathaniel's breathing, fast and heavy, filled the kitchen, but Liza wasn't done.

"She said no one here needed me anymore, but that she did. She loved me. She wanted me. We'd be happy together."

"You know that's not true, right? You know I need you."

She nodded. "Now I do. Because you're here and she's not. But I couldn't feel it then. I just wanted my life to end. I wanted everything to be over. And she showed me..."

"Showed you what, sweetheart?"

Her dark eyes darted to me, then away. "You had other children. And you were happy."

"Other children?"

Liza shut her mouth in a flat, firm line.

But I understood her meaning, so I finished the thought for her. "With me. That's what she tried with all the tutors you hired. That's why they didn't work out." I steeled myself against the waves of loss that threatened. It was all a horrible joke. The ghost had manipulated my interactions with Nathaniel the same way Jennifer had manipulated my relationship with Matt.

"I don't know what she showed the first one, but clearly she wanted Aimee to seduce you. And if that failed, maybe Aimee could kill you. If she could convince Liza that you had fallen for them, she could have what she's wanted all along—your daughter. Liza's love for you is the only thing that stands between this thing and the completion of her dream. She wants Liza, and to get her, you have to be removed in a way that Liza won't blame on her. She can't kill you because Liza would never forgive that. But if you had a completely mundane accident? Or ran off with a new bride and forgot about her? Liza might be vulnerable to persuasion."

He was shaking now and I reached out and laid a hand on his arm. The muscle bunched and trembled beneath my fingers.

"Who tries to convince a child that her father would be better off without her?"

"Liza has to come to her willingly. Whatever drives her won't be satisfied by snatching an unwilling victim."

"But it's okay to lie and even murder to make her willing?"

"It doesn't have to make sense to you, only to her."

"We're never going to figure this out." He shook his head.

"We are. Eat first and let's go get those photographs."

◊

WE WERE in and out of the master bedroom and back in the living room with four boxes of photographs and two ancient albums covered with olive green fabric within minutes. Nathaniel and I lifted the coffee table out of the way, leaving the papers atop it, and all three of us settled on the floor in front of the fireplace.

"What are you hoping to find?" he asked.

"Anything. She's here. Close." I pulled the first photo album into my lap. There, on heavy black paper I found an oval photograph of the woman I'd seen in the schoolroom right before I passed out. The same wide-shouldered outfit. The same erect posture, pale skin and fine bones. Black spots flickered around the edges of my vision and dizziness assailed. How could I have seen her? This was not the woman from the sketch made from the remains.

"My great-grandmother," Nathaniel said. "Mom has that same bone structure." He ruffled Liza's hair. "So do you, actually."

"Really?" She peered at the photograph and I longed to hug her tight. I'd underestimated the depth of her solitude. No wonder she hadn't wanted to let go of the ghost. "That's my great-great-grandmother?"

"It is."

"We'll come back and look at it in a few minutes, okay? I'd like to get through this and see if we can find any pictures of May." I hoped my voice didn't sound as strangled to them as it did to me.

The next few pages had more pictures of the woman, along with some of her husband. And then, at last, I found what I was looking for. The photographer had captured May kneeling at the edge of Wilton pond. Her long, black hair trailed into the water and tiny ripples echoed out from the ends. She was a beautiful girl, but her loneliness radiated from the page. Liza gasped, and I knew she felt that same oppressive emotion coming off the page.

"That must have been right after they adopted her," Nathaniel said. "She can't be more than nine or ten."

"She's so *lonely*," Liza whispered.

A few pages later, the twins appeared. Photographs became more frequent after that, with several crammed on each page. I flipped through hurriedly, slowing only for those pages that prominently featured May. Though she was often pictured caring for her younger sisters, she never lost that air of separation.

And then, in the second book, came the funeral. Black cloaked figures huddled under a pale sky inside that tiny cemetery. I looked for May but did not see her among the mourners. It was Liza who figured out why.

"May must have died first." She pointed out the corner of one photo, where the stone cross was evident.

Nathaniel frowned. "First by a long shot. They didn't get that headstone in a week."

"It's not engraved. Or if it was, the engraving's worn off. So it wouldn't have taken as long as a custom one."

Nathaniel nodded thoughtfully. "No. But if your daughter were ill with influenza, wouldn't you focus on her instead of on the one you could do nothing for? Would you worry about a headstone at all, especially for a kid you weren't planning on putting in your own family cemetery?"

"Maybe that's not May's grave after all." I was playing devil's advocate. It was May's grave. I knew it. I just didn't want to consider the implications of it being there already.

"It has to be. Look at this picture. She's not there but my grandmother is. And they haven't left empty spaces around Ellen's grave. They didn't think they'd need a spot for her sister. For either of her sisters."

The Ouija planchette flew up from the table where Liza

had set it and ripped across the page, sending photographs flying. Invisible hands tore the album from my hands and flung it at the fire. It bounced off the screen, which wobbled before falling to the floor in a clatter. Once again air gusted down the chimney, puffing smoke into the room before sucking it out, creating a vacuum that stole breath and sound. In the impossible silence, soundless voices shrieked and spun. Clear as a church bell, I heard my mother's admonition: *Maloney Jane, close the door!*

"I don't know how," I cried.

The light went out and the room disappeared and I was outside, looking up at the house from the shelter of the woods.

Close. So close. After all this time I was going to see her again. I screwed up my courage and dusted off my clothes, dirty from the long trip. I should wait until morning. It was only a few more hours. But I could not bear even another minute, so I left my bag beneath the sheltering oak, rubbed my hands to still the shivering— only partially from the cold—and approached the heavy wooden door.

My knock echoed inside—Imagine having a house so loud a sound might echo—and shortly thereafter footsteps approached. A tall man opened the door and down his hawk-like nose at me.

"Yes?"

I straightened to my full height. "I have come for my daughter."

"You have no child here," he said.

"Little Fawn," I insisted, though this was not the name her white father called her, nor the name I had given her in my heart. But when the churchmen came for her, after her father had kicked us out, they promised to call her Fawn. That much was allowed.

"Fawn!" I called. "Little Fawn, come to your mother!"

But he was shouting, too, and another man came, and one of them hit me, and it was Fawn's father all over again, the hitting and the hurting, and though I fought I was near unconscious when

when they dragged me over to the tree and laughed when they saw my bag and joked about my lack of power.

They flung a rope over a branch, then, and as it tightened around my neck, I looked up at the house and saw you in the window. And I made you the same promise I had made when they took you from me so many years before: I am coming for you, heart of my heart, and I will never stop.

"Molly!"

A sharp pain whipped across my right cheek and I blinked. We were standing by the broken window and for a second the scene outside remained superimposed over the library. When my vision cleared, my knees buckled and Nathaniel caught me, an arm around my waist, before I could fall into the glass on the floor. Liza was weeping and she flung herself at me, practically knocking me over. I couldn't understand the words beneath her sobs.

athaniel ushered both of us over to the sofa and Liza crawled into my lap. The trembling heat of her angular body against mine reminded me painfully of the times I'd held Ali in the forlorn days after Mama's death.

"It's okay," I assured her, my throat raw and achy as if I'd been screaming. "Liza, honey, it's all right." Was it? I was still processing the vision.

She burrowed deeply into me and did not look up, so I addressed Nathaniel.

"What happened?"

His skin looked waxy, scarcely alive, and when he spoke, it was the sound of a creaky hinge. "It was like upstairs."

My hand went to my neck, where new bruises were forming over the old ones.

Nathaniel reached for my hand, lacing his fingers with mine. "Don't. It's not good. How much do you remember?"

"The planchette came up by itself. The photo album hit the fireplace and then…then…did you hear anything?"

"No. Did you?"

How ridiculous would it sound? "I heard my mother."

"What did she say?"

"She wanted me to push the spirit away."

"That's what you meant when you said you didn't know how?"

"I said that aloud?"

"Several times. You shouted it, in fact. I tried to ask what you meant, but you couldn't hear me. You walked over to the window and stood there, muttering. I didn't want to wake you—it was as if you were sleepwalking, and I've heard it's a bad thing to wake a sleepwalker. But then you started gasping. I couldn't watch you…what happened upstairs, I couldn't go through that again. So I slapped you. I'm sorry."

I touched my cheek with my free hand, but the sting had subsided almost immediately. "Better than letting her strangle me." I couldn't help wondering, though, if his violence, restrained as it was, had served to confirm the spirit's association of him with his great-grandfather.

Liza's lips moved against my neck. "Did you see her?"

"I *was* her."

She pulled away and peered up at my face. "Then you know who she was!"

"May's mother."

"Good God," said Nathaniel.

"Remember what Adriana Livingston told us? Things left undone in life create unquiet spirits. In life, her daughter was stolen and she never had the opportunity to retrieve her. She wants a daughter. In particular, the daughter of the people who took hers."

A draft scuttled through the room and the shards of window glass clinked on the floor. The planchette, lying atop the board, stirred restlessly.

"I wasn't even born when May was stolen from her family!"

"Do ghosts understand time?" I picked up the planchette

and threw it through the crack in the curtains out into the thick, wet snow. The board and box I consigned to the fire, feeding the flames with the bellows be sure they burned. The door had opened before my arrival, but I would not wedge it wider.

Nathaniel let go of Liza and stood, pacing and rubbing his forehead. "I don't suppose it matters. Either she understands and doesn't care, or she doesn't understand. But how did she get here? Her daughter was in boarding school in Canada, for crying out loud. How did she ever find this house?"

"We may never know. But she did." The scene unspooled in my head. "She came at night and she raised a fuss and your great-grandfather, along with at least one other man, they killed her. She showed me one night in a dream, but I didn't understand what I was seeing until today. They beat her and hanged her and dumped her body in the pond." Again the taste of brackish water filled my nose and throat. "I don't think she was dead when she went in, either."

"My great-grandfather. Nathaniel. The hero of the fire. He stole her child and then he murdered her. No wonder she's out for revenge."

The temperature dropped and the wind pushed harder against the curtains. I thought about that small plastic piece outside, knocking to find a way in. The ash flew from the grate and whirled up into that same unnatural column I had faced upstairs. As one, Liza, Nathaniel and I backed away from it. A hail of glass flew at us and Nathaniel shoved me and Liza out of the way, taking the brunt of it on his left side.

"Stop! Just stop!" Liza wrenched herself from my grasp and took off. "Leave them alone! I'll come!"

"No!" I reached for her, but she was gone. Before Nathaniel and I could catch her she was out the door, which slammed hard behind her.

"Liza!" Nathaniel yanked on the knob, but the door remained stubbornly closed.

"Window!" I ran for the library. We pulled the drapes free of the broken window and climbed out into the white wilderness.

The wind howled, blowing us back against the house, flicking ice against skin in a prickling battery. Nathaniel called for Liza, but his words were snatched up and tossed away.

"The cemetery," I shouted. "She'll go to May's grave." He grabbed my hand in his good one and forged ahead through the blinding, blowing snow. The drifts clutched at my legs like clamoring hands. My eyes watered and the tears froze on my lashes. The air burned my sinuses and rippled all the way down to my lungs, but I would not stop. Could not stop.

As we approached the cemetery, the snow thickened to a white so heavy it appeared black. My legs disappeared into the gloom below the knee. I glanced back over my shoulder only to see that behind us light still filtered through the clouds. We were pushing into the heart of the storm.

A piece of ice flew out of the void and sliced through Nathaniel's cheek. Blood bloomed, shocking and red-black in the muted landscape. He cursed and wiped at it with his sleeve but did not slow.

I lost my vision completely a few steps later, and had no idea where we were. I had to trust that Nathaniel, who'd grown up on the property and had spent nights in the cemetery as a child in the midnight darkness, had enough muscle memory of the place to take us there.

Minutes, hours, days later, we reached the two crosses. I stumbled over a rock and landed shoulder-first on the iron cross. Pain screamed through me, shocking my spine, and it worsened when I leaned on the crossbar with my good hand and pushed myself up. The cold dulled the agony soon enough, but numbness, nausea and weakness came hard on its heels.

"Liza!" Nathaniel called.

I forced myself to my feet and felt around until I found the stone cross. Running my fingers down it, I found her huddled at the base.

"She's here! Liza, speak to me." I pulled her into my arms, using my good right arm to hold my left in place, trying to warm her against me. Nathaniel dropped beside us.

"She's so cold." A massive tremor rocked me. I wasn't going to be much use to her. "Liza, wake up and look at me. Please."

Her eyes opened and I reared back so quickly my head slammed into the stone cross behind me with a sickening thud. Something lived behind those eyes. Something dark and angry and filled with malice. Even in the strange, unnatural blizzard, I could tell that this was not the girl we knew.

"She is with me now. She wants to be."

"She doesn't. You forced her."

Nathaniel knelt beside us and cupped her face in his hands. "Liza, I know you're there. Come back to me, honey."

"She doesn't want to." Liza's lips moved out of sync with the words, like a soundtrack running a split-second behind. "She is my daughter, not yours."

"She's not," I said. "I know you hurt, and you're lonely, but this is Liza, not Little Fawn. And this is Nathaniel Prescott, not Nathaniel Fairchild. He's never hurt you, and he loves his daughter."

"She needs a mother," puppet Liza insisted.

"She needs a *life*. You'll kill her and she still won't be your daughter."

"She is not yours, either." Liza's white, bloodless lips twisted into a mocking grin, tearing a hole in my heart to mach the one in my shoulder.

"She's *mine.*" Nathaniel growled. "And she loves Molly. She loves both of us enough to sacrifice herself to save us. If you loved her, you'd honor her desires."

"You don't deserve her," not-Liza sneered.

"I know." And it was true, But that was the wonder of love. You could not earn it. It came or it did not. This mother-thing would understand that much. "But I love her. You love your daughter. You wish you could have kept her, looked after her, loved her in life. But you don't love Liza. Your daughter is here, buried beneath this cross." Suddenly I realized that the Wiltons must have volunteered to bury the "stranger" found in their pond. It would assuage their consciences while improving their reputation in town. Why else the second cross? "This is you, isn't it? Next to her. But I can't reunite you. I don't know how."

Those ancient eyes stared out at me for a long moment. My breath caught in my throat and not-Liza raised her hand to my neck, pushing me back against the cross. "If you love her so much, you could join us."

"Liza," Nathaniel begged, "please, sweetheart, push her out. You can do it. I need you to. Molly needs you to. I don't care what she told you about me succeeding without you, that won't happen. You're the only thing that's kept me going for the past two years. I need you. Every day. I know sometimes I looks as if I don't, but that's just fear. I'm afraid of doing the wrong thing and chasing you away, so I don't do anything at all. I'll do better, sweetheart, I promise. But I need you to come back to me. To fight."

The black pits of the not-Liza's eyes moved to his face for a moment, then back to mine.

"Liza," I choked out, "I know you want to help but this is not the way. You are not her daughter! Shake her off!"

"You know nothing of love," the not-Liza spat.

Nathaniel grabbed her and tried to wrench her away

from the headstone, away from me, but she kicked out and there was no way for him to get her without injuring her. The grip she had on my throat loosened, however, so I sucked in a breath of icy air and fought her the only way I could.

"Did you abandon your daughter?"

Her eyes blazed, hot enough to melt the snow around us and the fingers tightened on my throat once more. "No! She was stolen from me."

"You did what you thought was best when the school men came. She didn't disappear into the night, you gave her to them. You told them to call her Fawn. You made a mistake, but you made it out of love. That's all we can do in life. Love one another to the best of our ability. Humans make mistakes. Your daughter forgave you."

The heat died out of her face and a weary veil covered her features. The Liza we knew had disappeared beneath the visage of an old woman, haggard, angry, and bitter. "How do you know?"

"You saw your daughter the night Nathaniel Fairchild took your life. She saw you, too. She knows you were coming for her. At the end, she felt your love. Let go of your anger and you'll feel hers. You are so consumed with hate and your need for revenge that she can no longer find you. Let it go, remember how it felt to love her, and she will return to you.

"We don't know how to reunite you properly, but we'll do our best. I swear to you, We'll find out what was denied to you and do our best to make it right." It was a reckless promise—to promise Nathaniel's help to something that had tried to kill his daughter—but I believed he would honor it. So much had been taken from May and her mother. He of all people could understand it.

The pressure against my throat tightened and the not-

Liza laughed her familiar discordant cackle. "You expect me to believe that?"

I could not speak. Luckily, Nathaniel did. "What do you have to lose? You have stolen my daughter. Check on your own. See whether Molly is telling you the truth about that much. You have my word as well as hers that we will follow up to see that as much as possible is done to make things right. Believe me, we're going nowhere without Liza."

A second later, Liza's grip eased and Nathaniel pried her arm from my throat. Freezing air rushed into my lungs and I choked. Liza remained stiff in my lap for a long moment, waging some internal war. Then her body sagged.

"Give her to me," Nathaniel said.

I held on for one second before letting him take her. One last moment of connection to a child I'd come to consider my own.

"We're not through this yet." Nathaniel hiked her up in his arms. "Grab my waist. We have to get back to the house before we freeze to death out here."

My left arm, damaged by the iron cross, refused to function, so I clung to his belt with my frozen right fingers and set off after him in the dark.

THE FRONT DOOR stood wide open and the lights blazed into the night, calling us home. It should have been a relief, but even from my position I could tell that Liza had not moved, had not shifted in her father's arms the whole way back. If we could not save her, all this was for nothing.

Nathaniel laid her on the sofa and turned to stoke the fire, which had died back to nothing while we'd been gone. "Get a blanket. Or ten."

I went for the stairs as fast as I could, but I was having

trouble breathing, walking, seeing straight. My left arm, out of the brutal cold, began to throb. I staggered up the stairs into my room and gathered the duvet but when I straightened back up the world dimmed and I dropped to the floor. *Not yet not yet not yet.* All I had to do was make it back to Liza and then I could pass out. Then it wouldn't matter.

Of course it matters, my mother said. *It will always matter. She needs you.*

"I tried to close the door."

You did. But I can help you. Let me help you.

THE NEXT THING I KNEW, I was lying on the sofa in the living room while Nathaniel bandaged my shoulder with gauze from a first aid kit. The duvet I'd last seen upstairs was tucked around Liza, who had curled up in one of the wingback chairs.

"Why didn't you tell me you were hurt?" he asked.

Now that I was warm again, the tearing, searing pain had returned and it took everything I had not to cry. "I didn't think it mattered."

His hands stilled, then moved to cup my face. "It matters."

I glanced at the chair, my heart beating too fast for me to hold his gaze. "Is Liza okay?"

"She will be. That thing never wanted to hurt her."

"And you?"

"I'll be fine. Molly, look at me."

I did.

"I owe you more than I can ever repay."

My throat closed and those damnable tears filled my eyes. I blinked them back. "I don't need your thanks. Anyone would have done the same."

Liza's fuzzy voice interrupted us. "Molly?"

"Right here."

She slipped out of the chair and made her way over, the duvet a royal cloak trailing behind her, then dropped to her knees and threw her scrawny arms around my waist, resting her head against my chest.

"Be careful!" Nathaniel warned.

"She's fine." The words barely made it past the convulsive clog of emotions in my throat.

"I love you, too," she whispered to me.

Tears dripped from the corners of my eyes, running down my face. But my good arm was holding her, and I could not raise the other to wipe them away.

Nathaniel cleared his throat. "You should both be in the hospital. But I can't get you there. Not yet. When the storm breaks, I'll take the snowmobile and go for help."

Liza looked up. "I'm okay. Just cold. I could go make soup. That would taste good."

"I don't want us to split up."

She shook her head. "It's safe now. She's gone. She found her daughter."

"You know that for sure?" I asked.

She nodded. "They're happy. I can't feel them anymore. She was so sad. I didn't even realize, you know, that she was the one making me feel so bad. I thought it was me, creating her because I was feeling bad. But it started with her. It would be nice if we could help find their tribe, get the right people to help them properly."

I felt the tension seep out of Nathaniel as he squeezed his daughter in a tight hug. "We will. I promise. No more feeling bad without telling me, right?"

"Cross my heart." She suited action to words.

"Good. Still, I'll tell you what, I'll make soup, you stay here with Molly."

"You should both go." They needed the time together. "I'm about to fall asleep and won't be company for anyone."

They left the room then, and I felt my mother's presence. Not that cold, cancerous thing that had come to me in the early days of my stay, but the warm, loving woman I'd known in life. I waited, hoping I would see her, at least hear her, but she did not appear. The door was firmly closed. And yet I understood. She was waiting, just on the other side, in case the time had come for me to join her.

I closed my eyes and let myself drift, only to open them once more when a strange, ululating wail sliced through the room. Footsteps thundered up the hall from the kitchen and I heard the door wrenched open.

"Dad! It's a fire engine!"

Sure enough, a few minutes later, I heard stamping feet and men's voices. My eyelids were too heavy to lift and I could not focus well enough to hear entire conversations.

"...brother-in-law...trouble...insistent...snow...tire chains..."

Matt, I thought. Matt had called them. What a nice guy.

Then Nathaniel. "...left shoulder...blood loss...cold..."

And then they lifted me and the pain brought me screaming out of the drifting daze.

"Be careful!" Nathaniel shouted.

"She's up," said one of the firefighters. "Miss, can you walk? It might be less painful if you can." He helped me onto my feet, and then Nathaniel was holding me up, an arm under my good shoulder and around my waist.

"Slow, Molly."

I leaned heavily against him and let him guide me as my eyes drifted shut again.

HUMS AND BEEPS and white lights and the scent of antiseptic. A hospital room. Cool air, sterile, without personality. Or ghosts. I opened my eyes and found Nathaniel next to me. His face was longer, leaner, hollower than I'd ever seen it. Fear froze my heart.

"Liza? Is she okay?"

A grin broke across his face and suddenly he was young, handsome, his shoulders straight and unburdened. "She's great. Chattering, crocheting, driving the nurses crazy. One of them has taken her out for real food. The cafeteria here is pretty ghastly after a couple of meals."

"A couple of meals? How long have I been asleep?"

"Two days." He sucked in a deep breath. "I thought we were going to lose you. They told me…" He swallowed and shook his head.

"Told you?" My heart had not been damaged. Why was it beating so hard?

"They told me you'd make it, that you'd survive, but I couldn't let myself believe them." He sat gingerly on the edge of the bed. "I tried sending you away. More than once. You wouldn't go."

"No," I whispered.

"Now, I am going to ask you something entirely different." He took my good hand in both of his. "My daughter loves you. I love you. Please. Stay with us."

I tried to smile. "Don't confuse gratitude with love."

He shook his head. "I'm not. I swear it. But in case you're not sure, I'll hold you to your contract. Stay with us for a year. Let me prove it."

Unable to speak, I nodded.

"Ah," he said. "A silent communicator. I have some practice with that."

And then he kissed me, and it was everything I'd never allowed myself to hope for, and there was no need for words.

ACKNOWLEDGMENTS

I grew up loving Mary Stewart and Stephen King and they are the progenitors of this strange little book. But it's hard to write a book like this in today's world, and I have to thank an enormous number of people who helped with it.

My agent, Courtney Miller-Callihan, did not even flinch when I proposed it and did not shy away from the work of shepherding it through its many iterations.

This book was written at a rough time in my own life, and when I first submitted it to Theresa Stevens for editing I am honestly surprised she didn't send it back to me with "I think you accidentally sent me the rough draft."

My sensitivity reader—whose name I will not reveal here because if I got things wrong, the blame is entirely mine and I don't want her to be exposed to the Internet's scorn—gave me insight I was lacking into Romani culture in America.

Nina, Leanna, Tonda and so many others kept me going when I would have given up. You all are amazing.

And, of course, Mike, who lets me disappear for hours each day into my own separate world. Love you.

ABOUT THE AUTHOR

Laura K. Curtis gave up a life writing dry academic papers for writing decidedly less dry genre fiction. A member of RNA, MWA, ITW, and HWA, she has trouble settling into one lane. While she is best known as a writer of romantic suspense, she has also written contemporary romance novels and short crime fiction. Her first "weird" story was published in 2015's *Protectors 2: Heroes* anthology and she knew she'd found a new genre to love.

"It's easier to sell yourself if you only write in one genre," she tells people when speaking on branding at conferences, "I just can't make myself do it."

While the genre-hopping is natural for someone like Laura who comes from a family chock-full of ADHD, the conference circuit is an outgrowth of her background in education. She's taught middle school in New York, high school in St. Louis, and college in Texas, and loves speaking to groups about anything and everything.

facebook.com/authorlaurakcurtis

twitter.com/laurakcurtis

instagram.com/lauralkc

ALSO BY LAURA K. CURTIS

Twisted

Lost

Echoes

Mind Games

Toying With His Affections

Gaming the System